SPINETINGLERS

GHOULISH GHOST STORIES

KINGFISHER
a Houghton Mifflin Company imprint
222 Berkeley Street
Boston, Massachusetts 02116
www.houghtonmifflinbooks.com

First published in 1991
This edition published in 2007
2 4 6 8 10 9 7 5 3 1

LIBRARY OF CONGRESS CATALOGING–IN–PUBLICATION DATA
has been applied for.

ISBN 978-0-7534-6140-2

Printed in India
1TR/0207/THOM/MAR/70STORA/C

SPINETINGLERS

GHOULISH GHOST STORIES

COMPILED BY

ROBERT WESTALL

KINGFISHER

BOSTON

CONTENTS

THE KNOCK AT THE MANOR GATE

Franz Kafka

IT WAS SUMMER, a hot day. With my sister I was passing the gate of a great house on our way home. I cannot tell now whether she knocked on the gate out of mischief or out of absence of mind or merely threatened it with her hand and did not knock at all. A hundred paces farther on along the road, which here turned to the left, began the village. We did not know it very well, but no sooner had we passed the first house, when people appeared and made friendly or warning signs to us; they were themselves apparently terrified, bowed down with terror. They pointed toward the manor house that we had passed and reminded us of the knock on the gate. The proprietor of the manor would charge us with it; the interrogation would begin immediately. I remained quite calm and also tried to calm my sister's fears. Probably she had not struck the door at all, and if she had, it could never be proved. I tried to make this clear to the people around us; they listened to me but refrained from passing any opinion. Later they told me that not only my sister, but I, too, as her brother, would be charged. I nodded and smiled. We all gazed back at the manor, as one watches a distant smoke cloud and waits for the flames to appear. And right enough we presently saw horsemen riding in through the wide-open gate. Dust rose, concealing everything; only the tops of the tall spears glittered. And hardly had the troop vanished into the manor courtyard before they seemed to have turned their horses again, for they were already on their way to us. I urged my sister to leave me; I myself would set everything right. She refused to leave me. I told her that she should at least change, so as to appear in better clothes before these gentlemen. At last she obeyed and set out on the long road to our home. Already the horsemen were beside us, and even before dismounting, they inquired about my sister. She wasn't here at the moment, was the apprehensive reply, but she would come later. The answer was received with indifference; the important thing seemed their having found me. The chief members of the party appeared to be a young, lively fellow, who was a judge, and his silent assistant, who was named Assmann. I was commanded to enter the village inn. Shaking my head and hitching up my pants, I slowly began my statement, while the sharp eyes of the party scrutinized me. I still half believed that a word would be enough to free me, a city man, and with honor, too, from these peasant folks. But when I had stepped over the threshold of the inn, the judge, who had hastened in front and was already awaiting me, said, "I'm really sorry for this man." And it was beyond all possibility of doubt that by this he did not mean my present state, but something that was to happen to me. The room looked more like a prison cell than an inn parlor. Great stone flags on the floor, dark, quite bare walls, into one of which an iron rung was fixed, in the middle something that looked half a pallet, half an operating table.

Could I endure any other air than prison air now? That is the great question, or rather it would be if I still had any prospect of release.

YESTERDAY'S WITCH

Gahan Wilson

HER HOUSE SAT on a small rise, I remember, with a wide stretch of scraggly lawn between it and the ironwork fence that walled off her property from the sidewalk and the rest of the outside world. The windows of her house peered down at you through a thick tangle of oak-tree branches, and I can remember walking by and *knowing* that she was peering out at me and hunching up my shoulders because I couldn't help it, but never, ever, giving her the satisfaction of seeing me hurry because of fear.

To the adults, she was Miss Marble, but we children knew better. We knew that she had another name, though none of us knew just what it was, and we knew that she was a witch. I don't know who it was who first told me about Miss Marble being a witch; it might have been Billy Drew—I think it was—but I had already guessed in spite of being less than six. I grew up, all of us grew up, sure and certain of Miss Marble being a witch.

You never managed to get a clear view of Miss Marble, or I don't ever remember doing so, except that once. You just got peeks and hints. A quick glimpse of her wide, short body as she scuttled up the front porch steps; a brief hint of her brown-wrapped form behind a thick clump of bushes by the garage, where, it was said, an electric runabout sat rusting away; a sudden flash of her fantastically wrinkled face in the narrowing slot of a closing door, and that was all.

Fred Pulley claimed that he had gotten a good, long look at her one afternoon. She had been weeding or something, absorbed at digging in the ground and off-guard and careless even though she stood a mere few feet from the fence. Fred had fought down his impulse to keep on going by, and he had stood and studied her for as much as two or three minutes before she looked up and saw him and snarled and turned away.

We never tired of asking Fred about what he had seen.

"Her teeth, Fred," one of us would whisper—you almost always talked about Miss Marble in whispers—"Did you see her *teeth*?"

"They're long and yellow," Fred would say. "And they come to points at the ends. And I think I saw blood on them."

None of us really believed that Fred had seen Miss Marble, understand, and we certainly didn't believe that part about the blood, but we were so very curious about her, and when you're really curious about something, especially if you're a bunch of kids, you want to get all the information on the subject, even if you're sure that it's lies.

So we didn't believe what Fred Pulley said about Miss Marble having blood on her teeth, nor about the bones he said that he'd seen her pulling out of the ground, but we remembered it all the same, just in case, and it entered into any calculations that we made about Miss Marble.

Halloween was the time she figured most prominently in our thoughts, first because she was a witch, of course, and second because of a time-honored ritual among the neighborhood children concerning her and ourselves and that evening of the year. It was a kind of test by fire that every male child had to go through when he reached the age of 13—or to be shamed forever after. I have no idea when it originated. I only know that when I attained my 13th year and was thereby qualified and doomed for the ordeal, the rite was established beyond question.

I can remember putting on my costume for that memorable Halloween, an old Prince Albert coat and a papier-mâché mask that bore a satisfying likeness to a decayed cadaver, with the feeling that I was preparing myself for a great battle. I studied my reflection in the mirror, affixed by swivels to my bedroom bureau, and wondered gravely if I would be able to meet the challenge that this night would bring. Unsure, but determined, I picked up my brown paper shopping bag, which was very large so as to accommodate as much candy as possible, said goodbye to my mother and father and dog, and went out. I had not gone a block before I met George Watson and Billy Drew.

"Have you got anything yet?" asked Billy.

"No." I indicated the emptiness of my bag. "I just started."

"The same with us," said George. And then he looked at me carefully. "Are you ready?"

"Yes," I said, realizing that I had not been ready until that very moment and feeling an encouraging glow at knowing that I was. "I can do it, all right."

Mary Taylor and her little sister, Betty, came up, and so did Eddy Baker and Phil Myers and the Arthur brothers. I couldn't see where they all had come from, but it seemed as if every kid in the neighborhood was suddenly there, crowding around under the streetlight, costumes flapping in the wind, holding bags and boxes, and staring at me with glistening, curious eyes.

"Do you want to do it now," asked George, "or do you want to wait?"

George had done it the year before, and he had waited.

"I'll do it now," I said.

I began walking along the sidewalk, the others following after me. We crossed Garfield Street and Peabody Street, and that brought us to Baline Avenue, where we turned left. I could see Miss Marble's iron fence half a block ahead, but I was careful not to slow my pace. When we arrived at the fence, I walked to the gate with as firm a step as I could muster and put my hand upon its latch. The metal was cold and made me think of coffin handles and gravediggers' shovels. I pushed it down, and the gate swung open with a low, rusty groaning.

Now it was up to me alone. I was face-to-face with the ordeal. The basic terms of it were simple enough: walk down the crumbling path that led through the tall, dry grass to Miss Marble's porch, cross the porch, ring Miss Marble's bell, and escape. I had seen George Watson do it last year, and I had seen other brave souls do it before him. I knew that it was not an impossible task.

It was a chilly night with a strong, persistent wind and clouds scudding overhead. The moon was three fourths full, and it looked remarkably round and solid in the sky. I became suddenly aware, for the first time in my life, that it was a real *thing* up there. I wondered how many Halloweens it had looked down on and what it had seen.

I pulled the lapels of my Prince Albert coat close around me and started walking down Miss Marble's path. I walked because all of the others had run or skulked, and I was resolved to bring a new dignity to the test if I possibly could.

From afar, the house looked bleak and abandoned, a thing of cold blues and grays and greens, but as I came closer, a peculiar phenomenon began to assert itself. The windows, which from the sidewalk had seemed only to reflect the moon's glisten, now began to take on a warmer glow; the walls and porch, which had seemed all shriveled, peeling paint and leprous patches of rotting wood, now began to appear well kept. I swallowed and strained my eyes. I had been prepared for a growing feeling of menace, forever darker shadows, and this increasing evidence of warmth and tidiness absolutely baffled me.

By the time I reached the porch steps, the place had taken on a positively cozy feel. I now saw that the building was in excellent repair and that it was well painted with a smooth coat of reassuring cream. The light from the windows was now unmistakably cheerful, a ruddy, friendly, pumpkin kind of orange, suggesting crackling fireplaces all set and ready for toasting marshmallows. There was a very unwitchlike clump of corn fixed to the front door, and I was almost certain that I detected an odor of sugar and cinnamon wafting into the cold night air.

I stepped onto the porch, gaping. I had anticipated many awful possibilities during this past year. Never far from my mind had been the horrible pet that Miss Marble was said to own, a something-or-other that was all claws and scales and flew on wings with transparent webbing. Perhaps, I had thought, this thing would swoop down from the bare oak limbs and carry me off while my friends on the sidewalk screamed and screamed. Again, I had not dismissed the notion that Miss Marble might turn me into a frog with a little motion of her fingers and then step on me with her foot and squish me.

But here I was, feeling foolish, very young, crossing this friendly porch and smelling, I was sure of it now, sugar and cinnamon and cider, what's more, and butterscotch on top of that. I raised my hand to ring the bell and was astonished at myself for not being the least bit afraid when the door softly opened and there stood Miss Marble herself.

I looked at her, and she smiled at me. She was short and plump, and she wore an apron with a thick ruffle all along its edges, and her face was as smooth and red and shiny as an autumn apple. She wore bifocals on the tip of her tiny nose, and she had her white hair fixed in a perfectly round bun in the exact center of the top of her head. Delicious odors wafted around her from the open door, and I peered greedily past her.

"Well," she said in a mild, old voice, "I am so glad that someone has at last come to have a treat. I've waited so many years, and each year I've been ready, but nobody's come."

She stood to one side, and I could see a table in the hall piled with candy and nuts and bowls of fruit and platefuls of pies and muffins and cakes, all of it shining and glittering in the warm, golden glow that seemed everywhere. I heard Miss Marble chuckle warmly.

"Why don't you call your friends in? I'm sure that there will be plenty for all."

I turned and looked down the path and saw them, huddled in the moonlight by the gate, hunched wide-eyed over their boxes and bags. I felt a sort of generous pity for them. I walked to the steps and waved.

"Come on! It's all right!"

They would not budge.

"May I show them something?"

She nodded yes, and I went into the house and got an enormous orange-frosted cake with lots of golden sugar pumpkins on its sides.

"Look," I cried, lifting up the cake into the moonlight. "Look at this! And she's got lots more! She always had, but we never asked for it!"

George was the first through the gate, as I knew he would be. Billy came next, and then Eddy, and then the rest. They came slowly, at first, as timid as mice, but then the smells of chocolate and tangerines and brown sugar got to their noses, and they came faster. By the time they had arrived at the porch, they had lost their fear, the same as I, but their astonished faces showed me how I must have looked to Miss Marble when she'd opened the door.

"Come in, children. I'm so glad you've all come at last!"

None of us had ever seen such candy or dared to dream of such cookies and cakes. We circled the table in the hall, awed by its contents, clutching our bags.

"Take all you want, children. It's all for you."

Little Betty was the first to reach out. She got a gumdrop as big as a plum and was about to pop it into her mouth when Miss Marble said, "Oh, no, dear, don't eat it now. That's not the way you do it with tricks and treats. You wait till you get out on the sidewalk, and then you go ahead and gobble it up. Just put it in your bag for now, sweetie."

Betty was not all that pleased with the idea of putting off the eating of her gumdrop, but she did as Miss Marble asked and plopped it into her bag and quickly followed it by other items such as licorice cats and apples dipped in caramel and nuts lumped together with some lovely-looking brown stuff, and soon all of the other children, myself very much included, were doing the same, filling our bags and boxes industriously, giving the task of clearing the table as rapidly as possible our entire attention.

Soon, amazingly soon, we had done it. True, there was the occasional peanut, and now and then a largish crumb survived, but, by and large, the job was done. What was left was fit only for rats and roaches, I thought, and then I was puzzled by the thought. Where had such an unpleasant idea come from?

How our bags bulged! How they strained to hold what we had stuffed inside them! How wonderfully heavy they were to hold!

Miss Marble was at the door now, holding it open and smiling at us.

"You must come back next year, sweeties, and I will give you more of the same."

We trooped out, some of us giving the table one last glance just to make sure, and then we headed down the path, Miss Marble waving goodbye to us. The long, dead grass at the sides of the path brushed stiffly against our bags, making strange hissing sounds. I felt as cold as if I had been standing in the chilly night air all along and not comforted by the cozy warmth inside Miss Marble's house. The moon was higher now and seemed, I didn't know how or why, to be mocking us.

I heard Mary Taylor scolding her little sister: "She said not to eat any till we got to the sidewalk!"

"I don't care. I want some!"

The wind had gotten stronger, and I could hear the stiff tree branches growl high up over our heads. The fence seemed far away, and I wondered why it was taking us so long to get to it. I looked back at the house, and my mouth went dry when I saw that it was gray and old and dark once more and that the only light from its windows were reflections of the pale moon.

Suddenly little Betty Taylor began to cry, first in small, choking sobs and then in loud wails. George Watson said, "What's wrong?" and then there was a pause, and then George cursed and threw Betty's bag over the lawn toward the house and his own box after it. They landed with a strange rustling slither that made the small hairs on the back of my neck stand up. I let go of my own bag, and it flopped, bulging, into the grass by my feet. It looked like a huge, pale toad with a gaping, grinning mouth.

One by one the others rid themselves of what they carried. Some of the younger ones, whimpering, would not let go, but the older children gently separated them from the things that they clutched.

I opened the gate and held it while the rest filed out onto the sidewalk. I followed them and closed the gate firmly. We stood and looked into the darkness beyond the fence. Here and there one of our abandoned boxes or bags seemed to glimmer faintly; some of them moved, I'll swear it, though others claimed that it was just an illusion produced by the waving grass. All of us heard the high, thin laughter of the witch.

A LEGION MARCHING BY

John Hynam

JOHN MIZENAS WAS a remarkable man. I have not seen him for 30 years, but I do not forget him. His children are married and have children of their own, and time has been kind to his beloved Judith. Can one remain the friend of a man whom one has not seen for a generation? I believe it is possible, for I only have to think for a moment, and I can recall his voice, his manner, his laughter, his seriousness; he was a man of spirit and of positive outlook; add to this a long though now faraway friendship, and I believe that you have sufficient reason—that I have sufficient reason—for keeping his memory green.

It was in the summer of—no, I will not say which summer, because this particular time is so long ago, and the distance—I use the word advisedly—between then and now has a tendency to frighten me. This particular day had been so full of sun and drowsiness and sandwiches and fiercely bright bottles of soda and moorhens and wagtails and fish that we came home in the twilight half drugged with all the free favors of nature. I was sleepy as we took our time (that word again!), climbing the cart track from the Dene valley up to the Heastor road; it was all open fields and clumps of bushes in those days, given over entirely to the service of the small wild creatures that frequented the thick hedges and, from time to time, dared to cross the road that twists down the hill to Heastor village, with the great woods on your left as you come up from the valley.

John was in front of me. Instead of going directly down the road, he crossed over and moved a little to the right, where he leaned on the fence and looked out over the green corn that was losing its color in the fading light. So I crossed and leaned with him. I didn't speak, because I knew that he was going to find the right words. That was John, a finder and a speaker of the right words.

"Marvelous," he said. And I just waited.

He pointed. "Even with the corn near full high, you still see it."

I followed his pointing finger. "Oh, yes. The Roman road."

He stayed leaning, very still now, as though movement might shatter part of his thought.

"Marvelous," I said. I did not think it was sycophantic to repeat what he said. It was the right word, after all.

"All those years, Tom. All those years ago. Angles, Saxons, Danes, and Normans. Winter cold and summer heat, plowing and replowing, century after century. And it's still there." He used the voice that he naturally used when there was something of magic and mystery in his mind; it had a kind of reverent tone, and it never failed to grip me.

But the grip relaxed, and my next words showed the difference in temperament between us. I said, "Anything'll last if it's well made." The accountant's reply to the poet.

We had eaten our sandwiches at around noon, and now my stomach was sending out signals. I was going to suggest that the best thing to do was get home and see what was for supper, but I didn't. John could indicate an idea with the tiniest inflexion, and I held my tongue.

"The legions," he said, softly, "can't you imagine them, Tom?"

19

I spoke quietly too. "I'll let you imagine them. You're better at it than I am." I knew what was going on, now. He had mentioned it a few months ago, obliquely, not committing himself, not then.

"The transports, the broad-wheeled supply wagons; their accoutrements, shields, pylums, their leather and bronze, the men at the head carrying the standards. Can't you see them?"

"Can you?"

He smiled. I asked, "Is it supposed to be tonight, then?"

"Supposed to be?"

"You mean that you believe it and I don't?"

He turned and faced me squarely. "Let's stay and see them. Now. Tonight is the night. Let's stay!"

"So you do believe it?"

"I'm going to stay and see if I believe it. Once every thirty years, they say, you can see the legion marching north. They pass west of Fenborough, but this stretch, here, is the only place where they can be seen. ..." The words seemed to drift across my mind and fade into the cooling evening. "Stay, Tom," he said, and I did not know if it was a request or a command.

I looked into the growing dark and saw bats and an owl and heard little squeaks and scurries. I thought of my mother getting anxious, but I didn't mention her. I said, "Yes," and we climbed the fence, walking almost waist deep in the border of meadow grass that surrounded the burgeoning wheat. He led; I followed. At length he stopped around five yards from the wall that enclosed the woods and around the same distance from where the long hump of the road was visible, as straight as a sword.

"Let's sit, then," John said.

We sat. "I can't see over this grass," I said.

"You won't have to," he replied, and it took me a few seconds to see what he meant.

I cannot tell how long we stayed, waiting. The Heastor church clock tolled ten. Men would be coming out of The Oak and The Bluebell and The Gordon Arms at this time. The old clock's announcement was all that we heard. There was no traffic at all on the road. It seemed to be an especial kind of stillness.

Faintly, a rumble came to our ears. It was only a train running into Fenborough East station, along the line that shared the valley with the Dene river. Then the fading rumble of the train seemed to blend into a different, more irregular kind of rumble, coming from down the slope and through the woods. My face asked, "Is it?" and John nodded. There was no doubt in his mind, and, therefore, I did not doubt either.

The rumbling grew, adding a regular rhythm and an erratic jingle; the woods began to fade, as though it was giving way to day in the midst of night. We could hear the marching feet; John felt, I am sure, how I was feeling, expectant, tense, but *delighted*. . . .

We saw them.

When I was a boy, I used to enjoy the fine historical drawings of an artist named Fortunino Matania; I liked in particular the way he drew the Romans, and I was filled with joy to discover that he was right—the soldiers, marching in the past and showing themselves in a scrap of our present time, were just what I expected, except that they always seemed larger in Matania's pictures, for his Roman women were usually Junoesque and his men six footers. These men were, on average, around five foot five or six, but tough and wiry.

First came the standard-bearers, each wearing a tiger skin on head and shoulders and each carrying a legion's emblem. I was childishly pleased to see the "S. P. Q. R." on the standards, but was puzzled by the fact that they carried two emblems, one of an eagle and the other of a stag's head. Were they two half legions? I had a feeling that I would never know.

After these two rode the commander, erect, proud, his helmet carrying a brush of green plumes, and then the soldiers, centurions spacing the hundreds. They were marching at ease, talking, and we strained to catch their words. To my ears, if what they spoke was Latin, then it was a very different Latin from the language that we learned in school.

John whispered, "Some of them are Britons. Do you see?"

In our time, it was dark; in theirs was a soft glow of sunshine. I said, "Are they the group saying words over to each other? That's what it sounds like."

The soldiers marched in front of us, marched from and into the eternal past. John said, "I think that some of them are British born, and they are recruits trying to learn army Latin. That's what the laughter is about."

Satisfaction and pleasure were in my mind; there was no fear.

Then John scared me. He suddenly stood and shouted, "Hail Caesar, hail Caesar!" A centurion looked straight at us and paused for a moment in his step and then turned and marched on. At the end of the column rumbled the baggage wagons, lumbering and broad of wheel. In some of them we saw women; they might have been wives or merely camp followers. Two red-haired Britons were in charge of water carts, pulled by donkeys or mules, I did not know which. Finally came the rear guard, around 50 men, a junior officer on his horse, and some mounted Britons riding small, thick ponies; these were the scouts, but, by the easy way they rode and by the way in which they stayed together, they were not expecting any trouble in this part of the Roman Empire.

Then the light of a day long past filtered away and left us in our present night. We walked home, not speaking, not even saying good night when we parted.

For me, mathematics was and still is childishly easy. I got a good science degree and then my accountant's qualifications, and I entered the world of commerce. I loved one woman, who married someone else. Henceforward I was a bachelor, with my own house and a good housekeeper. I kept my love of fishing and added to that a fair hand at watercolor painting.

John, inevitably, was of nobler stuff. He studied classical languages at Oxford University, obtained a first-class honors degree, and for his brilliance became a miserably paid teacher. It never bothered him; he could finish a day's work worn out, and the next morning he was refreshed as though by a secret mountain stream. He met Judith while at Oxford; they got married, and their children were Rosalind, Juliet, and Sebastian, all three as wise as their father and as beautiful as their mother. They seemed ideally happy; how could Judith and her children know that John was willing to forsake them for an unsubstantial idea, for a drifting ephemera? When he studied in his spare time for a history degree—which he achieved brilliantly, as expected—how could they interpret the signs?

After around 21 years, we both returned to Heastor. John was a classics teacher at an independent school in Fenborough, and I was an actuary for and a director of Hewall Engineering, a Fenborough company with a good reputation. John's wife and kids just about adopted me as an uncle. Perhaps it was because there was a shortage of uncles. But I did not visit too often, because I was afraid of my strong attraction to Judith. She was such a prize; any man would have gone overboard for her, and more than once I thought that John did not appreciate her and what a wonderful person she was. Sometimes, after a visit, I would lie awake and think of her for hours on end as a woman whom I would have liked to take as a wife. Had she been mine, I would have made her the heart and center of my life.

It was a hot summer. Heastor remained as it had always been, no public housing estates, just a village in which the most recent building had been built 30 years before. The bushy lanes still led down into the valley of the Dene, and boys of ten and 11 still went fishing. The Roman road was still there, defiant in its green clothing as it ran parallel to the Fenborough road, having ascended the hill by a different and wooded route.

I was in the garden one evening, doing battle with the greenflies on the roses. The gate sounded, and I looked up to see Judith coming across the lawn.

"Hello, Tom."

"Hello and welcome," I said. "I was just thinking about a pint of cider. Will you join me?"

"That sounds lovely."

I drew two pints from the barrel in the little dark scullery and carried them out to the lawn, where Judith had seated herself at the rickety old table in the corner. She took a long pull at her tankard. "Isn't that beautiful—a real country drink."

"I've always thought so," I said. I put down my tankard. "How's the family?"

"Fine."

And I knew at once that all was not fine. The greater the love, the less can truth be dissembled.

She watched an ant walk over the old tabletop, and then she said, "Tom, have you—noticed—anything about John lately?"

I wondered if she knew that, when I came to visit them and she was present, I hardly noticed John. I said, "What's worrying you, Judith?"

She stared into her tankard, took another long drink, and then said, "There's a barrier."

I waited.

"There's something on his mind."

"He's a very intelligent man and somewhat obsessive. Sometimes his interests take priority. Then, he needs only himself."

"Yes. He is so intelligent."

"I would say that you are equally intelligent," I said, and this was not flattery. She was the wife of John, even if she was not always as loved and appreciated as I thought right.

"Things were pretty good, until the beginning of this year," she said. "Now, something's changed. I feel that it's something that has been dormant for a long time, and now, here it is. Dormant."

"The body renews itself every seven years. Does the mind do that too?"

"Dormant." I could see that the word had a grip on her mind. She repeated it and seemed to hope that I would go on talking. I did not. After a moment she finished her cider with a swift finality seldom seen in women.

She rose with a smile. "Thanks for talking, Tom."

"You've got nothing to thank me for."

"Watch him," she said, "and tell me what you think."

"I can't promise anything. This is intimate ground; this is husband-and-wife stuff. Fools rush in, Judith."

She smiled. I watched her go. I was not happy.

The next time I visited, John took me aside. He was filled with a dream, an idea. Their children were playing with those of Dr. Barnett, whose wife was also visiting.

"Come with me, Tom. I've got something to show you."

So, on that warm summer evening, we went together down to the smaller of the two sheds at the bottom of the garden. Here, in the musty dried-earth smell, he unlocked a rough old chest, made of pine. He took from the chest clothes that seemed to be made of rabbit skins, and thonged sandals, and a rough undershirt of a wide weave, and a large-bladed weapon somewhere between a sword and a machete. He could see that I was puzzled.

His eyes were shining. "I'd dress in them for you," he said, "but someone might come."

"What's that stuff for? A play?"

He grinned. "You could say that."

I just stared at him. I was beginning to remember.

"You and I saw them, as boys, thirty years ago."

"The legion."

"Yes."

My mind raced around all the possibilities, but, as ever, he saw more than I did. "You're going to—"

"Watch the legion go by. Every thirty years. We know the story."

"Then, these clothes—"

"Don't you remember, Tom, how I cried, 'Hail Caesar'— but it was the wrong language? Now if I, dressed as a Briton, call to them in their own language and say that I want to join them . . . don't you see?"

For at least a minute, I was incapable of answering him. I was wondering how this man, whom I thought that I knew so well, had nurtured this idea for 30 years. I did not see what he thought he was achieving. But, then, he was the poet, and I was only the accountant.

"John, don't do it."

"It's just an experiment."

"Except that you don't know what you're experimenting with. To say the least, it's a very unscientific approach."

"So, how would you go about doing it?"

"I wouldn't," I snapped, "and I don't think you should either."

"Thirty years ago tomorrow night?"

"You could be miles out in your calculations—"

"Oh, Tom, you disappoint me! I'm no mathematician, but I figured that out. What do you say—let's both try it!"

He saw by my face that I was set against the idea and tried with more emotion to stir me into the way that he was going. "Thirty years ago, we were kids. Can't we do better,

27

now? . . . Tom, I'm talking about an old friendship."

"How would you like me to tell Judith about this?"

He smiled and shook his head. "You wouldn't do that."

I knew then what sort of a coward I was. I watched him put the skin clothes and the knife away and lock the box. He straightened and said, "You'd never betray a confidence, Tom." He was expecting a reply; stubborn, I tried not to reply, but I knew that he was right, so at last I said, "No. I won't tell. But I beg you not to do this."

All he did was shake his head and chuckle.

Less than 48 hours later, the police were out looking for John Mizenas. They spread their net wider and wider, until, at last, inevitably, they decided that he couldn't be found, and so they called off the search. The news value diminished, until John Mizenas was forgotten by all except for a handful of people in Fenborough and Heastor.

I kept my promise, but my mind would not rest. I even feared to meet the possible truth that John Mizenas had met the Romans and joined them and had marched with them into the dangerous past, where, perhaps, with his knowledge of languages, he had possibly found a place for his scholarship. As John knew Latin, it would take him around a week to master the sound they gave it, and after that . . .

But this was mere rambling. For me, there was the deep personal agony of knowing that Judith and the children regarded me as a member of the family. I did not doubt that if, after a respectable interval, I proposed marriage, I would be accepted. I was even sure that in Heastor it would be regarded as a good and happy thing if I married Judith.

I was 44; she was 33. John was missing and would later be "presumed dead." After that, there was no impediment.

Except that I could not bring myself to believe that John was dead. His ghost did not visit me, I received no supernatural message, but knowing what I did, I could not bring myself to say the words to Judith.

But if I was not forthcoming, someone else was. Dr. Barnett's wife died suddenly, and a year after, he married Judith, and it was soon a happy case of "yours, mine, and ours" with the increasing family. Now the children of three marriages are grown up, and Judith, in her 60s, is still beautiful, because her mind is open and her spirit is ready for laughter.

I am still a bachelor, not too crusty, I hope, and reasonably sociable. I am over 70, but I still have something to look forward to.

Come with me, and I will show you.

Here you see a rough suit of skins and some dateless underwear, good leather shoes, made by hand, and a cloak, and a sturdy staff. And see how patriarchal I look, having let my beard grow to its present length. Don't I look the part? And when I go up the hill tonight and wait for them to come as I stand by the old road, I shall have enough knowledge of Latin to speak to them. I shall look for John Mizenas. He may not be there. He may still be 40 years old, as he was on the night that he disappeared, or he may be only four years younger than myself. But I must go up there, and wait, and see the legion marching by.

THE LAWYER AND THE GHOST

Charles Dickens

I KNEW A man—40 years ago—who took an old, damp, rotten set of chambers in one of the most ancient inns that had been shut up and empty for years and years before. There were lots of stories about the place, and it certainly was far from being a cheerful one; but he was poor and the rooms were cheap, and that would have been quite a sufficient reason, if they had been ten times worse than they really were.

The man was obliged to take some moldering fixtures, and, among the rest, was a great lumbering wooden press for papers with large glass doors and a green curtain inside—a pretty useless thing, for he had no papers to put in it; and as to his clothes, he carried them about with him, and that wasn't very hard work either.

Well, he moved in all of his furniture—it wasn't quite a truck full—and had sprinkled it about the room, so as to make the four chairs look as much like a dozen as possible, and was sitting down before the fire at night, drinking the first glass of two gallons of whisky that he had ordered on credit, wondering whether it would ever be paid for, if so, in how many years' time, when his eyes encountered the glass doors of the wooden press.

"Ah," says he, speaking aloud to the press, having nothing else to speak to. "If it wouldn't cost more to break up your old carcass than it would ever be worth afterward, I'd have a fire out of you in less than no time."

He had hardly spoken the words when a sound resembling a faint groan appeared to issue from the interior of the case; it startled him at first, but thinking that it must be some young fellow in the next chamber who had been dining out, he put his feet on the fender and raised the poker to stir the fire.

At that moment, the sound was repeated, and one of the glass doors slowly opened, disclosing a pale figure in soiled and worn apparel, standing erect in the press. The figure was tall and thin and the countenance expressive of care and anxiety, but there was something in the hue of the skin and gaunt and unearthly appearance of the whole form that no being of this world was ever seen to wear.

"Who are you?" said the new tenant, turning very pale, poising the poker in his hand, however, and taking a very decent aim at the countenance of the figure. "Who are you?"

"Don't throw that poker at me," replied the form. "If you hurled it with ever so sure an aim, it would pass through me, without resistance, and expend its force on the wood behind. I am a spirit!"

"And, pray, what do you want here?" faltered the tenant.

"In this room," replied the apparition, "my worldly ruin was worked, and I and my children beggared. In this room, when I had died of grief and long-deferred hope, two wily harpies divided the wealth for which I had contested during a wretched existence and of which, at last, not one farthing was left for my unhappy descendants. I terrified them from the spot and since that day have prowled by night—the only period at which I can revisit the earth—

about the scenes of my long misery. This apartment is mine: leave it to me!"

"If you insist upon making your appearance here," said the tenant, who had had time to collect his presence of mind, "I shall give up possession with the greatest pleasure, but I should like to ask you one question, if you will allow me."

"Say on," said the apparition, sternly.

"Well," said the tenant, "it does appear to me somewhat inconsistent that when you have an opportunity of visiting the fairest spots of earth—for I suppose that space is nothing to you—you should always return exactly to the very places where you have been most miserable."

"Egad, that's very true; I never thought of that before," said the ghost.

"You see, sir," pursued the tenant, "this is a very uncomfortable room. From the appearance of that press, I should be disposed to say that it is not wholly free from bugs; and I really think you might find more comfortable quarters, to say nothing of the climate of London, which is extremely disagreeable."

"You are very right, sir," said the ghost politely. "It never struck me till now; I'll try a change of air directly."

In fact, he began to vanish as he spoke: his legs, indeed, had quite disappeared!

"And if, sir," said the tenant, calling after him, "if you *would* have the goodness to suggest to the other ladies and gentlemen who are now engaged in haunting old empty houses that they might be much more comfortable elsewhere, you will confer a very great benefit on society."

"I will," replied the ghost. "We must be dull fellows, very dull fellows, indeed; I can't imagine how we can have been so stupid."

With these words, the spirit disappeared, and what is rather remarkable, he never came back again.

THE GHOST WHO WAS AFRAID OF BEING BAGGED

Anonymous Indian story

ONCE UPON A time there lived a barber who had a wife. They did not live happily together, as the wife always complained that she did not have enough to eat. The wife used to often say to her mate, "If you did not have the means to support a wife, why did you marry me? People who do have the means should not indulge in the luxury of a wife. When I was in my father's house, I had plenty to eat, but it seems that I have come to your house to fast. Widows only fast; I have become a widow in your lifetime." She was not content with mere words; she got very angry one day and struck her husband with the broomstick of the house. Stung with shame on account of his wife's reproach and beating, he left his house with the implements of his craft and vowed never to return and see his wife's face again till he had become rich. He went from village to village and toward nightfall came to the outskirts of a forest. He laid himself down at the foot of a tree and spent many a sad hour bemoaning his hard lot.

It so chanced that the tree, at the foot of which the barber was lying down, was dwelt in by a ghost. The ghost, seeing a human being at the foot of the tree, naturally thought of destroying him. With this intention, the ghost appeared from the tree and, with outspread arms and a gaping mouth, stood like a tall palm tree before the barber and said, "Now, barber, I am going to destroy you. Who will protect you?" The barber, though quaking in every limb through fear and his hair standing erect, did not lose his presence of mind, but with promptitude and shrewdness replied, "Oh, spirit, you will destroy me! Wait a while, and I'll show you how many ghosts I have captured this very night and put inside my bag; and very glad am I to find you here, as I will have one more ghost in my bag." So saying, the barber produced from his bag a small mirror that he always carried around with him along with his razors, his whetstone, his strop, and other utensils, to enable his customers to see whether their beards had been well shaved or not. He stood up, placed the mirror right up against the face of the ghost, and said, "Here you see one ghost that I have seized and bagged; I am going to put you also in the bag to keep this ghost company." The ghost, seeing his own face in the mirror, was convinced of the truth of what the barber had said and was filled with fear. He said to the barber, "Oh, sir barber, I'll do whatever you bid me, only do not put me inside your bag. I'll give you whatever you want." The barber said, "You ghosts are a faithless set; there is no trusting you. You will promise and not give what you promise." "Oh, sir," replied the ghost, "be merciful to me; I'll bring to you whatever you order; and if I do not bring it, then put me inside your bag." "Very well," said the barber. "Bring me just now one thousand gold mohurs; and by tomorrow night you must raise a granary in my house and fill it with paddy. Go and get the gold mohurs immediately, and if you fail to do my bidding, you will certainly be put inside my bag." The ghost gladly consented to the conditions. He went away and in the course of a short time returned with a bag containing 1,000 gold mohurs. The barber was delighted beyond measure at the sight of the gold mohurs. He then told the ghost to see to it that by the following night a granary was erected in his house and filled with paddy.

It was during the small hours of the morning that the barber, loaded with the heavy treasure, knocked at the door of his house. His wife, who reproached herself for having in a fit of rage struck her husband with a broomstick, got out of bed and unbolted the door. Her surprise was great when she saw her husband pour out of the bag a glittering pile of gold mohurs.

The next night, the poor devil, through fear of being bagged, raised a large granary in the barber's house and spent the livelong night carrying on his back large packages of paddy till the granary was filled to the brim. The uncle of this terrified ghost, seeing his worthy nephew carrying on his back loads of paddy, asked what was the matter. The ghost related what had happened. The uncle-ghost then said, "You fool, you think that the barber can bag you! The barber is a cunning fellow; he has cheated you, like a simpleton as you are." "You doubt," said the nephew-ghost, "the power of the barber! Come and see." The uncle-ghost then went to the barber's house and peeped inside it through a window. The barber, perceiving from the blast of wind that the arrival of the ghost had produced that a ghost was at the window, placed full before it the self-same mirror, saying, "Come now—I'll put you also inside the bag." The uncle-ghost, seeing his own face in the mirror, got quite frightened and promised that very night to raise another granary and to fill it, not this time with paddy, but with rice. So in two nights the barber became a rich man and lived happily with his wife begetting sons and daughters.

SCHOOL FOR GHOSTS

Adapted by Vida Derry from a story by Pu Sung-Ling

WHEN YANG SHIEN heard about the haunted house, once the home of a high official, but now empty and deserted, he decided that he would approach the owner to allow him to live there as a caretaker, for it was just the sort of home that Yang had dreamed that one day he would own.

At first the high official would not hear of it. "Young man," he said, "no one has been able to live there for years. The spirits that occupy it are such that they bring trouble to anyone who stays in the house."

"I am prepared to risk that. It is a great pity that such a lovely house should be left to spirits that care nothing if it falls into ruins. I will look after it for you."

The older man shrugged his shoulders. "I have nothing to lose, young man. I have warned you, and seeing that you still insist, you can have the key. But at the first sign of trouble, you must leave. Otherwise, I would not want to be responsible for you."

Yang was jubilant and immediately moved his belongings into his new home. He had to make several journeys back and forth, carrying everything himself, for he could not afford to hire a cart, and it was past sunset when he returned with his last load.

Yang's books were his pride and joy, and he had carefully placed them upon a table that he had decided would be admirable for his studies, but when he returned with his last load, they were no longer there. He hunted high and low, but they were not to be found in the house, and there was no sign of anyone having broken in. When, however, he returned to the room where he had left the missing books, they were back on the table. Puzzled, but happier now at the return of his most precious possessions, he went to the kitchen to cook some rice for his supper, and when he returned to his room, where he thought that he would read a while before retiring, he found that his books had again vanished. He then heard the patter of light footsteps and saw two beautiful young girls carrying his books in their arms. They were laughing together as they quietly replaced the books on the table.

They turned around and gazed straight at him, looking so human in the half light of dusk that he could hardly believe that they were ghosts at all; but knowing that they were, he turned his head away and would not return their saucy looks. Whereupon they laughed at him and came closer.

Yang's heart bumped against his ribs with fear as he remembered the warning of the owner of the house. One of the girls prodded his body with her finger. The other one stroked his face, and they started walking around him trying to make him look at them, touching him and laughing as they did so.

Yang had now revised his disbelief in spirits, and if he had not seen them with his own eyes walk right through the door just now, he would not have believed that they were ghosts. However, they seemed as harmless as little children, and he decided to treat them as such.

"Get out of my sight, you silly ghosts," he exclaimed. "How dare you come here to disturb me?" He made his voice sound as angry and belligerent as he possibly could. All the same, he did not expect them to take fright and scuttle away as quickly as they did.

His confidence returned, Yang lit a lamp and began to read, but all the time he was aware of other presences in the room and conscious of flitting shadows in the dark corners. He tried to concentrate on his book, but could not quite ignore those now quiet but eerie spirits that were around him. He soon gave up trying to read and got ready for bed.

He was very tired after his busy day, but no sooner had he closed his eyes than he was disturbed by a tickling sensation on his nose. Many times he brushed away whatever was tickling him, but it always returned. Eventually he sneezed, and in the darkness he heard sounds of suppressed laughter. He got up, lit a candle, and went back to bed again, closing his eyes and listening.

Presently he heard a faint sound, and he opened his eyes. One of the girls was coming toward him with a feather in her delicate little hand. Immediately, he jumped out of bed and shouted at her, and she ran away. Eventually he managed to get to sleep, only to be awakened by a tickling sensation, this time on his ear. And so it went on all night. He couldn't get any sleep owing to the wretched little ghosts until dawn, and then all was peaceful, and he relapsed into a deep sleep, not waking until long past noon.

The rest of the day was quiet and normal, and Yang did some cleaning, arranging everything to his liking. Then he settled down to study, realizing that he would probably be plagued again by his ghostly visitors after sunset. He was reading when he became aware of a presence, and looking up from his book, he beheld his beautiful visitors of the previous night watching him. He ignored them and continued reading. Then suddenly one of them came up to him and closed his book.

He jumped up in anger. "Am I to have no peace in this house?" he shouted. "I have important work to do, so go away."

They ran off, but no sooner had he returned to his book than they returned. Yang held onto his book, determined to continue his reading, but one of them came up behind him and put her cool hands over his eyes. Again he jumped up in anger, but they only laughed at him. So he tried a different approach.

"I have work to do and must study to pass my examinations," he told them in a friendly manner. "So why don't you be good girls and leave me in peace? Go and do something useful."

This approach surprised them, and they stopped laughing and looked at him in a contemplative way. One of them whispered in the other's ear, and they both smiled sweetly at him and then left the room. Presently he heard sounds of activity in the kitchen, and he went back to his work, thankful that he was getting a little peace at last.

Around half an hour later the two pretty ghosts came back and started to lay out a meal on the low table. It all looked delicious, but even though Yang was hungry, he was a little dubious about eating a meal cooked by ghosts. They might poison him! He thanked them and told them how clever he thought they were. "But I am not hungry," he said, going back to his book.

"If you do not trust us, how can you expect us to be good?" asked the one who seemed to be the elder of the two.

Yang looked up in surprise, for she had spoken in a sweet, tinkling voice. "Of course I trust you," he felt obliged to reply.

"Then if you trust us, you will eat the food that we have labored to prepare for you."

Yang thought that if he refused to eat, he would continue to be plagued by them and would be unable to stay there. He took up a bowl of rice and chopsticks and tasted some of the food, and, feeling no ill effects, he pronounced it excellent and perfectly cooked, and the two little ghosts were delighted.

After he had finished his meal, they sat together and talked, but they would say little about themselves. He learned that the name of the older one was Ching-Yen and the younger one was Shai-Lu; but of their families they would tell him nothing, saying that as they were only spirits, his interest in them could not be marriage—therefore why was he so curious?

"As I never thought to meet such charming spirits when I came here, it is natural that I am curious about you, especially as we are to live together in this house."

To this Ching-Yen replied, "Fortunately for you, the other spirits that occupied this house have been recalled to the world below by the Black Judge, while we await whatever fate is in store for us. But if you wish to stay here, we will continue to serve you."

And so Yang was able to settle down and work, and the girls—for he could no longer think of them as ghosts—came every evening after sunset and cleaned and cooked for him, taking an interest in his work, disturbing him no longer, and he was very happy.

One day he had to go out and did not return until well after sunset. He found the younger girl, Shai-Lu, seated at his desk laboriously copying from the book that he had been transcribing. She showed him what she had been doing, and he praised it. "But there is much room for improvement," he told her with a smile, "and, if you like, I will teach you."

Shai-Lu was delighted at the suggestion, and Yang, sitting her on his knee, held her hand and showed her how to hold the brush correctly. Just then, Ching-Yen came into the room, and, on seeing them thus, her face flushed up to the roots of her shiny black hair as though she was jealous of the younger girl.

On seeing this, Yang set Shai-Lu on her feet again and offered his knee to Ching-Yen. "Let me see how well you can wield the brush, my dear," he said to her, and smilingly the girl wrote with Yang guiding her wrist.

Seeing that they were both very interested, Yang gave them each a piece of paper and told them to copy a verse, and while they labored at their tasks, he was able to continue with his own studies. When they had finished, they brought their work to him, and he graded them. The younger girl's work got the higher grades, and again Yang had to placate Ching-Yen with encouraging words, telling her that if she worked hard, she would soon improve.

Thus Yang became the teacher to the two young ghosts, and when their writing improved, he taught them how to read. They were apt students, and once they had grasped anything, they did not forget it.

One evening Ching-Yen brought her young brother, Song, a handsome youth of around 16 years, but also, alas, like his attractive sister, a ghost, having departed this life at a tender age. Could Song also be Yang's student? Yang agreed, and Song proved to be a very intelligent boy. Before long he was reading the classics and writing poems.

Yang was delighted with the success of his school for ghosts. The lessons kept these naughty spirits occupied and out of mischief, and Yang was able to continue with his studies and also earn a little money writing poems of satire on current affairs, which became quite well known, but not always popular.

Eventually the day came when Yang had to leave to take his examinations and say goodbye to his phantom students. He was gratified to find how badly they took his news. The girls wept, and Song was full of forebodings, begging him not to go. "The gods are not with you at this time," he said, "and if you go now, some dreadful calamity will befall you."

But Yang would not listen and the next day left the house to keep his appointment with the examiner. When Yang arrived in the capital, he learned that his works of satire had enraged a prefect of great influence in the district, and his examiner, far from being sympathetic, accused Yang of improper conduct. Yang was thrown into prison, and, penniless, without food, becoming weaker every day, he wished that he had taken heed of Song's warning.

One night he thought that he was dreaming when he saw Ching-Yen, but when she gave him food, he knew that it was really her. She told him that his examiner had been bribed to accuse him of improper conduct and that her brother, Song, had gone to the court to plead for his release. She would return the next night to tell him how Song had fared.

When she had left, he ate the food, which gave him new strength and hope. But Ching-Yen did not return the following night as she had promised. Neither did she come the next night or the next, and Yang became even weaker—all hope gone.

Then one night Shai-Lu came to him, but she was very sad and downcast. She told him that Song's request for Yang's release had fallen on deaf ears, and he also had been taken into custody. Bad luck had also befallen Ching-Yen, who on her way back from visiting Yang had been accosted by the Black Judge and had been carried off to be his concubine, but, refusing to submit, she, too, had been imprisoned.

Yang, as weak as he was, tried to console Shai-Lu, taking the blame upon himself. She gave him some money so that he could buy food and then left him, saying that she must go back to watch over Song.

The next day Yang was brought before the Judge, who asked him who was the young man named Song Tsai who had pleaded for his release. Yang, not wanting to cause any more trouble for his spirit students, pretended that he did not know, whereupon the Judge told him that the young man had been brought before him to be beaten, but, throwing himself upon the ground, he had disappeared. Yang still stayed silent, and the Judge, thinking that Song's disappearance was a sign to indicate Yang's innocence, told him that he was free to go.

Yang could hardly believe his good fortune. He went

back to his house as quickly as he could, arriving there just after dusk, but no one was there to greet him. When he went to bed that night, he could hear the sound of weeping, but when he got up and lit his candle, he could see no one.

Henceforth Yang often heard in the night the sound of quiet weeping, and it made him feel very sad and helpless. He was not visited by his little ghost maidens anymore, and he missed them very much and often thought of them when he sat alone at his studies in the evening. He thought of taking a wife, but how could he afford to do so when he had not yet passed his examinations? He began to work harder than ever, dreaming of the wife he would be able to have one day, and she always looked like either Ching-Yen or Shai-Lu.

One night the sound of weeping was louder than usual, but it came from outside the house. Yang got up and went to the door to investigate. A young girl was there. He asked her from whence she came.

"I have traveled a long way, and now I am so tired that I cannot walk another step. I was told that you would give me refuge."

Yang invited her inside and saw that she was very beautiful, with lovely eyes and teeth like pearls. "Who told you to come to me?" he asked, thinking how pale she looked and wondering if she was another ghost.

But the girl fell at his feet with exhaustion, and he lifted her onto his bed. He watched over her all through the night, and in the morning when she awoke he made porridge for her. He knew now that she was not a ghost, and yet she had talked in her sleep, calling him by name and reciting verses that had been written by his spirit students and known only by him. He was mystified and could hardly wait to ask her again how she had come to him and from where.

"I only know that I was very sick, indeed close to death, when a girl came to me and told me of Yang and his teachings. She said that you needed me and that I must come to you. She seemed to enter my body and give me the strength, and here I am."

Yang was amazed at what he heard and asked, "Did the girl who came to you tell you her name?"

"She told me her name was Shai-Lu. Do you know of her?"

"Yes, I know of her. Did she say anything else?"

The girl blushed and lowered her eyes. "She said that you would want to take me for your wife."

And Yang knew that nothing would make him happier. "But," he said to her regretfully, "your family would not want you to marry a poor man."

"I will not marry anyone but you," she told him.

And so a messenger was sent to the girl's parents, who soon came to take her away, but she would not go with them, and therefore they had to agree to the marriage, which took place the next day.

But one thing marred their happiness, and that was the sound of weeping that haunted the house every evening, until they were blessed with their first child, and then the weeping ceased.

The child was a girl, and she strongly resembled Ching-Yen.

THE LITTLE YELLOW DOG

Mary Williams

IN MY MIND I called him my sandman, because I always saw him at bedtime, from my window, when my Aunt Daphne had left me and gone downstairs. He was a small grayish-yellow man, like the beach itself in the twilight, when the sea and sky became one . . . merging toward the dim uncertain lines of dunes tufted with beards of rushes.

My aunt's seaside house stood high up on the dunes, with only a small cluster of chalets and cottages straggling behind it to the village of Wyck-on-Sea. So I had a clear view from my window, and I always knew exactly when the old man would appear . . . immediately after the church clock had struck eight. The tower of the church poked up from the left on the seaside of the hamlet, and I knew, with the odd instinct of children, that he came from there.

I was only seven years old, and the old man was my secret, like the little yellow dog. The dog, though, was my daytime companion. We played hide-and-seek in the sand hills, and I only mentioned him once when my aunt came to find me for dinner and said, "Who were you calling to, Johnny?"

"The little yellow dog," I said. "Look, there he goes." He was racing ahead, his rear end, with its fuzzy, funny tail quickly disappearing around a hump of the dunes. But my aunt, who was peering closely, said, "There's *no* little yellow dog. You're making things up again. You mustn't. It's really silly."

She wasn't pretending. She just didn't see him. That's why

47

I didn't tell her about the sandman, because I knew that it would be the same with him.

The shore at Wyck was wide and lonely, stretching for half a mile to the sea when the tide was low, leaving just a few pools behind by occasional rocks and humps of mud.

Except for the dunes, everywhere around Wyck-on-Sea was flat. The roads and gardens seemed always filmed by thin sand, where poppies and star-shaped yellow daisies grew profusely, in wild abandon. Dykes cut through the countryside, making a patchwork of fields rich with ripening corn and oats. There were butterflies, too; hundreds of tiny blue butterflies flying and drifting on the hot air that was tangy with the smell of brine, seaweed, sweetbriar, and the bitter, strange smell of the yellow daisy.

It was all so long ago; yet I can still see in my mind clearly that dancing, laughing, raggedy-looking pup and the more mysterious figure of the sandy-looking old man as he passed each evening along the beach, with his head turned up from his rounded back, his thin, longish hair and beard blowing in the wind like the rushes of the dunes. Although I could not see his expression, I knew that he was looking for something. Once when I could not sleep, I got out of bed later and went to the window. He was returning then from where he had been; his figure greenish gold in the moonlight, only more bent, as though he was saddened by great disappointment.

He walked . . . almost drifted along, with head bowed toward the glittering sand, and when he reached the bend where the path led to the church, the shadows closed in on him, and he was there no more.

The next day was sunny again; and when I told my aunt

that I was going to the beach, she looked at me doubtfully for a moment and then remarked, "All right, Johnny. Yes, it's a lovely day. Later, perhaps, I'll join you; so don't hide and pretend that you're playing silly games with your make-believe little yellow dog."

I didn't promise; I just nodded and was presently running through a valley of dunes with the blue butterflies all around me, the yellow daisies smelling, and the sand warm on my bare toes.

The tide was halfway out, and I wandered around for a while, picking up razor shells and some of the tiny pink ones that had holes in them, which I was collecting to give to my sister Mary when I went home. She was recovering from the chickenpox and would like them, I knew, if I could find enough for her to make a necklace.

I hadn't been out long when the little dog came racing toward me over a breakwater from the direction where the old man walked each evening. There was a funny little building there . . . a ruin . . . just under the sand hills, which someone said had been used in the war. The little dog was whitish-gold from the sand, and when he jumped up at me, laughing, I could see the sand on his tongue, in his eyes, and on the shaggy brows falling over them. He never barked; and this, I thought, was why my aunt didn't believe in him. But, then, ours was a secret relationship, and barking would have given the show away.

"Come on . . ." I called, starting to run with him beside me. "You hide, and I'll find you. . . ." Generally he bounded off when I said that, but this time he didn't; he just turned back in the direction that he'd come from, paused, looked at me, and then went on again. It happened several times, until at last I followed, a bit grudgingly, because the dunes thinned that way and weren't nearly so good for hide-and-seek, merging eventually into a part called The Warren, half sand, half earth and grass, and riddled with rabbit holes.

There weren't so many blue butterflies there, and quite suddenly as we approached the ruin, the sun went in, leaving the air cool with a thin wind shivering from the sea. The little dog hurried ahead, but I knew that he wasn't playing hide-and-seek anymore, although once, for a few seconds, his shaggy form became lost in the gray light, and I felt suddenly sad with the odd kind of loss that only a child could feel . . . as though all of the magic had gone for good . . . all of the magic that I'd known of those summer haunted hours with the little yellow dog.

Then I saw him again: a shadowed shape slipping into the darkness of the derelict tumbled doorway.

I went in after him. He looked around once and then started digging with his two front paws, digging with a hungry urgency that I knew in some way must be terribly important.

"All right," I said, thinking of a buried treasure. "I'll help." And my brief depression seemed to lift a little.

How long we scraped in the sand and earth I don't know. There'd been an exceptionally high tide that night, which had sucked a good deal of ground away, leaving rubble exposed that could have been hidden for years. Large chunks of coastline were being taken by the sea from time to time; my aunt had told me about a church and two empty cottages farther on that had fallen and disappeared; that's why she didn't like me playing on the beach when the water was up.

I remembered this in my feverish attempts to help the little dog. He didn't seem to notice me anymore, and he wasn't laughing or playing, not even for a moment . . . just scrape, scrape . . . sniffing and scratching, until very gradually I began to get not only tired, but afraid, sensing intuitively that the end of the adventure could be something less pleasant than pirates' gold.

So I got up, shook my clothes, and wiped the sandy dust from my eyes, knees, and hands.

"I'm going," I said. "There's nothing there, anyway. It's a stupid game. I'm going home."

I turned my head to look at him, but he wasn't there. He'd gone. I was sorry and sad and wanted to cry. He must have heard me when I was fixing and cleaning myself and taken off without my noticing. I called and called, but there was no response. There was nothing left but the lonely shore outside the ruin, the far-off sea that had turned from blue to gray, and the lonely trek back across the sand, which seemed bereft without the little yellow dog.

Early that afternoon, I took my pail and shovel and, when my aunt questioned me, told her that I was going to dig on the beach. "Don't be long, then," she said. "The tide's turned. If you're not back by three, I shall come and get you."

I went out, and as I cut through the dunes, the blue butterflies were there again, and the sun was warm, diamonded gold and silver under the brilliant sky. But there was no little yellow dog, and he didn't even come when I reached the ruined hut or whatever it was and started to dig with my shovel.

I was hot, and soon my shirt was sticking to my back with

perspiration. I could feel rivulets of sweat trickling from my forehead, over my eyes, and down my face. But the place where I found it, at last, was cold and damp from the rain and the sea, and the thing was shining white beneath the clinging rubble of dust.

I fetched some water in my bucket from a nearby pool and threw it over the curled-up shape. Then I stood staring. I wasn't frightened . . . just awed . . . The skeleton in an odd kind of way was beautiful in its perfection of bone structure, lying there as if in a long sleep . . . the skeleton that could so easily have been that of a little yellow dog.

I moved it very gently a few inches to the door of the ruined building, went out, and then looked back. In the sunlight, the bones glistened clear and pale, like ivory. Perhaps I cried a little then—I don't know. But after the brief pause I walked on toward my aunt's house, not turning, not wanting to see anymore, grateful only for the sunshine and the distant sound of the waves breaking, for being alive in a world of summertime filled with blue butterflies and starred clumps of yellow daisy flowers.

That night I watched from my window as usual and saw the sandy old man walking along the shore. He was hurrying this time, with his head turned to the twilit sky . . . or perhaps it was the wind at his back that made me think so . . . the wind and the thin clouds of fine sand blown upward toward the dunes. I went back to bed, but I was restless and wakeful; and in around an hour . . . it must have been an hour because I heard the church clock chiming nine . . . I got up and crossed to the window again.

The moon was just spreading its path of silver across the

sea, gathering in radiance until the whole scene was a brilliant pattern of light and slipping shadows. It was then that I saw the old man returning, with something under one arm. Something that looked like a sack. And as he passed, the color of the evening seemed to lift and change, momentarily bathing the bent figure in a quivering glow of rose. Everything suddenly was mysteriously warm and comforting; and I knew then, knew something that was beyond understanding or the need to understand.

A minute later the enhanced translucence of the sky faded once more into the pallor of moon-washed dusk. The figure of the old man with his burden slipped inside the looming shadow of the church, and everything was still and motionless and curiously bereft.

Presently I went back to bed. I was tired and slept well. When I awoke, the morning sun was already streaking through the curtains.

I got up, dressed, and went downstairs very quietly so that my aunt, who was in the kitchen, would not hear me. Then I let myself out the front door and made my way by the dunes to the church. The gate was half open; I went through and up the path where the gravestones stood on either side, emerging gray and chillingly remote from the grass, only tipped yet with a glimmer of morning light; but the little yellow daisies were there and a few poppies shedding their scarlet petals on the faint drift of wind.

It did not take me long to find the old man's resting place. I recognized it from the curled-up, carefully arranged skeleton of the little yellow dog that lay innocently close to a mound of grass topped by a simple stone.

With a lump in my throat, I went closer and read the epitaph:

Sacred to the memory of William Thomas, born 1869, died 1939.

And lower down, smaller, and more frailly inscribed:

In life he dearly loved his dog and died mourning him.

Just then two tiny butterflies flew down from the sky. I held out my hand, and one fluttered and rested there for a second, velvet-bright in the morning dew.

Then I turned and went back to the house.

Later, when I'd had breakfast, I returned to the churchyard. The pearly white skeleton no longer lay by the grassy mound. But a gardener was cleaning up, and I wondered if he'd moved it away. It didn't matter, because I felt that everything was all right.

And that night I knew.

I saw them from my window, walking along the sand just below the dunes. But the old man seemed taller, more erect, and gold in the golden light of evening, as gold as the little yellow dog trotting happily by his side. Once my sandman stopped and threw a stick, and I watched the little dog bound on after it, laughing, I was sure, as he'd laughed with me. I stayed at the window, staring after them until the fading sky enfolded them, leaving nothing behind but the wide expanse of beach below the sand hills where the rushes blew.

I never saw them again; and no one else ever knew what had happened. In any case, no one really cared except for me; the secret was mine alone . . . mine, the sandman's, and the little yellow dog's, who had been lost in the dunes, rabbiting probably.

Sometimes, even now, after so many years, I look back and remember, reclaimed by that other world of blue butterflies and yellow daisies . . . the world of childhood, where dreams so often have a potency for transcending physical reality and perhaps more of truth.

Who knows?

I, for one, am not prepared to answer.

THE PIPER AT THE GATES OF DAWN

Kenneth Grahame *from* The Wind in the Willows

Portly, Otter's youngest child, is lost. Rat and Mole decide to row up the river at night and look for him. . . .

THEY GOT THE boat out, and the Rat took the sculls, paddling with caution. Out in midstream there was a clear, narrow track that faintly reflected the sky; but wherever shadows fell on the water from bank, bush, or tree, they were as solid to all appearances as the banks themselves, and the Mole had to steer with judgment accordingly. Dark and deserted as it was, the night was full of small noises, song and chatter and rustling, telling of the busy little population that were up and about, plying their trades and vocations through the night till sunshine should fall on them at last and send them off to their well-earned repose. The water's own noises, too, were more apparent than by day, its gurglings and "cloops" more unexpected and near at hand.

The line of the horizon was clear and hard against the sky. At last, over the rim of the waiting earth, the moon lifted with slow majesty till it swung clear of the horizon and rode off, free of moorings; and once more they began to see surfaces—meadows widespread, and quiet gardens, and the river itself from bank to bank, all softly disclosed, all washed clean of mystery and terror, all radiant again as by day, but with a difference.

Fastening their boat to a willow, the friends landed in

this silent, silver kingdom and patiently explored the hedges, the hollow trees, the runnels and their little culverts, the ditches and dry waterways. Embarking again and crossing over, they worked their way up the stream in this manner, while the moon, serene and detached in a cloudless sky, did what she could, though so far off, to help them in their quest, till her hour came and she sank earthward reluctantly and left them, and mystery once more held field and river.

Then a change began. The horizon became clearer, field and tree came more into sight, and somehow with a different look; the mystery began to drop away from them. A bird piped suddenly and was still; and a light breeze sprang up and set the reeds and bulrushes rustling. Rat, who was in the stern of the boat while Mole sculled, sat up suddenly and listened with a passionate intentness. Mole, who with gentle strokes was just keeping the boat moving while he scanned the banks with care, looked at him with curiosity.

"It's gone!" The Rat sighed, sinking back in his seat again. "So beautiful and strange and new! Since it was to end so soon, I almost wish that I had never heard it. For it has roused a longing in me that is pain, and nothing seems worthwhile but just to hear that sound once more and go on listening to it forever. No! There it is again!" he cried, alert once more. Entranced, he was silent for a long space, spellbound.

"Now it passes on, and I begin to lose it," he said presently. "Oh, Mole! The beauty of it! The merry bubble and joy, the thin, clear, happy call of the distant piping! Such music I never dreamed of, and the call in it is stronger even than the music is sweet! Row on, Mole, row! For the music and the call must be for us."

The Mole, greatly wondering, obeyed. "I hear nothing myself," he said, "but the wind playing in the reeds and rushes and osiers."

The Rat never answered. Rapt, transported, trembling, he was possessed in all of his senses by this new divine thing that caught up his helpless soul and swung and dandled it, a powerless but happy infant in a strong, sustaining grasp.

In silence, Mole rowed steadily, and soon they came to a point where the river divided, a long backwater branching off to one side. With a slight movement of his head, Rat, who had long dropped the rudder lines, directed the rower to take the backwater. The creeping tide of light gained and gained, and now they could see the color of the flowers that gemmed the water's edge.

"Clearer and nearer still," cried the Rat joyously. "Now you must surely hear it! Ah—at last—I see you do!"

Breathless and transfixed, the Mole stopped rowing as that glad piping broke on him like a wave, caught him up, and possessed him utterly. He saw the tears on his comrade's cheeks and bowed his head and understood. For a space they hung there, brushed by the purple loosestrife that fringed the bank; then the clear, imperious summons that marched hand in hand with the intoxicating melody imposed its will on Mole, and mechanically he bent to his oars again. And the light grew steadily stronger, but no birds sang as they were wont to do at the approach of dawn; and but for the heavenly music all was marvelously still.

On either side of them as they glided onward, the rich meadow grass seemed that morning of a freshness and greenness unsurpassable. Never had they noticed the roses so vivid, the fireweed so riotous, the meadowsweet so odorous and pervading. Then the murmur of the approaching weir began to hold the air, and they felt a consciousness that they were nearing the end, whatever it might be.

A wide half circle of foam and glinting lights and shining shoulders of green water, the great weir closed the backwater from bank to bank, troubled all the quiet surface with twirling eddies and floating foam streaks, and deadened all other sounds with its solemn and soothing rumble. In midmost of the stream, embraced in the weir's shimmering arm spread, a small island lay anchored, fringed close with willows and silver birches and alders.

Slowly, but with no doubt or hesitation whatever, and in something of a solemn expectancy, the two animals passed through the broken, tumultuous water and moored their boat at the flowery margin of the island. In silence they landed and pushed through the blossoms and scented herbage and undergrowth that led up to the level ground, till they stood on a little lawn of a marvelous green, set around with Nature's own orchard trees—crab apple, wild cherry, and sloe.

"This is the place of my song dream, the place the music played to me," whispered the Rat, as if in a trance. "Here, in this holy place, here if anywhere, surely we shall find Him!"

Then suddenly the Mole felt a great awe fall upon him, an awe that turned his muscles to water, bowed his head, and rooted his feet to the ground. It was no panic terror—indeed, he felt wonderfully at peace and happy—but it was an awe that smote and held him, and, without seeing, he knew it could only mean that some august presence was very, very near. With difficulty, he turned to look for his friend and saw him at his side, cowed, stricken, and trembling violently. And still there was utter silence in the populous bird-haunted branches around them; and still the light grew and grew.

Perhaps he would never have dared to raise his eyes, but that, though the piping was now hushed, the call and the summons seemed still dominant and imperious. He might not refuse, were Death himself waiting to strike him instantly, once he had looked with mortal eye on things rightly kept hidden. Trembling, he obeyed and raised his humble head; and then, in that utter clearness of the imminent dawn, while Nature, flushed with fullness of incredible color, seemed to hold her breath for the event, he looked in the very eyes of the Friend and Helper; saw the backward sweep of the curved horns, gleaming in the growing daylight; saw the stern, hooked nose between the kindly eyes that were looking down on them humorously, while the bearded mouth broke into a half smile at the corners; saw the rippling muscles on the arm that lay across the broad chest, the long, supple hand still holding the panpipes only just fallen away from the parted lips; saw the splendid curves of the shaggy limbs disposed in majestic ease on the sward; saw, last of all, nestling between his very hooves, sleeping soundly in entire peace and contentment, the little, round, chubby, childish form of the baby otter. All this he saw, for one moment breathless and intense, vivid on the morning sky; and still, as he looked, he lived; and still, as he lived, he wondered.

"Rat!" he found breath to whisper, shaking. "Are you afraid?"

"Afraid?" murmured the Rat, his eyes shining with unutterable love. "Afraid! Of *Him*? Oh, never, never! And yet—and yet—oh, Mole, I am afraid!"

Then the two animals, crouching to the earth, bowed their heads and did worship.

Sudden and magnificent, the sun's broad golden disk showed itself over the horizon facing them; and the first rays, shooting across the level water meadows, took the animals full in the eyes and dazzled them. When they were able to look once more, the Vision had vanished, and the air was full of the carol of birds that hailed the dawn.

As they stared blankly, in dumb misery deepening as they slowly realized all they had seen and all they had lost, a capricious little breeze, dancing up from the surface of the water, tossed the aspens, shook the dewy roses, and blew lightly and caressingly in their faces, and with its soft touch came instant oblivion. For this is the last best gift that the kindly demigod is careful to bestow on those to whom he has revealed himself in their helping: the gift of forgetfulness. Lest the awful remembrance should remain and grow and overshadow mirth and pleasure and the great haunting memory should spoil all of the afterlives of little animals helped out of difficulties, in order that they should be as happy and lighthearted as before.

Mole rubbed his eyes and stared at Rat, who was looking around him in a puzzled sort of way. "I beg your pardon; what did you say, Rat?" he asked.

"I think I was only remarking," said Rat slowly, "that this

was the right sort of place and that here, if anywhere, we should find him. And look! Why, there he is, the little fellow!" And with a cry of delight, he ran toward the slumbering Portly.

But Mole stood still a moment, held in thought. As one wakened suddenly from a beautiful dream who struggles to recall it and can recapture nothing but a dim sense of the beauty of it. Till that, too, fades away in its turn, and the dreamer bitterly accepts the hard, cold waking and all of its penalties; so Mole, after struggling with his memory for a brief space, shook his head sadly and followed the Rat.

Portly woke up with a joyous squeak and wiggled with pleasure at the sight of his father's friends, who had played with him so often in past days. In a moment, however, his face grew blank, and he fell to hunting around in a circle with a pleading whine. As a child who has fallen happily asleep in his nurse's arms and wakes to find himself alone and laid in a strange place, and searches corners and cupboards, and runs from room to room, despair growing silently in his heart, even so Portly searched the island and searched, dogged and unwearying, till at last the black moment came for giving it up and sitting down and crying bitterly.

The Mole ran quickly to comfort the little animal; but Rat, lingering, looked long and doubtfully at certain hoof marks deep in the sward.

"Some—great—animal—has been here," he murmured slowly and thoughtfully and stood musing, musing, his mind strangely stirred.

"Come along, Rat!" called the Mole. "Think of poor Otter, waiting up there by the ford!"

Portly had soon been comforted by the promise of a treat—a jaunt on the river in Mr. Rat's real boat; and the two animals conducted him to the water's side, placed him securely between them in the bottom of the boat, and paddled off down the backwater.

"I feel strangely tired, Rat," said the Mole, leaning wearily over his oars as the boat drifted. "It's being up all night, you'll say, perhaps; but that's nothing. We do as much half the nights of the week, at this time of the year. No; I feel as if I had been through something very exciting and rather terrible, and it was just over; and yet nothing particular has happened."

THE LILIES

Alison Prince

I STOPPED AT the chapel on my way home from school to see if they had been throwing their flowers away again. It was an ugly building made of bricks as dark as ox liver, with an iron railing in front of it with spikes on top. My mother said it looked as if it was meant for cold storage rather than worship. The chapel seemed black and awful to me, like the smell of gas or like the rubber galoshes that Mrs. Parfitt across the street wore over her shoes on wet days. But I had to see about the flowers.

I pushed the iron gate open and went around the side of the building. Its windows were high up, and there were slabs of stone in the wall commemorating the death of people with names like Edwin Pugh and Gladys Bowker. A neat, sad little row of lobelia plants set among granite chips looked up at me mournfully, but the salvias planted behind them didn't say a word. Salvias, though brave souls, are sadly lacking in imagination.

Outside the back door of the chapel there was a garbage can. I took off the lid and looked in. Sure enough, on top of a pile of used cardboard beakers, there were three dead lilies. Their long, white blooms were brown and shriveled now, and their stems were slimy from being in water too long. I lifted them out carefully.

The back door opened, and the Reverend Evans came out. His face knotted in a frown when he saw me. "Sarah

Mulloy, you are at it again!" he said angrily. I dropped the lid back on the can and fled. "I'll be coming to see your mother!" he shouted after me. "What you are doing is pagan, do you hear me? Pagan!"

I ran down the street with my hair flying out behind me and the dead lilies flopping up and down in my arms. The terraces of houses seemed to bump up and down with me as I ran, jogging behind their stone steps and clipped privet hedges as if they were alive, instead of dozing with half-shut eyes behind their curtained windows. Welsh houses were never considered to be respectable unless their curtains were kept almost closed. On the downhill side of the street the land fell away to the disused railroad and the greened-over slag heaps, and on the other side the mountain reared up against the sky.

I hated the Reverend Evans. I hated the way that his black jacket was too small for him, with the sleeves too short so that his wrists poked out and made his brown-mottled hands seem even bigger. I hated the collar that cut into his thick neck and the pale, square face and the gray hair sticking up in a crest like an angry parrot.

I turned up the hill between the co-op and the Black Bull, where the doorsteps were high at one corner and low at the other because of the steep slope, and then turned left past Mrs. Parfitt's. Our house was the last on that narrow street. There was nothing after us except the mountain. I could see my mother in the garden—at least I could see the top half of her above the waist-high lupines and Canterbury bells. Her head was bent as she stooped to talk to the flowers, and strands of hair were escaping as always from the pinned-up mass of it. She looked up and saw me. "There you are, my darling!" she called. She had never lost her Irish accent, although it was years since she and my father had come across from Ireland in search of work. I had been born here, and my father lay buried in the steep cemetery behind the Catholic church; but my mother had never become Welsh. She made her way between the flowers to see what I carried.

"Ah, the poor souls," she said when she saw the lilies. She gathered them gently from me and set off around the side of the house to the backyard, sloping away up the hill. At the end was our graveyard. A spade leaned against the wall, and I took it and began to dig a hole big enough to accommodate the lilies. When it was done, my mother knelt down and laid the dead flowers in it. "From earth you came, to earth you shall return," she said. "And God's blessing be upon you." I said, "Amen," and then shoveled the earth back on top of the lilies. We wrote their name and the date on a small white marker and stuck it in the earth to show where they lay. Our graveyard was full of such markers, like a field of small plastic tombstones.

"What's for dinner?" I asked, dusting my hands.

"I think we'll have scrambled eggs," my mother said.

We had just finished when there was a banging at the front door.

"Will you listen to that?" said my mother, not moving. "Who could it be, coming to the front? That door has never been opened in years."

"I'll go and tell them to come around the back," I said, getting up, but with a sinking of the heart, for something told me that it would be the Reverend Evans. Sure enough, it was. His black coat was tightly buttoned, and his large face was grim. He followed me around to the kitchen door, but his eyes were darting around, and instead of coming in, he stopped and said, "I want you to show me the place."

"What place?" I asked, although I knew what people said about us. And I knew that he listened.

"The place where you bury these flowers," he said. "There has been a lot of wild talk going on. People murmur of witchcraft. It's bad for the village."

My mother had come to the kitchen door in time to hear this. "The village!" she said with contempt. "All scrubbed white doorsteps and drawn curtains, but devil a one of them has a good word to say about another. They're a black-hearted, treacherous bunch. Don't be talking to me about the village."

The flowers were listening, and they shrank together a little. There was a bad feeling from the man with his angry hair and his pale, bulging eyes.

"We only lay the flowers to rest," I told him. "So that their bodies return to the soil and their souls return to God, from whence they came."

"Sacrilege!" shouted the Reverend Evans, raising a quivering fist against the sky. "I will not have pagan rites conducted in this village! Where is the place? I will find it!" He charged up the sloping yard like a black bull and stopped as if poleaxed when he came to the graveyard.

"Disgusting!" he said between clenched teeth, and beads of sweat stood out on his forehead. "A parody of human decency!"

He grabbed the spade that stood against the wall and

started to swipe wildly at the little plastic gravestones, scattering them aside and cutting gouges in the earth. A thin cry went up from the foxgloves and the shaggy red poppies and was echoed along the gray leaves of the alyssum and through the wild thyme that grew between the flagstones, until the whole garden vibrated in protest.

My mother wasted no words. She reached out a brown hand and grabbed the spade, and for a few seconds she and the Reverend Evans were locked in a tussle for its possession. But my mother was used to hard work, and she was stronger than the flabby man for whom a smile was a taxing of the muscles. She wrested the spade away from him, and its sudden loss threw him off balance. He grabbed for support at a great sunflower whose face was turned to the sky as if trying not to look at the man, but its thick, hairy stem broke in his grasp. He fell awkwardly, flinging his hand up as if to grab at something else, and the back of his head smacked against the wall with a sound like the breaking of a huge hard-boiled egg.

"Ohhhh," breathed the flowers in a waft of scent and relief. "The stupid man," said my mother, staring down at the Reverend Evans, who lay like a sack of soot among the plastic gravestones. "He should have stayed down there in his chapel."

It was very quiet. The broken-off sunflower lay across the black-clad chest, smiling blandly up at the sky. Its broad, dinner-plate face was studded with ripening seeds, so it had no resentment. I knelt down and looked carefully at the Reverend Evans. His face was very white, and it didn't have any meaning. He seemed to have turned into a thing instead of a person. A trickle of blood was making its way over the back of his stiff collar to soak into the earth. The plants would like that, I thought. As good as a dead rat in a leek trench.

My mother stood leaning on the spade, looking down at the black heap of a man. "When I die," she said thoughtfully, "you must bury me here."

"Not in the churchyard?" I asked. "Not with my father?" But I knew what she meant.

"It would be such a pity to waste me," she said and ran her finger gently up the wide-open bells of the campanula that leaned against her apron.

It took us a long time to bury the Reverend Evans. Not only was he very large, but redisposing the mortal remains of the flowers already in the graveyard was time-consuming. At last it was all done, and the earth was raked smooth between the neat rows of little plastic gravestones. The presence of the man had created quite a hump.

I sat back on my heels. It was almost dark. "Shouldn't we put a marker in for him?" I said.

My mother looked faintly puzzled. "But he is fertilizer, child," she said. So we put the tools away in the shed and went inside for a mug of cocoa before bed.

I felt a little worried. The house plants did their best to console me, holding up the gentle patterning of their leaves and stretching their petals wide despite the lateness of the night, but I was fearful of what the morning would bring. I had good reason to fear the village people, for the children I went to school with had all been told by their parents that my mother was a witch. And I, the witch's child, was the one whose hands were burned with hot match ends behind the cycle shed, to see if it hurt. I had no friends at school. Although each face was different, made individual by a freckled nose or a missing tooth, the eyes were all the same, lit with a cruel curiosity. Tomorrow was Saturday, a blessed respite from torment. I could stay with the flowers, and they would heal the wounds of the week with the simple truth of their existence. But what of the Reverend Evans? People would come looking for him.

"Don't look so worried, my darling," said my mother as I picked up my candle to go to bed. "God is in the garden. It is vain of us to be troubled when he knows everything." And I kissed her and went up the stairs with the candle shadows leaping on either side of me, up to my little room where the morning glory had wandered in through my window under the thatch and now waited with closed buds for the dawn.

The sun was streaming in when I woke up. The morning glory had opened her china-blue flowers, and I ran to the window and looked out. My mother was at the end of the garden beside the graveyard, on her knees. Her hands were clasped and her head bent in prayer. That was strange, I thought. She would hardly pray for the soul of the Reverend Evans. One did not pray for fertilizer. I put on my dress and ran downstairs.

As I approached the graveyard, I saw why my mother was kneeling. The earth that we had left raked and bare the night before was green with young plants. Poppies and sweet Williams, snapdragons and pansies, and love-in-a-mist were all thrusting their way upward, growing from their dead parents before our very eyes. And chief among them all were the pale spears of the three white lilies that I had brought home only yesterday from the garbage can behind the chapel. I could not believe what I saw. The God of our garden had truly wrought a miracle. I met my mother's eyes and found in her face the same astonishment and gratitude that I felt myself. And there was, too, the same effort to suppress an unspeakable giggle.

"The lilies," I began carefully. "We put them—" I could not say it.

My mother composed her lips to banish any hint of a smile before she completed my sentence. "Underneath the Reverend Evans," she said with precision. "Yes." We stared in silence at the sharp tips of the lily shoots, already a hand span tall. Then my mother got to her feet, dusted the earth from her long skirt, and went back to the kitchen with me, for she had left a batch of bread dough proving before the fire.

They never found the Reverend Evans, although ours was one of the first houses that the police came to. They searched the cottage and then went into the garden and stood there in their thick serge uniforms, staring around. The flowers stared back rather rudely, but the policemen did not notice. "What would you be looking for?" my mother asked them, and the fat policeman whose chin strap made pink grooves down the sides of his face said, "Signs of recent digging."

The flowers tittered among themselves. There was not an inch of soil to be seen between them, and the graveyard in particular was smothered with blooms of amazing size and opulence. The policeman's unhappy gaze rested on the three tall spikes of white lilies that stood like cathedral spires among the shorter plants. There was a brooding inwardness about them that would arrest the attention of anyone with the wit to see it. The policeman nodded at them grudgingly. "Nice, those," he said. "Sort of . . . pure." And then he and his partner trudged across the street to Mrs. Parfitt's.

Time went by, and at last I was able to leave school. I sold vegetables from a little stall at our gate, for the plants were glad to see their fruit put to its natural use as food for other living beings. But the barbarians who asked me to cut my flowers for them were turned away with no words wasted. Dry grasses and the beautiful skeletons of honesty they were welcome to, but nobody could make me slice through the stem of one of my living friends.

One warm evening I found my mother lying in the garden among the flowers, quiet and still, while the snow-in-summer touched her lips and her eyes with its silver fingers. I wept for the loss of her, and the flowers respected my grief. But they told me that time is unimportant and that death is only part of the pattern of growing and consuming and rebirth, and after a while their wisdom made me calm. I knew what I had to do. "It would be a pity to waste me," she had said.

I suppose that I should have waited until dark. The villagers who came for a pound of tomatoes and a cucumber stared when they saw me digging so deeply in the new graveyard that we had made where the end of the path used to be, and they did not seem to like the sight of my mother lying there among the flowers. A little while later the policemen came and brought with them some men wearing long, white coats. I was very angry with them, because they started to interfere with what I was doing, and it was no business of theirs. They dragged me away from my half-dug grave and stabbed me in the arm with something sharp. I was not in the least bit tired, for the sun still shone in the sky and it was nowhere near bedtime, but sleep came swimming over me. I cried out, and the white lilies remembered how I had saved them from their death behind the chapel and leaned toward me anxiously. I clutched their smooth stems, but I fell down, down, past the rosettes of the hollyhocks and past their strong leaves and even past the startled little rock rose, down to a darkness like that of the earth itself.

I woke in this strange place where the sky is hard and white and terribly close. All of my flowers had come with me, and the white walls were alive with them, touching me gently with leaf and tendril. After a while the people in white coats came in and stood around my bed, talking. They moved through strong stems and fleshy green leaves as if the room was empty, and the flowers laughed to see it.

My hands were aching, and when I looked to see why this was, I found that I was gripping the stems of the three white lilies with all of my strength. The people noticed this and tried to uncurl my fingers so that they could take away my lilies, but I screamed and held on tightly, and at last the people went away.

When I was alone again, the flowers wept. I stared at the hard, white, man-made sky that was so close above my head and knew that beyond it was the sun. I felt the strength of the lilies in my hands and the host of flowers crowded around me, dew-wet with their tears. Yes, they said. Yes. The strength of the lilies can penetrate all obstacles. Remember the Reverend Evans.

I got up from the bed where I had woken and laid the lilies carefully on the white sheet. Their dying faces smiled up. Trust us, they said. We will free you from this place. Carefully, I climbed back onto the bed and carefully lay down with the lilies underneath me, their heads below my heart.

A gale of fragrance comes from my flowers, for soon we will be out in the real world again, in God's blue, endless sky. Already the skin in the middle of my back is pricked by the spear-sharp tips of the growing lilies.

THE EMISSARY

Ray Bradbury

MARTIN KNEW THAT it was autumn again, for Dog ran into the house bringing wind and frost and a smell of apples turned to cider under trees. In dark clock springs of hair, Dog fetched goldenrod, dust of farewell summer, acorn husk, hair of squirrel, feather of departed robin, sawdust from fresh-cut cordwood, and leaves like charcoals shaken from a blaze of maple trees. Dog jumped. Showers of brittle fern, blackberry vine, marsh grass sprang over the bed where Martin shouted. No doubt, no doubt of it at all, this incredible beast was October!

"Here, boy, here!"

And Dog settled to warm Martin's body with all of the bonfires and subtle burnings of the season, to fill the room with soft or heavy, wet or dry odors of far traveling. In the spring, he smelled of lilac, iris, lawn-mowed grass; in the summer, ice-cream-mustached, he came pungent with firecrackers, Roman candles, pinwheels, baked by the sun. But autumn! Autumn!

"Dog, what's it like outside?"

And lying there, Dog told as he always told. Lying there, Martin found autumn as in the old days before sickness bleached him white on his bed. Here was his contact, his carryall, the quick-moving part of himself that he sent with a yell to run and return, circle and scent, collect and deliver the time and texture of worlds in town, country, by creek, river, lake, down cellar, up attic, in closet or coal bin. Ten dozen times a day he was gifted with sunflower seed, cinder path, milkweed, horse chestnut, or full-flame smell of pumpkin. Through the loomings of the universe, Dog shuttled; the design was hidden in his pelt. Put out your hand; it was there. . . .

"And where did you go this morning?"

But he knew without hearing where Dog had rattled down hills where autumn lay in cereal crispness, where children lay in funeral pyres, in rustling heaps, the leaf-buried but watchful dead, as Dog and the world blew by. Martin trembled his fingers, searched the thick fur, read the long journey. Through stubbled fields, over glitters of ravine creeks, down marbled spreads of cemetery yards, into woods. In the great season of spices and rare incense, now Martin ran through his emissary, around, about, and home!

The bedroom door opened.

"That dog of yours is in trouble again."

Mother brought in a tray of fruit salad, cocoa, and toast, her blue eyes snapping.

"Mother . . ."

"Always digging places. Dug a hole in Miss Tarkin's garden this morning. She's spittin' mad. That's the fourth hole he's dug there this week."

"Maybe he's looking for something."

"Fiddlesticks! He's too darned curious. If he doesn't behave, he'll be locked up."

Martin looked at this woman as if she was a stranger.

"Oh, you wouldn't do that! How would I learn anything? How would I find out things if Dog didn't tell me?"

Mom's voice was quieter. "Is that what he does—tell you things?"

"There's nothing I don't know when he goes out and around and back, *nothing* I can't find out from him!"

They both sat looking at Dog and the dry strewings of mold and seeds over the quilt.

"Well, if he'll just stop digging where he shouldn't, he can run all he wants," said Mother.

"Here, boy, here!"

And Martin snapped a tin note to the dog's collar:

MY OWNER IS MARTIN SMITH—TEN YEARS OLD—SICK IN BED—VISITORS WELCOME.

Dog barked. Mother opened the downstairs door and let him out.

Martin sat listening.

Far off and away you could hear Dog in the quiet autumn rain that was falling now. You could hear the barking-jingling fade, rise, fade again as he cut down alley, over lawn, to fetch back Mr. Holloway and the oiled metallic smell of the delicate snowflake-interiored watches he repaired in his home shop. Or maybe he would bring Mr. Jacobs, the grocer, whose clothes were rich with lettuce, celery, tomatoes, and the secret canned and hidden smell of red demons stamped on cans of deviled ham. Mr. Jacobs and his unseen pink-meat devils waved often from the yard below. Or Dog brought Mr. Jackson, Mrs. Gillespie, Mr. Smith, Mrs. Holmes, *any* friend or near friend, encountered, cornered, begged, worried, and at last shepherded home for lunch or tea and cakes.

Now, listening, Martin heard Dog below, with footsteps

moving in a light rain behind him. The downstairs bell rang. Mom opened the door; light voices murmured. Martin sat forward, face shining. The stair boards creaked. A young woman's voice laughed quietly. Miss Haight, of course, his teacher from school!

The bedroom door sprang open.

Martin had company.

Morning, afternoon, evening, dawn, and dusk, Sun and Moon circled with Dog, who faithfully reported temperatures of turf and air, color of earth and tree, consistency of mist or rain, but—most important of all—brought back again and again—Miss Haight.

On Saturday, Sunday, and Monday, she baked Martin orange-frosted cupcakes, brought him library books about dinosaurs and cavemen. On Tuesday, Wednesday, and Thursday, somehow he beat her at dominoes, somehow she lost at checkers, and soon, she cried, he'd defeat her handsomely at chess. On Friday, Saturday, and Sunday, they talked and never stopped talking, and she was so young and laughing and handsome, and her hair was a soft, shining brown like the season outside the window, and she walked clear, clean, and quick, a heartbeat warm in the bitter afternoon when he heard it. Above all, she had the secret of signs and could read and interpret Dog and the symbols that she searched out and plucked forth from his coat with her miraculous fingers. Eyes shut, softly laughing, in a gypsy's voice, she divined the world from the treasures in her hands.

And on Monday afternoon, Miss Haight was dead.

Martin sat up in bed, slowly.

"Dead?" he whispered.

Dead, said his mother, yes, dead, killed in a car accident a mile out of town. Dead, yes, dead, which meant cold to Martin, which meant silence and whiteness and winter coming long before its time. Dead, silent, cold, white. The thoughts circled around, blew down, and settled in whispers.

Martin held Dog, thinking, and turned to the wall. The lady with the autumn-colored hair. The lady with the laughter that was very gentle and never made fun and the eyes that watched your mouth to see everything you ever said. The other-half-of-autumn lady, who told what was left untold by Dog about the world. The heartbeat at the still center of a gray afternoon. The heartbeat fading . . .

"Mom? What do they do in the graveyard, Mom, under the ground? Just lay there?"

"*Lie* there."

"Lie there? Is that *all* they do? It doesn't sound like much fun."

"For goodness sake, it's not supposed to be fun."

"Why don't they jump up and run around once in a while if they get tired lying there? God's pretty silly—"

"Martin!"

"Well, you'd think that he'd treat people better than to tell them to lie still forever. That's impossible. Nobody can do it! I tried once. Dog tries. I tell him, 'Dead Dog!' He plays dead a while and then gets sick and tired and wags his tail or opens one eye and looks at me, bored. Boy, I bet sometimes those graveyard people do the same, huh, Dog?"

Dog barked.

"Be still with that kind of talk!" said Mother.

Martin looked off into space.

"Bet that's exactly what they do," he said.

Autumn burned the trees bare, and Dog ran still farther around, fording creek, prowling graveyard as was his custom, and back in the dusk to fire off volleys of barking that shook windows wherever he turned.

In the late last days of October, Dog began to act as if the wind had changed and blew from a strange country. He stood quivering on the porch below. He whined, his eyes fixed at the empty land beyond town. He brought no visitors for Martin. He stood for hours each day, as if leashed, trembling, and then shot away straight, as if someone had called. Each night, he returned later, with no one following. Each night, Martin sank deeper and deeper into his pillow.

"Well, people are busy," said Mother. "They haven't got time to notice the tag that Dog carries. Or they mean to come to visit, but forget."

But there was more to it than that. There was the fevered shining in Dog's eyes and his whimpering tic late at night, in some private dream. His shivering in the dark, under the bed. The way he sometimes stood for half the night, looking at Martin as if some great and impossible secret was his and he knew no way to tell it save by savagely thumping his tail or turning in endless circles, never to lie down, spinning and spinning again.

On October 13th, Dog ran out and didn't come back at all, even when after supper Martin heard his parents call and call. The hour grew late; the streets and sidewalks stood empty; the air moved cold around the house, and there was nothing, nothing.

Long after midnight, Martin lay watching the world beyond the cool, clear glass windows. Now there was not even autumn, for there was no Dog to fetch it in. There would be no winter, for who could bring the snow to melt in your hands? Father, Mother? No, not the same. They couldn't play the game with its special secrets and rules, its sounds and pantomimes. No more seasons. No more time. The go-between, the emissary, was lost to the wild throngings of civilization, poisoned, stolen, hit by a car, left somewhere in a culvert. . . .

Sobbing, Martin turned his face to his pillow. The world was a picture under glass, untouchable. The world was dead.

Martin twisted in bed, and in three days the last Halloween pumpkins were rotting in trash cans, papier-mâché skulls and witches were burned on bonfires, and ghosts were stacked on shelves with other linens until next year.

To Martin, Halloween had been nothing more than one evening when tin horns cried off in the cold autumn stars, children blew like goblin leaves along the flinty walks, flinging their heads, or cabbages, at porches, soap-writing names or similar magic symbols on icy windows. All of it as distant, unfathomable, and nightmarish as a puppet show seen from so many miles away that there is no sound or meaning.

For three days in November, Martin watched alternate light and shadow sift across his ceiling. The fire pageant was over forever; autumn lay in cold ashes. Martin sank deeper, yet deeper in white marble layers of bed, motionless, listening, always listening. . . .

On Friday evening, his parents kissed him good night

and walked out of the house into the hushed cathedral weather toward a motion-picture show. Miss Tarkin from next door stayed on in the parlor below until Martin called down that he was sleepy and then took her knitting home.

In silence, Martin lay following the great move of stars down a clear and moonlit sky, remembering nights such as this when he'd spanned the town with Dog ahead, behind, around, about, tracking the green-plush ravine, lapping slumberous streams gone milky with the fullness of the moon, leaping cemetery gravetones while whispering the marble names; on, quickly on, through shaved meadows where the only motion was the off-on quivering of stars, to streets where shadows would not stand aside for you but crowded all the sidewalks for mile on mile. Run now, run! Chasing, being chased by bitter smoke, fog, mist, wind, ghost of mind, fright of memory; home, safe, sound, snug-warm, asleep . . .

Nine o'clock.

Chime. The drowsy clock in the deep stairwell below. Chime.

Dog, come home and run the world with you. Dog, bring a thistle with frost on it or bring nothing else but the wind. Dog, where *are* you? Oh, listen, now, I'll call.

Martin held his breath.

Way off somewhere—a sound.

Martin rose up, trembling.

There, again—the sound.

So small a sound, like a sharp needle point brushing the sky, long miles and many miles away.

The dreamy echo of a dog—barking.

The sound of a dog crossing fields and farms, dirt roads, and rabbit paths, running, running, letting out great barks of steam, cracking the night. The sound of a circling dog that came and went, lifted and faded, opened up, shut in, moved forward, went back, as if the animal was kept by someone on a fantastically long chain. As if the dog was running and someone whistled under the chestnut trees, in mold shadow, tar shadow, moon shadow, walking, and the dog circled back and sprang out again toward home.

Dog! Martin thought, Oh, Dog, come home, boy! Listen, oh, listen, where have you *been*? Come on, boy, make tracks!

Five, ten, 15 minutes; close, very close, the bark, the sound. Martin cried out, thrust his feet from the bed, leaned to the window. Dog! Listen, boy! Dog! Dog! He said it over and over. Dog! Dog! Wicked Dog, run off and gone all these days! Bad Dog, good Dog, home, boy, hurry, and bring what you can!

Close now, close, up the street, barking, to knock clapboard house fronts with sound, whirl iron roosters on rooftops in the moon, firing off volleys—Dog! now at the door below . . .

Martin shivered.

Should he run—let Dog in or wait for Mom and Dad? Wait? Oh, God, wait? But what if Dog ran off again? No, he'd go down, snatch the door wide, yell, grab Dog in, and run upstairs so fast, laughing, crying, holding so tight that . . .

Dog stopped barking.

Hey! Martin almost broke the window, jerking it.

Silence. As if someone had told Dog to hush now, hush, hush.

A full minute passed. Martin clenched his fists.

Below, a faint whimpering.

Then, slowly, the downstairs front door opened. Someone was kind enough to have opened the door for Dog. Of course! Dog had brought Mr. Jacobs or Mr. Gillespie or Miss Tarkin, or . . .

The downstairs door shut.

Dog raced upstairs, whining, flung himself on the bed.

"Dog, Dog, where have you *been*, what have you *done*? Dog, Dog!"

And he crushed Dog hard and long to himself, weeping. Dog, Dog. He laughed and shouted. Dog! But after a moment he stopped laughing and crying, suddenly.

He pulled away. He held the animal and looked at him, eyes widening.

The odor coming from Dog was different.

It was a smell of strange earth. It was a smell of night within night, the smell of digging down deep in shadows through earth that had lain cheek by jowl with things that were long hidden and decayed. A stinking and rancid soil fell away in clods of dissolution from Dog's muzzle and paws. He had dug deep. He had dug very deep indeed. That *was* it, wasn't it? Wasn't it? *Wasn't it!*

What kind of message was this from Dog? What could such a message mean? The stench—the ripe and awful cemetery earth.

Dog was a bad dog, digging where he shouldn't. Dog was a good dog, always making friends. Dog loved people. Dog brought them home.

And now, moving up the dark hall stairs, at intervals

came the sound of feet, one foot dragged after the other, painfully, slowly, slowly, slowly.

Dog shivered. A rain of strange night earth fell seething on the bed.

Dog turned.

The bedroom door whispered in.

Martin had company.

JOHN PETTIGREW'S MIRROR

Ruth Manning-Sanders

THIS IS A story that my grandmother told me; nobody need believe it unless they wish, but everybody may believe it who will.

Well then, long ago there lived in a small seaside town an honest basket maker named John Pettigrew. He lived alone, for he had neither wife nor child, only an old shrew of a married cousin, Sarah Polgraine, who came in to cook and clean for him. John was as accustomed to Sarah's grumblings and scoldings as he was to the voice of the sea, and he did not notice them unless he was obliged to. He was grateful to her for looking after him, and, being thoroughly good-natured himself and inclined to think well of his fellows, he had a conviction that, underneath it all, Sarah was a good sort.

Underneath it all, *everyone* was a good sort, so it seemed to John; but, when he tried to tell Sarah this, she would sniff and say, "That's all *you* know!" And then she would point out everyone's faults and failings and tell John to "just look" at this, that, and the other one of their acquaintance! And John would shake his head and say, "That's a cockeyed way of looking, Cousin Sarah!" And Sarah would sniff again and say that her eyes saw plainly enough, and if some old fools would learn to face the facts, it would be more satisfactory for all concerned. But then John would chuckle. "You're better than your words, Sarah, *I* know!" And with that he would leave her and go out to the yard where he worked and where

86

the sound of her scolding voice reached him only faintly.

This yard of John's was built against the sea wall; there was a shed in it for wet weather and plenty of sunshine when the skies were clear; and there he would spend his days among the ozier bundles and the big and little baskets, of which some were severely practical and some cunningly decorated, according to his mood and fancy. A leisurely yet useful life was John's, with plenty of time for contemplation and for an occasional tune on his mouth organ when his fingers grew tired or his mind felt the need for refreshment.

One stormy afternoon in the late summer, John took a sack and went down to the seashore in search of wreck wood. The shore was littered with shining brown ribbons of seaweed, and the wood that he gathered was all tangled up with sand and shells. Great waves staggered and broke along the shore, and the run of them swirled up around John's feet so that sometimes he was ankle-deep and sometimes high and dry. From the tops of the breakers an off-sea wind flung foam into his eyes. The low and watery sun, shooting its rays from amid rapidly moving storm clouds, brightened the foam and flung wide mirrors of light across the backs and among the hollows of the mountainous waves that rose and fell beyond the breakers. And in these waves two seals, an old one and a young one, were merrily playing. Up they floated like things of cork, and down they dived as swift as birds flying; and when they dived, John saw the shadow of their bodies through the waves, and when they floated up, he saw their big eyes shining.

Blessed creatures! thought John. No need to ask if you are happy! And they do say that all of the wisdom of the deep unsearchable flows through your oily noddles!

A powerful gust of wind set him stumbling backward. The sun vanished in the gathering storm; between two close-packed clouds a wan fork of lightning flashed through the gray air; thunder rolled, echoing among the rocks; a deluge of rain dropped its murky curtains between John and all else; and through this curtain came the roar of the unsearchable deep where the seals played.

Time this old man was safe indoors! thought John. And he slung his sack over his shoulder and made for home.

What a night to be sure! In all of his long life John could not remember such another one. The wind boomed in the chimney, and the smoke blew down it; the light in the lamp jumped and flared and sooted the lamp glass. The windows shook and clattered as the rain lashed them. The wind flung itself against the door like a wild beast determined to get in; and, at every thud that the door gave, all of the crocks on the dresser set up a protesting rattle. From every crack and hole came shrieks, whistles, hootings, flutings, and trumpetings; and behind all sounded the steady roar of the sea, crazed and billowing, dementedly leaping the wall beyond John's yard and washing in among his ozier bundles and piles of baskets—even volleying under the kitchen door in a series of crazy chuckles and lunatic snickerings, which added their small frenzy to the general hubbub.

John set a sandbag against the door and hung up a blower in front of the fire. The storm seized the house in its fists and shook it, like a man rattling a dice box.

But the house is built upon a rock, thought John; and, offering up a prayer for those "that do business in deep waters," he put on his spectacles and took down his Bible.

"They mount up to the heaven; they go down again to the deeps. . . . They reel to and fro, and stagger like a drunken man, and are at their wits' end. Then they cry. . . ."

Bang! Crash! A wave hit the kitchen door with the roar of a cannon. And—hearken!—out there, a strange cry that was neither bleat, nor bark, nor the groan of a man. One cry, and then no more. If 'twere a fiend from hell, thought John, on such a night a man must open his door to it. And, laying his spectacles between the leaves of his Bible, he kicked the sandbag aside and pulled back the door.

The wind came into the kitchen with a whoop and a gallop; the lamp flared and went out; the fire roared, and the blower clattered on to the hearthstone. A wave leaped ghostly at the yard wall. John stopped in a pool of water, felt a fur-coated bundle lying there, dragged it over the threshold, slammed the door, and relit the lamp.

Then he stared at the fur-coated bundle. It was a young seal; its eyes were glazed, its hinder feet curled up, and its fore flippers sprawling. Dead and gone! thought John. And a while back so prettily playing! I guarantee your mammy told you to stay clear of the breakers. But youth is headstrong—and see what comes of it! He shook his head and stooped to run his hand over the gray, sodden body.

Hello, hello! What was this? The body gave a hump and a wiggle under John's caressing hand; a flipper waggled; the lackluster eyes kindled. The young seal was looking up at John Pettigrew with eyes of unutterable wisdom.

"Oh, well, come on, then, if that's the case, little fellow!" A delighted John lifted the seal in his arms and laid it carefully in front of the fire.

It was a merry evening they spent after that, John and his new companion. The little seal drank milk from a bottle and ate the fish that was meant for John's supper. And John, remembering that seals are fond of music, played it a tune on his mouth organ, and the little fellow clapped with his flippers and bleated for more. More milk, or more fish, or more tunes? John couldn't be sure; so he plied it with all three.

And then they both fell asleep, the seal on the hearthrug and John on the settle; for this was the first house companion he had ever possessed, and he didn't feel like going upstairs and leaving it lonesome.

But, in his dreams, an old seal came to him, and the tears were flowing from her eyes in silver streams; and it seemed to John that if he didn't stop the flow of those tears, they would presently drown the whole world. So, in the morning, when the wind had dropped and the sea heaved gray and sullen, as if in sulky apology for the havoc that it had caused, John carried his new friend through the wreckage in his yard, and over the bricks of fallen chimneys and the slates of torn roofs out in the street, and among piles of blown sand and great heaps of stones and seaweed, down to the shore, and there he pushed the little fellow out into the sea.

The little fellow spun around and around like a rudderless boat, as if it had forgotten which way to steer itself. And then it struggled out of the water and bleated after John; and when John turned for home, the little fellow came flipping and humping up the sand so fast that it reached the yard gate as soon as John did. So then John borrowed a boat, and rowed a long way out to sea, and dropped the little fellow gently overboard—and there was the little fellow spinning around and around once more and crying out so loud that half the town could hear it. And so pitiful was its cry that John was obliged to take it inside the boat again.

It came into John's mind, then, that perhaps the young seal was still suffering in some way from the bang that the breakers had given it and that it didn't feel able to fend for itself. "If only I could catch a glimpse of your mammy," he said, "I should know what to do." He looked this way and that over the sparkling water, but all he saw was a couple of gulls, circling and mewing. "Seal, mammy seal!" he called. But there was no answer.

"I don't know what may be in her mind—exactly," said John. "But I do think I'll have to care for you a while longer." And with that he pulled for home, while the young seal lay contentedly in the bottom of the boat and watched him with its wise eyes.

"Now," said Sarah Polgraine, "you can shoot the creature; and I'll make me a fur tippet for Sundays."

"I've never handled a gun in my life," said John with a chuckle. "And I don't intend to handle one now."

So then Sarah, who coveted the sealskin, carried on alarmingly and said that John couldn't keep an outlandish creature like that around the place and that if he was afraid to handle a gun, he could use a sharp knife. And it came into John's mind, then, that though both he and Sarah were looking at the little seal, yet they were seeing different things. *She* was seeing a fur tippet, and *he* was seeing a dearly loved child. So he told her his dream about the tears that might presently drown the whole world, and Sarah said, "Stuff and nonsense!" But it seemed to John that the young seal understood and nodded its head in approval. He went into the yard, cleaned up the mess that the storm had made, and set to work again; and the little seal watched him with its shining eyes. And when John crossed the yard, it crossed the yard; and when John sat at his trade, it lay at his feet; and when John played on his mouth organ, it made happy sounds and clapped with its flippers; and when John threw a ball, it caught the ball on its nose and spun it up and caught it again, which was very pretty to watch; and in the evenings it lay on the hearthrug and gazed at the fire; and so things went on for some days.

But John, much as he joyed in the company of his little friend, couldn't get the dream of an old seal with tear-streaming eyes out of his mind; and every day, when his work was done, he went down to the shore and looked into the gray, or the green, or the blue water for sight of the one that had shed those tears. And the little seal went with him, but it looked at John and not at the water.

And then, one day, through a wave as green and clear as glass, John saw the shape of a swimmer; and up came a round, glistening head, turning this way and that, as if in search of something. "There's your mammy at last," said John, "and it's into the water you go, my beauty, and no nonsense this time!"

And, so saying, he picked up the little fellow, and waded out as far as he could, and flung his playmate from him. Then he made a run for dry ground and hid behind a rock, with just his head poked out to watch what would happen. And first there was the young seal spinning around and around like a rudderless boat and crying after John; and then, out to sea, there was the old seal reared upright through a green wave and calling after the young one; and then there was the young one swimming out toward the green wave; and then there was nothing but the tossing water; and then a lifting wave bore the shapes of two swimmers in its bosom, and, as they floated up on the wave's crest, John saw their big eyes shining.

And now there was John going home, rejoicing that he had done right, but with a lonely feeling in his heart.

And is that the end of the story? No, indeed! Though it has taken some time in the telling, it is only the beginning; and what follows is what you may believe or not believe, as you will.

The next Sunday, John took a walk by the seashore. He wasn't exactly looking for the seals, you understand, but he was thinking about them—picturing to himself what life would be like in the deep places of ocean and of the things to be seen there, which no man has ever seen. And, all of a sudden, the thought came to him that man knew but little, and thought less, of the strangeness and power and glory of creation, and he took his mouth organ out of his pocket and began to play a hymn. Well, he hadn't played more than a bar of that hymn when, down in the bright water just beneath him, he saw the old seal swimming and balancing something on her nose. It wasn't a ball; but what it was John could not tell, for as she tossed it up and caught it again, it spun so quickly and flashed so magnificently that it made John's eyes water to look at it. And then—whiz!—it was flying through the air toward John, and he caught it in his two hands.

It was a small, round mirror—and such a mirror! The frame was fashioned like a garland of flowers, and the heart of each flower was a great pearl, the petals were rubies and sapphires, and the leaves emeralds. John turned it this way and that in admiration, till it chanced that he turned it so that its glass reflected the sea; and there beneath him he saw not a seal, but a beautiful woman with a child in her arms. The child wore a little crown of gold, and he stretched out his arms and waved to John, and the woman smiled at John very sweetly, and then they both disappeared under the water. And John stood staring into the mirror as if he couldn't believe his eyes.

He slanted the mirror to the sky and saw the clouds; they *were* clouds, you understand, and yet they were also palaces and towers, and great white swans, and majestic old men in snowy garments. He slanted the mirror to the earth and saw the flowers and the bushes; they *were* flowers and bushes, but the stems of the flowers were birds, and the leaves were wings, and every branch was a king with a jeweled crown. Oh, thought John, as he made for home, I shall never be tired of looking in *this* mirror! And, looking into it once again, he chanced to see his own face reflected; and he tucked the mirror hastily into his pocket, for he was almost ashamed to look at the glory and brightness, the majesty and beauty, of the lordly one who gazed kindly back at him.

Over against the sea wall he passed a group of old men in their Sunday clothes, lounging to watch the water; some of them were squinty, some potbellied and bandy, some sad, some foolish. I wonder now, thought John, what the mirror will make of this bunch! So he took it out of his pocket and slanted it upon them. And there they were—lords of the earth, every one of them: strong and straight, and handsome and brave, and dressed fit for the kingdom of heaven.

"If that's the way it is," said John to himself, "not only I, but all of the town, would be better for a peep into the mirror." And he got a strong nail and hung the mirror on his front door, which was always shut, because he never went in that way.

You may be sure that there was soon a crowd around the door, everyone jostling and pushing to have a look at themselves. Nobody knew quite what to make of what they saw: giddy girls came up and looked and went away hushed and awestruck; old men and women looked and walked down the street holding their heads high and smiling to themselves; young men looked and walked off as proud and solemn as priests at a sacrifice. And in the dawn, when the street was empty, a thief came by and coveted the frame for its precious stones; but, as he reached to unhook the mirror from its nail, he saw his face reflected, and it was the face of an angel. So he left the mirror where it was and tiptoed away; because, of course, angels are not thieves.

It would take too long to tell of all the people who looked into John Pettigrew's mirror and of what they saw there; but be sure that whoever looked saw nothing but beauty and goodness, because there was nothing else to see. And it wasn't long before there wasn't an evil, or a selfish, or a sick, or an angry person left in the town, because everyone remembered what they were really like and behaved accordingly. The prison was empty, the law courts were turned into a dancing school, and the policemen, after yawning for a while at street corners, got tired of doing nothing and took to growing strawberries. The mayor, by common consent, was left in authority; and if any citizen for a moment forgot himself and behaved foolishly, the mayor had but to order that he take a peep into John Pettigrew's mirror, and after that there was no more trouble with him.

There was only one person in the town who wasn't quite happy, and that was Sarah Polgraine. She was so used to grumbling and complaining, scolding and finding fault, that now, when everything was perfect and there was nobody left to find fault with, she felt like a pricked bubble. For what was the use of her having lived such an exemplary life, and worked herself to skin and bone, and done so much for John Pettigrew and a host of others, if it didn't give her the satisfaction of knowing herself to be more virtuous than anybody else in the town? All this nonsense about reflections in a mirror! *She* knew what people were like, and she knew what she was like, without any lying mirror to tell her! And so, every time she passed John Pettigrew's front door, Sarah Polgraine shut her eyes. For it seemed to her that the mirror had robbed her of her one pleasure in life.

That was an unhappy feeling to live with; and the unhappy feeling grew and grew, until there was no putting up with it. So one winter morning, when the wind was blowing half a hurricane and the sea was gray and angry, she rose with the first streak of daylight and ran to John Pettigrew's house and, shutting her eyes, unhooked the mirror, tucked it under her shawl, and went and stood on a rock by the seashore to throw the tiresome thing back to the deep places where it had come from. The wind was blowing so hard that she almost lost her balance, but she raised her arm and threw; and there was the mirror now, flashing out over the water with its myriad-colored jewels agleam in the rising sun. But, just as it left her hand, it happened that Sarah Polgraine for the first time saw her face reflected in it; and though it was but for a spinning second that she saw that face, certainly it was not the face of a woman who could do such an evil thing, and she began to weep bitterly and cried out in a loud voice, "Oh, what have I done? Give it back! Give it back!"

Then the round, glistening head of the old seal appeared on the top of a wave, balancing the mirror on her nose; and first she spun the mirror up and caught it, and then she gave it a toss and sent it flying back over the water to Sarah Polgraine.

Sarah Polgraine stretched out her hands; but what with the tears that were streaming from her eyes and the wind that was blowing her hair across them, she couldn't see anything clearly, and, instead of catching the mirror, she let it slip through her fingers. It was dashed against a rock and broke into a hundred pieces.

Sarah Polgraine scrambled off the rock and set up such a loud wailing that soon half the town was on the seashore. Some began to gather up the splinters, and they were the sensible ones, for in the fragments that they picked up they could still see, though cracked and piecemeal, the image of their glory reflected. Others began to blame Sarah Polgraine; and, as soon as they did that, she began to justify herself and clean forgot the face that she had seen for one spinning second in the mirror. And soon the place was echoing with angry voices and hot words, such as had not been heard in the town for many a long day. One man picked up the jeweled frame and said that he would have that, anyway; but another tried to wrench it from him, and then there were blows, as well as angry words. Hitting and snarling, the two of them fell off the rock into the sea, and there might have been murder done, had not a policeman, peacefully at work on the strawberry bed in his garden, heard the racket and come running to take up his official duties once again.

And so, it wasn't very long before the townspeople went back to their old ways, as if no such thing as a mirror from the unsearchable deep had ever hung outside John Pettigrew's door to show them a different image of themselves: the quarrelsome quarreled, the drunkards drank, the giglots giggled, and the thieves stole; the law courts were reopened, and the policemen put on their helmets and stood on street corners. In fact, as Sarah Polgraine said, it was shameful the way that people went on, and what the world was coming to she *couldn't* think!

Only the sensible ones, John Pettigrew among them, each cherished his piece of broken mirror and, by taking a peep into it now and then, carried the image of a lordly one in their minds and in their hearts.

Yes, that's the end of the story; except that whenever, as a young girl, things went crisscrossed with me and life seemed all awry, my grandmother, who was a wise and peace-loving old body, would smile and shake her head over my glum face and say, "Ah, child, you'd think differently if you could take a peep into John Pettigrew's mirror."

SREDNI VASHTAR

Saki (H. H. Munro)

CONRADIN WAS TEN, and the doctor had pronounced that the boy would not live another five years. The doctor counted for little, but his opinion was endorsed by Mrs. de Ropp, who counted for almost everything. Mrs. de Ropp was Conradin's cousin and guardian, and in his eyes she represented those three fifths of the world that are necessary and disagreeable and real; the other two fifths were summed up in himself and his imagination. Without his imagination, Conradin would have succumbed to Mrs. de Ropp long ago.

Mrs. de Ropp would never have confessed that she disliked Conradin, though thwarting him "for his good" was a duty that she did not find especially irksome. Conradin hated her with a desperate sincerity that he was perfectly able to mask. Such few pleasures as he could contrive gained an added relish from the likelihood that they would be displeasing to his guardian, and from the realm of his imagination she was locked out—an unclean thing.

In the dull, cheerless garden, overlooked by so many windows that were ready to open with a message not to do this or that or a reminder that medicines were due, he found little attraction. The few fruit trees were set jealously apart from his plucking, as though they were rare specimens; it would have been difficult to find a market gardener who would have offered ten shillings for their entire produce. In a forgotten corner, however, almost hidden behind a dismal shrubbery, was a disused tool shed, and within its walls Conradin found a haven. He had peopled it with a legion of familiar phantoms, evoked partly from history and partly from his own brain, but it also boasted two inmates of flesh and blood. In one corner lived a ragged-plumaged Houdan hen, on which the boy lavished an affection that had scarcely another outlet. Farther back in the gloom stood a large hutch with iron bars, the abode of a large polecat ferret, which a friendly butcher boy had once smuggled in, cage and all, in exchange for a long-secreted hoard of small silver. Conradin was dreadfully afraid of the lithe, sharp-fanged beast, but it was his most treasured possession. Its very presence in the shed was a secret and fearful joy, to be kept scrupulously from the knowledge of the Woman, as he privately dubbed his cousin. And one day he spun the beast a wonderful name, and from that moment it grew into a god and a religion. The Woman indulged in religion once a week at a church nearby and took Conradin with her, but to him the church service was alien. Every Thursday, in the dim and musty silence of the tool shed, he worshiped before the wooden hutch where dwelled Sredni Vashtar, the great ferret. Red flowers in their season and scarlet berries in the wintertime were offered at his shrine, for he was a god who laid some special stress on the fierce, impatient side of things, as opposed to the Woman's religion. And on great festivals, powdered nutmeg was scattered in front of his hutch, an important feature of the offering being that the nutmeg had to be stolen. These festivals were irregular and were chiefly appointed to celebrate some passing event. When Mrs. de Ropp suffered an acute toothache for three days, Conradin kept up the festival during the entire three days and almost succeeded in persuading himself that Sredni Vashtar was personally responsible for the toothache. If the malady had lasted for another day, the supply of nutmeg would have given out.

The Houdan hen was never drawn into the cult of Sredni Vashtar. Conradin had long ago settled that she was an Anabaptist. He did not pretend to have the remotest knowledge as to what an Anabaptist was, but he privately hoped that it was dashing and not very respectable.

After a while, Conradin's absorption in the tool shed began to attract the notice of his guardian. "It is not good for him to be puttering down there in all weathers," she promptly decided, and at breakfast one morning she announced that the Houdan hen had been sold and taken away overnight. With her shortsighted eyes she peered at Conradin, waiting for an outbreak of rage and sorrow, which she was ready to rebuke. But Conradin said nothing: there was nothing to be said. Something perhaps in his white-set face gave her a momentary qualm, for at lunch that afternoon there was toast on the table, a delicacy that she usually banned on the ground that it was bad for him, also because the making of it "gave trouble," a deadly offense in the middle-class feminine eye.

"I thought you liked toast," she exclaimed with an injured air, observing that he did not touch it.

"Sometimes," said Conradin.

In the shed that evening there was an innovation in the worship of the hutch god. Conradin had been wont to chant his praises; tonight he asked a boon.

"Do one thing for me, Sredni Vashtar."

The thing was not specified. As Sredni Vashtar was a god, he must be supposed to know. And choking back a sob as he looked at that other empty corner, Conradin went back to the world he so hated.

And every night, in the welcome darkness of his bedroom, and every evening in the dusk of the tool shed, Conradin's bitter litany went up: "Do one thing for me, Sredni Vashtar."

Mrs. de Ropp noticed that the visits to the shed did not cease, and one day she made a further journey of inspection.

"What are you keeping in that locked hutch?" she asked. "I believe it's guinea pigs. I'll have them all cleared away."

Conradin shut his lips tight, but the Woman ransacked his bedroom till she found the carefully hidden key and forthwith marched down to the shed. It was a cold afternoon, and Conradin had been bidden to keep to the house. From the farthest window of the dining room the door of the shed could just be seen beyond the corner of the shrubbery, and there Conradin stationed himself. He saw the Woman enter, and then he imagined her opening the door of the sacred hutch and peering down with her shortsighted eyes into the thick straw bed where his god lay hidden. Perhaps she would prod at the straw in her clumsy impatience. And Conradin fervently breathed his prayer for the last time. But he knew as he prayed that he did not believe. He knew that the Woman would come out presently with that pursed smile that he loathed so well on her face and that in an hour or two the gardener would carry away his wonderful god, a god no longer, but a simple brown ferret in a hutch. And he knew that the Woman would triumph always as she triumphed now and that he would grow ever more sickly under her pestering and domineering and superior wisdom, till one day nothing would matter much more with him, and the doctor would be proved right. And in the sting and misery of his defeat, he began to chant loudly and defiantly the hymn of his threatened idol:

Sredni Vashtar went forth.
His thoughts were red thoughts, and his teeth were white.
His enemies called for peace, but he brought them death.
Sredni Vashtar the Beautiful.

And then all of a sudden he stopped his chanting and drew closer to the windowpane. The door of the shed still stood ajar as it had been left, and the minutes were slipping by. They were long minutes, but they slipped by nevertheless. He watched the starlings running and flying in little parties across the lawn; he counted them over and over again, with one eye always on that swinging door. A sour-faced maid came in to set the table for lunch, and still Conradin stood and waited and watched. Hope had crept by inches into his heart, and now a look of triumph began to blaze in his eyes that had only known the wistful patience of defeat. Under his breath he began once again the paean of victory and devastation. And presently his eyes were rewarded: out through that doorway came a long, low, yellow-and-brown beast, with eyes a-blink at the waning daylight and dark, wet stains around the fur of jaws and throat. Conradin dropped on his knees. The great polecat ferret made its way down to a small brook at the foot of the garden, drank for a moment, and then crossed a little plank bridge and was lost to sight in the bushes. Such was the passing of Sredni Vashtar.

"Lunch is ready," said the sour-faced maid. "Where is the mistress?"

"She went down to the shed some time ago," said Conradin.

And while the maid went to summon her mistress to lunch, Conradin fished a toasting fork out of the sideboard drawer and proceeded to toast himself a piece of bread. And during the toasting of it and the buttering of it with much butter and the slow enjoyment of eating it, Conradin listened to the noises and silences beyond the dining room door. The loud, foolish screaming of the maid, the answering chorus of wondering ejaculations from the kitchen region, the scuttering footsteps and hurried calls for outside help, and then, after a lull, the scared sobbings and the shuffling steps of those who bore a heavy burden into the house.

"Whoever will break it to the poor child? I couldn't for the life of me!" exclaimed a shrill voice. And while they debated the matter among themselves, Conradin made himself another piece of toast.

MISS MOUNTAIN

Philippa Pearce

WHATEVER ELSE MIGHT be spring-cleaned in Grandmother's house, it was never her box room. Old Mrs. Robinson lived in a house with only two rooms upstairs, besides the bathroom: one was her bedroom; the other, the box room. This room fascinated her grandchildren, Daisy and Jim. It was around eight feet by six and so full of stuff that even to open the door properly was difficult. If you forced it open enough to poke your head around, you saw a positive mountain of things reaching almost to the ceiling—old suitcases, bulging cardboard boxes of all shapes and sizes, stringed-up piles of magazines, cascades of old curtains, and a worm-eaten chair or two.

Grandmother was teased about the state of her box room. She retorted with spirit: "There isn't as much stuff as there seems to be, because it's all piled up on the spare bed. The room's really a guest room. I'm only waiting for a bit of time to clear it."

Then everybody would laugh—Daisy and Jim and their father, who was Grandmother's son, and their mother, who was her daughter-in-law. Grandmother would join in the laughter. She always laughed a lot, even at herself.

If they went on to suggest lending a hand in the clearing of the box room, Grandmother stopped laughing to say, "I'd rather do it myself, thank you, when I have a bit of time." But she never seemed to have that bit.

She was the nicest of grandmothers: rosy to look at, and plump, and somehow cozy. She liked to spoil her grandchildren. Daisy and Jim lived in a neighborhood only just around the corner from Grandmother's little house, so they were always visiting her, and she them.

Then suddenly everything was going to change.

The children's father got another job that would mean the whole family moving out of the area, leaving Grandmother behind.

"Goodness me!" Grandmother said, cheerful about most things. "It isn't the end of the world! I can come and visit you for the day."

"Not just for the day," said young Mrs. Robinson, who was very fond of her mother-in-law. "You must come and stay—often."

"And the children shall come and stay with me," Grandmother said.

"Where shall we sleep?" Jim asked.

"You'll have to clear the guest room," Daisy said.

"Yes, of course," said her grandmother, but for a moment looked as if she had not quite foreseen that and regretted the whole idea. But really the clearing out of the box room ought to have been done years and years ago.

Grandmother said that she preferred to do all the work herself; but everyone insisted that it would be too much for her. In the end she agreed to let Daisy and Jim help her. Perhaps she thought that they would be easier to manage than their parents.

How much the box room held was amazing; and everything had to be brought out and sorted carefully. A lot went straight into the garbage; some things—such as the bundles of magazines and the curtains—went to the church hall for the next thrift sale; the chairs went onto the bonfire. Grandmother went through all of the suitcases and got rid of everything; the suitcases themselves were only fit to be given away. The cardboard boxes, Grandmother said, were going to be more difficult, so for the moment they were piled up in a corner of her bedroom.

They sorted and cleared for several days. Sure enough, under the mountain, there really had been a bed—narrow, but wide enough for Daisy (who was older and larger than Jim), and there was a mattress on it and pillows and blankets (only one moth-eaten enough for the garbage). Grandmother made the bed up at once with sheets and pillowcases from her linen closet.

"There!" she said. "My guest room!"

Daisy and Jim loved it. The room seemed so small and private, with old-fashioned wallpaper that must have been there before Grandmother moved in, all those years ago. The window looked over the yard and received the morning sun. (Of course, that meant that in the evenings the room got dark early.)

All that remained was to clear the cardboard boxes that were still in Grandmother's own bedroom. She said that she could do this herself in the evenings when the children had gone home. But Daisy thought that her grandmother already looked tired. She made her sit down in a chair, and the two children began going through the boxes for her. "We'll show you everything as we come to it," Daisy said.

Grandmother sighed.

For the first half hour, everything went out to the garbage—the cardboard boxes themselves and their contents, which turned out to be certificates of this and that and old programs and brochures and other souvenirs. Then they came to boxes of photographs, some of them framed. These delayed the children.

"Look, Daisy!" said Jim. "What a fat little girl!"

"Here she is again," said Daisy. "Just a little bit older and even fatter."

"It's me," said their grandmother and leaned forward from her chair to dart a hand between the two children and take the photographs and tear them in halves as trash.

"Grandmother!" they protested; but it was too late.

They found a framed wedding group of long ago with gentlemen in high-buttoned jackets and ladies wearing long dresses and hats toppling with feathers and flowers and fruit and bows.

"Was this your wedding, Grandmother?"

Grandmother said, "I'm not as old as *that*. I wasn't thought of then. That was the wedding of my mother and father."

The children peered. "So that's our great-grandfather and our great-grandmother . . ."

"And a couple of your great-great-aunts as bridesmaids," said their grandmother. She snorted. "I preferred not to go in for bridesmaids." She found them a photograph of her own wedding, with everybody still looking very strange and old-fashioned, but clearly their grandmother did not think so.

The children thought that the quaint wedding group of their great-grandparents would suit the little guest room. With their grandmother's agreement, they hung it there. All of the other photographs went down to the garbage.

The last of the cardboard boxes was a squarish one, from which Daisy now drew out a barrel-shaped container. The staves of the barrel, the bands encircling them, and the lid were all made of the same tarnished metal.

Grandmother said, "That's a cookie jar."

"Is it real silver?" asked Daisy.

"Yes," said Grandmother.

"How grand!" said Jim.

"Yes," said Grandmother. "Very valuable."

Daisy set the cookie jar respectfully on the floor where they could all admire it.

"It was in our house when I was a child," said Grandmother. "I never liked it."

"There's a curly 'H' on it," said Jim.

"For 'Hill,'" said Grandmother. "That was our last name. But I hated that cookie jar. I've always meant to get rid of it."

"Please, Grandmother!" cried Daisy. "You could stand it on the sideboard downstairs. It would look so nice. I'll polish up the silver." Their grandmother still stared unforgivingly at the jar. "Think, Grandmother; you could keep cookies in it for when we come to stay. Our favorite ones. I like chocolate chip best."

"I like pink sugar wafers," said Jim.

"Promise you'll keep it, Grandmother, to keep our cookies in," said Daisy.

Grandmother stopped looking at the cookie jar and looked at her grandchildren instead. Suddenly she jumped up to hug them. "Oh, yes!" she said. "For, after all, I'm lucky. Very, very lucky. I've got a guest room and two grandchildren who want to come and stay with me!"

The little guest room, so small and private, was ready for its first guest.

The first guest was Jim. Perhaps by rights it should have been Daisy, because she was the elder, but Jim was the one likely to be a nuisance during the family's move. So the night before the move and the first night after were spent by Jim in his grandmother's guest room. Then his father drove over and brought him back to their new home.

In the new house, everyone was tired with the work of getting things straight and might have been short-tempered with Jim's little-boy bounciness. But Jim was quieter than usual. They asked whether he had had a good time with his grandmother. Yes, he had gone shopping with her, and she had bought him a multicolored pen; and he had had sparklers in the yard after dark and peaches for both of his suppers; and Grandmother had had pink sugar wafers for him—his favorite.

"You're lucky to have a grandmother like that," said his mother.

"Reminds me of my own granny," said his father, "your grandmother's mother. She was a good sort too."

That night Daisy and Jim had to share a bedroom, because Daisy's room wasn't ready yet. Jim went to bed and asked his mother to leave the landing light on and the door ajar. "I thought you'd given that up," she said. "You're a big boy now." But she let him have his way.

Later, when Daisy came up, he was still awake.

Daisy said, "I'll be in my own room tomorrow night."

"I don't mind sharing."

Daisy got into bed.

"Daisy . . ."

"What?"

"I don't want to sleep here alone tomorrow night."

"But—but, Jim, you always sleep alone!" There was no reply from the other bed. "Jim, you're just being silly!"

Still no reply; and yet a little noise. Daisy listened carefully—Jim was crying.

She got out of bed and went to him. "What is it?"

"Nothing."

"It must be something."

"No, it's not. It's nothing."

Daisy knew Jim. He could be very obstinate. Perhaps he would never tell her about whatever it was.

"You'd feel better if you told me, Jim."

"No, I wouldn't."

He was crying so much that she put her arms around him. It struck her that he was shivering.

"Are you cold, Jim?"

"No."

"Then why are you shivering? You're not afraid of something?"

In answer, Jim gave a kind of gasp. "Leave me alone."

Daisy was extremely irritated—and curious, too. "Go on— say something. I won't leave you alone till you say something."

Still he did not speak; and Daisy amended: "If you say something, I won't argue—I'll go back to bed and leave you alone. But you must say something—something that is something."

Jim collected himself and said carefully, "I don't want to stay the night in Grandmother's house again—ever." He turned over in bed with his back to Daisy.

Daisy stared at him, opened her mouth, remembered her promise, shut up, went back to bed, and lay there to think. She tried to think what might have happened during Jim's visit to make him feel as he did. It occurred to her that she might find out when her turn for a visit came. . . .

How odd of Jim. There could be nothing to be afraid of at night in the house of the coziest, rosiest, plumpest of grandmothers.

The moment she fell asleep, she was standing on her grandmother's front doorstep, her suitcase in her hand. She had already knocked. The door opened just as usual; there stood her grandmother, just as usual. But no, not as usual. Her grandmother peered at Daisy as if at a stranger. "Yes?" she said. "I'm Daisy Robinson," said Daisy. "I'm your granddaughter. I've come to stay the night." Without a word, her grandmother stood aside to let her enter. At once Daisy began to mount the stairs that led to that early-shadowed little guest room. She already saw the door ajar, waiting for her. Behind her, downstairs she could hear her grandmother securing the front door for the night—the lock, the bolts, the chain: she shut the two of them in together for the night. Daisy could hear her grandmother's little laugh: she was chuckling to herself.

The rest of the dream—if there was any—had vanished by the time Daisy woke up in the morning. All she knew of it was that she was glad she could not remember it.

Daisy told no one about Jim, mostly because there was so little to tell. He seemed all right again, anyway. By that evening the bedrooms had been sorted out so that Jim had his to himself. Without protest, he went to sleep alone. It's true that he screamed in the night so that his mother had to go to him, but all children have nightmares sometimes. By the next night he had resumed his usual sound sleeping.

So, Jim had been making a strange fuss about nothing, Daisy thought; or perhaps he'd gotten used to the idea of whatever there might have been; or—not the most comfortable idea for Daisy—he had been able to shut it from his mind because he was now a safe distance from Grandmother's little guest room.

Their grandmother came to stay. She was her usual cheerful self, and everyone enjoyed the visit; Jim seemed to enjoy her company as much as usual. At the end of her visit, Grandmother said, "Well, which of you two is coming to sleep in my guest room next?"

Jim said, "It's Daisy's turn."

"That's very fair of you, Jim," their mother said approvingly. Daisy looked at Jim; but Jim stubbornly looked past her. She knew that he would not have agreed to go under any circumstances.

Only a few weeks later, Daisy went.

With her suitcase, she stood on her grandmother's doorstep. Twice she raised a hand to the knocker and twice let it fall. The third time, she really knocked. She heard the patter of her grandmother's feet approaching. The door opened, and there was Grandmother, and all the uneasy feelings that Jim had given her vanished away. Her grandmother was laughing for joy at her coming, and the house seemed to welcome her. Even from the doorway Daisy could see into the living room, where the electric light had not yet been turned on. An open fire burned brightly, and by the fireplace stood a tea table with the china on it shining in the firelight, and beyond that glowed the polish of the sideboard with the objects on it all giving as much glow or glitter as they could.

They had tea with hard-boiled eggs and salad, as time was getting on, and this had to be afternoon tea and supper together.

"Anything more you fancy, Daisy, dear?"

Daisy looked over to the sideboard, to the cookie jar. "Pink sugar wafers?" she said.

"What an idea!" said her grandmother. "They're not *your* favorite cookies!"

Daisy went over to the cookie jar and put her hand in. "Go on, dear, take whatever you find, as many as you want. I like you to do that."

Daisy drew out a chocolate-chip cookie. "Grandmother, you're wonderful! You never forget anything."

Grandmother sighed. "Sometimes I wish I was more forgetful."

Daisy laughed and munched.

Later, they went to bed. They stood side by side looking into the little guest room. With the curtains drawn and the bedside light glowing a pink shade from inside, the room looked as cozy and rosy as Grandmother herself. "I hope you sleep well, my dear," said her grandmother and talked about the number of blankets and the number of pillows and the possibility of noise from neighboring houses. Sometimes people had late parties.

"Did the neighbors disturb Jim?" Daisy asked suddenly.

"No," said her grandmother. "At least—he's a poor sleeper for such a young child, isn't he? He slept badly here."

Daisy glanced sideways to see her grandmother's expression when she had said this. She found her grandmother stealing a sideways glance at her. They both looked away at once, pretending nothing had happened.

"Remember," said Grandmother, "if you want anything, I'm just across the landing." She kissed Daisy good night.

Daisy decided not to think about that sideways glance tonight. She went to bed, slipped easily downhill into sleep, and slept.

Something woke her. She wasn't sure that it had been a noise, but surely it must have been. She lay very still, her eyes open, her ears listening. Before going to bed, she had pulled back the curtains so that she would wake to the morning sun. Now it was night, without moon or stars, and all of the lights of the surrounding houses had been extinguished.

She waited to hear a repetition of noise in the house, but there was none. She knew what she was expecting to hear: the creak of a stair. There was nothing, but she became sure, all the same, that someone was creeping downstairs.

It could be—it *must* be—her grandmother going downstairs for something. She would go quietly, for fear of waking Daisy. But would she manage to go so very, very quietly?

Whoever it was would have reached the foot of the stairs by now. Still no noise.

It must be her grandmother; and yet Daisy felt that it wasn't her grandmother. And yet again she felt that it was her grandmother.

She must know. She called "Grandmother!", pitching her voice high to reach the bottom of the stairs. The sound she made came out screamlike.

Almost at once she heard her grandmother's bedroom door open and the quick, soft sound of her feet bringing her across to the guest room.

"Here I am, dear!"

"I thought I heard—I thought you were going downstairs, Grandmother."

Grandmother seemed—well, agitated. "Oh, did you? Sometimes I need a drink of water in the night, and sometimes I do go downstairs for it."

"But it wasn't you. You came from your bedroom just now, not back up the stairs."

"What sharp ears you have, dear!"

"I didn't exactly *hear* anyone going downstairs, anyway," Daisy said slowly.

"So it was all a mistake. That's all right, then, isn't it?"

Not a mistake; more of a muddle, Daisy thought. But she let herself be kissed good night again, and her light was turned off. Her grandmother went back to bed. There was quiet in the house: not only no unusual sound, but no feel of anything unusual. Daisy slept until the morning sunshine.

The daytime was made as delightful for Daisy as her grandmother had made it for Jim. But evening came and night; and this night was much worse than the previous one.

Daisy woke up and lay awake, knowing that someone was creeping downstairs again. But it's my imagination, she told herself; how can I know, when I hear nothing?

Whoever it was reached the bottom of the stairs and crossed the hall to the living room door. Had Grandmother left that door closed or open when she went to bed? It did not matter. Whoever it was had entered the living room and was moving across to the sideboard.

What was happening down there in the dark and the silence?

Suddenly there was no more silence. From downstairs there was a shrill scream, which turned into a crying and sobbing, both terrified and terrifying.

Hardly knowing what she was doing, Daisy was out of bed, through her bedroom door, across the landing to her grandmother's room. The door was closed; she had to pause an instant to open it, and in that instant she realized that the crying from downstairs had stopped.

She was inside her grandmother's bedroom. The bedside light was on, and Grandmother, flustered, had just sat up in bed. Daisy said, "That crying!"

"It was me," said her grandmother.

"Oh, no, no, no, no!" Daisy contradicted her grandmother with fury. She glared at her in fury and terror: the nicest grandmother in the world was concealing something, lying. What kind of grandmother was she then—sly, perhaps treacherous? Wicked?

At the look on Daisy's face, Grandmother shrank back among the pillows. She hid her face in her hands. Between the fingers Daisy saw tears beginning to roll down over the dry, old skin. Grandmother was crying, with gasping sobs, and her crying was not all that different, but much quieter, from the crying that Daisy had heard downstairs.

In the middle of her crying, Grandmother managed to say, "Oh, Daisy!" and stretched out her hands toward her, begging her.

Daisy looked searchingly at her grandmother; and her

grandmother met her gaze. Daisy took the outstretched hands and stroked them. She calmed herself even while she calmed her grandmother. "I'll make us a pot of tea," she said. "I'll bring it up here."

"No," said her grandmother. "I'll come down. We'll have it downstairs, and I'll tell you—I'll tell you—" She began to cry again.

Daisy was no longer afraid. She went downstairs into the kitchen to boil a kettle. As she went, she turned on the living room light and switched on an electric fire. Everything was exactly as usual. The door had been shut.

From downstairs she heard her grandmother getting up and then coming out of her bedroom. She did not come directly downstairs. Daisy heard her cross the landing into the guest room, spend a few moments there, and then come down.

Daisy carried the tea on a tray into the living room; she took the cookie jar off the sideboard and put it on the tray, in case Grandmother wanted something to eat with her tea. Grandmother was already waiting for her. She had brought downstairs with her the framed wedding photograph from Daisy's bedroom and set it where they could both see it. Daisy asked no questions.

They sat together and sipped their tea. Daisy also nibbled on a cookie; her grandmother had shaken her head and shuddered when Daisy offered her the cookie jar.

"Now I'll tell you," said Grandmother. She paused, while she steadied herself, visibly. "I brought the wedding photo down so that I could *show* you."

Again she paused, for much longer; so Daisy said, "Your mother looked sweet as a bride."

"I never knew her," said Grandmother. "She died when I was very young."

Daisy said, "But Dad knew her! He talks about his granny."

"That was my stepmother; his step-grandmother."

Now something seemed plain to Daisy. "A stepmother—poor Grandmother!"

"No," said Grandmother. "It wasn't like that at all. My stepmother—only I never really think of her as my stepmother, just as my mother—she was a darling."

"Then—?"

"They're both in the group," said Grandmother. "My mother as the bride. My stepmother—as she later became—as one of the bridesmaids. The bridesmaids were my two aunts: one my mother's sister, whom my father married after my mother's death, and the other my father's sister."

Daisy studied the photograph. Now that she knew that one of the bridesmaids was the bride's sister, it was easy to see which one: there was the same plumpness with prettiness.

The other bridesmaid was tall, thin, and quite glum-looking. There was a resemblance between her and the bridegroom, but not such a striking one.

"When my mother died," said Grandmother, "I was a very little girl, still babyish in my ways, no doubt. My father had to get someone to look after me and run the house. He was in business and away at his office all day.

"He asked his sister to come—the other bridesmaid."

Daisy looked at the thin bridesmaid and wondered.

"She'd always been very fond of my father, I believe, and jealous of his having gotten married. Perhaps she was glad that my mother had died; perhaps she would have been glad if I had never been born. She would have had my father all to herself then. She hated me."

"Grandmother!"

"Oh, yes, she hated me. I didn't fully understand it then. I just thought I had suddenly become stupid and disobedient and dirty and everything that—as it seemed to me—anyone would hate. I daresay I was rather a nasty little girl: I became so. One of the worst things was—"

Grandmother stopped speaking, shaded her face with her hand.

"Go on."

"It won't seem terrible to you. You may just laugh. Aunt used to sneer. When she sneered, that made it worse."

"But what was it?"

"I ate."

"Well, but . . . "

"I ate whenever I could. I ate enormously at meals, and I ate between meals. Aunt used to point it out to my father and put a tape measure around where she said my waist should be as I sat at the table. I've always been plump, like my mother's side of the family. I grew fat—terribly fat.

"Our last name was Hill. There were two Miss Hills in the house, my aunt and myself. But Aunt said that there need be no confusion. She was Miss Hill; I was Miss Mountain. She called me Miss Mountain, unless my father was present. She would leave notes to me, addressed to Miss Mountain. Once my father found one and asked her about it, and she pretended that it was just a little joke between us. But it wasn't a joke—or if it was, it was a cruel, cruel one."

"Couldn't you just have eaten less and grown thinner and

spoiled her game?" asked Daisy.

"You don't understand. Her teasing me made me eat even more. I took to stealing food. I'd slip out to the pantry after Sunday dinner and tear the crisp pieces of fat off the meat while it was still warm. Or I'd take raisins out of the jar in the cupboard. Or I'd pare off bits of cheese. Even a slice of dry bread, if there was nothing else. Once I ate dog biscuits from the shelf above the kennel.

"Of course, sooner or later, Aunt realized what was happening. She began to expect it and took a delight in catching me. If she couldn't catch me at it, she would prevent me. She took to locking the kitchen door at night, because she knew I went down then to the cupboard and pantry.

"Then I found the cookie jar."

"This very cookie jar?"

"Yes. It always stood on the sideboard with graham crackers in it—just the plainest of cookies, to be eaten with fruit. Well, I didn't mind that. I used to creep down for a graham cracker or two in the middle of the night."

"In this house?"

"Goodness, no! We lived a hundred miles from here, and the house has been pulled down now, I believe.

"Anyway, I used to creep down, as I've said. I dared not put on any light, although I was terribly afraid of the dark—I had become afraid of so many things by then. I felt my way into the room and across to the sideboard and along it. The sideboard was rather grand, with a mirror, and all kinds of grand utensils were kept on it: the silver cream jug, a pair of silver candlesticks, the silver-rimmed breadboard with the silver-handled bread knife. I felt among them until I found

the cookie jar. Then I took off the lid and put my hand in."
She paused.

"Go on, Grandmother."

"I did that trip once, twice, perhaps three times. The third or fourth time seemed just as usual. As usual, I was shaking with fright, both at the crime I was committing and at the blackness in which I had to commit it. I had felt my way to the cookie jar. I lifted the lid with my left hand, as usual. Very carefully, as usual, I slipped my right hand into the jar. I had thought that there would be crackers at the top; but there were not. I had to reach toward the bottom—down—down—down—and then my fingers touched something, and at once there was something—oh, it seemed like an explosion!—something snapped at me, caught my fingers, held them in a bitter grip, causing me pain, but much more than pain: terror. I screamed and screamed and sobbed and cried.

"Footsteps came hurrying down the stairs, lights appeared, people were rushing into the dining room where I was. My father, my aunt, the maid—they all stood looking at me, a fat little girl in her nightgown, screaming, with her right hand extended and a mousetrap dangling from the fingers.

"My father and the servant were bewildered; but I could see that my aunt was not taken by surprise. She had been expecting this, waiting for it. Now she burst into loud laughter. I couldn't bear it. With my left hand I caught up the silver-handled bread knife from the sideboard, and I went for her."

"You killed her?"

"No, of course not. I was in such a mess with screaming and crying, and the knife was in my left hand, and my aunt sidestepped, and my father rushed in and took hold of me and grabbed the knife from me. Then he prized the mousetrap off my other hand.

"All this time I never stopped crying. I think I was deliberately crying myself sick. Through my crying I heard my father and my aunt talking, and I heard my father asking my aunt how there came to be a mousetrap inside the cookie jar.

"The next day either I was sick or I pretended to be—there wasn't much difference, anyway. I stayed all day in bed with the curtains drawn. The maid brought me bread and milk to eat. My aunt did not come to see me. My father came in the morning before he went to his office and in the evening when he got home. On both occasions I pretended to be asleep.

"The day after that I got up. The fingers of my right hand were still red where the trap had snapped across them, and I rubbed them to make them even redder. I didn't want to be well. I showed them to the maid. Not only were the fingers red, but two of the fingernails had turned black. The maid called my father in—he was just on his way to work. He said that the doctor should see them, and the maid could take me there that afternoon on foot. Exercise would do me good, and change. He looked at me as if he was about to say more, but he did not. He did not mention my aunt—who would have been the person to take me to see the doctor, ordinarily—and there was still no sign of her.

"The maid took me. The doctor said my fingers had been badly bruised by the blow of the mousetrap, but nothing worse. The fingernails would grow right. I was disappointed. I had hoped that my finger bones were broken, that my fingertips would drop off. I wanted to be sent to the hospital. I didn't want to go home and be well and go on as before—

little Miss Mountain as before.

"I walked home with the maid.

"As we neared our house, I saw a woman turn in at our gateway. When we reached the gate, she was walking up the long path to the front door. Now, I've said I never knew my own mother, to remember; but when I saw the back view of that young woman—she *stumped* along a little, as stoutish people often do—I knew that that was exactly what my mother had looked like. I didn't think beyond that; that was enough for me. I ran after her, as fast as I could; and as she reached the front door, I ran into her. She lost her balance, she gave a cry between alarm and laughter, and she sat down suddenly on the front doorstep, and I tumbled on top of her, and felt her arms around me, and burrowed into her, among the folds of all the clothing that women wore in those days. I always remember the plump softness and warmth of her body and how sweet it was. I cried and cried for joy, and she hugged me.

"That was my other aunt, the other bridesmaid—my mother's sister. My father had telegraphed for her to come from the other side of England, and she had come. My father had already sent my thin aunt packing—I never saw her again. My plump aunt moved in as the housekeeper, and our house was filled with laughter and happiness and love. Within the year, my father had married her. She had no child of her own by him, so I was her only child. She loved me, and I her."

"Did you—did you manage to become less stout?" Daisy asked delicately.

"I suppose I must have. Anyway, I stopped stealing food. And the cookie jar disappeared off the sideboard—my new mother put it away, after she'd heard the story, I suppose. Out of sight, out of mind: I forgot it. Or at least I pretended to myself that I'd forgotten it. But whenever it turns up, I remember. I remember too well."

"I've heard of haunted houses," said Daisy thoughtfully. "But never of a haunted cookie jar. I don't think it would be haunted if you weren't there to remember, you know."

"I daresay."

"Will you get rid of it, Grandmother? Otherwise Jim will never come to stay again; and I—I—"

"You don't think I haven't wanted to get rid of it, child?" cried her grandmother. "Your grandfather wouldn't let me; your father wouldn't let me. But, no—that was never the real explanation. Then, I couldn't bring myself to give them my reasons—to tell the whole story; and so the memory has held me, like a trap. Now I've told the story; now I'm free; now the cookie jar can go."

"Will you sell it, Grandmother? It must be worth a lot of money."

"No doubt."

"I wonder how much money you'll get and what you'll spend it on, Grandmother . . ."

Grandmother did not answer.

The next morning, Daisy woke to sunshine and the sound of her Grandmother already up and about downstairs. Daisy dressed quickly and went down. The front door was wide-open, and her grandmother stood outside on the doorstep, looking at something farther up the street. There was the sound of a heavy vehicle droning its way slowly along the street, going away.

Daisy joined her grandmother on the doorstep and looked where she was looking. The weekly garbage truck was droning its way along; it had almost reached the end of the street. The men were slinging into it the last of the trash that the householders had put out for them overnight or early that morning. The two rows of great metal teeth at the back of the truck opened and closed slowly, mercilessly, on whatever had been thrown into that huge maw.

Grandmother said, "There it goes," and at once Daisy knew what "it" was. "Done up in a plastic bag with my empty bottles and cans and the old fish-stick carton and broken eggshells and I don't know what else. Bad company—serves it right." The truck began to turn the corner. "I've hated it," said Grandmother. "And now it's being scrunched to pieces. Smashed to smithereens." Fiercely she spoke; and Daisy remembered the little girl who had snatched up a bread knife in anger.

The truck had turned the corner.

Gone.

Grandmother put her arm around Daisy and laughed. She said, "Daisy, dear, always remember that one can keep chocolate-chip cookies and pink sugar wafers for friends in any old jar."

WAS IT A DREAM?

Guy de Maupassant

I HAD LOVED her madly!

Yesterday I returned to Paris, and when I saw my room again—our room, our bed, our furniture, everything that remains of the life of a human being after death—I was seized by such a violent attack of fresh grief that I felt like opening the window and throwing myself out into the street. I could not remain between these walls, which had sheltered her, which retained a thousand atoms of her, of her skin and of her breath. I took up my hat to make my escape, and just as I reached the door, I passed the large glass in the hall, which she had put there so that she might look at herself every day from head to foot as she went out, from her little boots to her bonnet.

I stopped short in front of that mirror in which she had so often been reflected—so often, so often, that it must have retained her reflection. I was standing there trembling, with my eyes fixed on the glass—on that flat, profound, empty glass—that had contained her entirely and had possessed her as much as I. I felt as if I loved that glass. I touched it; it was cold. Sorrowful mirror, burning mirror, horrible mirror, to make men suffer such torments! Happy is the man whose heart forgets everything that it has contained.

I went out without knowing it toward the cemetery. I found her simple grave, a white marble cross, with these few words:

She loved, was loved, and died.

She is there below. I sobbed with my forehead on the ground, and I stopped there for a long time. Then I saw it was getting dark, and a strange, insane wish, the wish of a despairing lover, seized me. I wished to pass the night weeping on her grave. But I should be seen and driven out. How was I to manage? I was cunning and got up and began to roam that city of the dead. I walked and walked. How small this city is in comparison with the city in which we live. And yet how much more numerous the dead are than the living. We need high houses, wide streets, and much room. And for all of the generations of the dead, there is scarcely anything. The earth takes them back. Adieu!

At the end of the cemetery, I was in its oldest part, where the crosses themselves are decayed. It is full of untended roses, of strong and dark cypress trees—a sad and beautiful garden.

I was perfectly alone. So I crouched under a green tree and hid myself amid the thick and somber branches.

When it was very dark, I left my refuge and began to walk softly. I wandered around for a long time, but could not find her tomb again. I went on with extended arms, knocking against the tombs with my hands, my feet, my knees, my chest, even with my head, without being able to find her. I groped around like a blind man; I felt the stones, the crosses, the iron railings, and the wreaths of faded flowers. I read the names with my fingers. I could not find her again!

There was no moon. What a night! I was horribly frightened in those narrow paths between two rows of graves. I sat down on one of them, for I could not walk any longer; my knees were so weak. I could hear my heart beat!

And I heard something else as well. What? A confused, nameless noise. Was the noise in my head, in the impenetrable night, or beneath the mysterious earth? I looked all around me: I was paralyzed with terror, cold with fright, ready to shout out, ready to die.

Suddenly it seemed to me that the slab of marble on which I was sitting was moving. As if it was being raised. With a bound, I sprang onto the neighboring grave, and I distinctly saw the stone that I had just left rise upright. Then the dead person appeared, pushing the stone back with its bent back. I saw it quite clearly, although the night was so dark. On the cross I could read:

Here lies Jacques Olivant, who died at the age of fifty-one.
He loved his family, was kind and honourable,
and died in the grace of the Lord.

The dead man also read what was inscribed on the gravestone; then he picked up a stone off the path, a little pointed stone, and began to scrape the letters carefully. He slowly effaced them, and with the hollows of his eyes, he looked at the place where they had been engraved. Then, with the tip of the bone that had been his forefinger, he wrote in luminous letters:

Here reposes Jacques Olivant, who died at the age of fifty-one.
He hastened his father's death by his unkindness, as he
wished to inherit his fortune; he tortured his wife, tormented
his children, deceived his neighbors, robbed everyone he could,
and died miserable.

When he had finished writing, the dead man stood motionless, looking at his work. On turning around I saw that all of the graves were open, that all of the dead had emerged, and that all had effaced the lines inscribed on their gravestones by their relations, substituting the truth instead. And I saw that all had been tormentors of their neighbors— malicious, dishonest, hypocrites, liars, rogues; that they had stolen, deceived, performed every disgraceful, every abominable, action, these good fathers, these faithful wives, these devoted sons, these chaste daughters, these honest tradesmen. They were all writing at the same time, on the threshold of their eternal abode, the truth, the terrible and the holy truth, of which everybody was ignorant or pretended to be ignorant while they were alive.

I thought that *she* also must have written something on her gravestone; and now, running without any fear, I went toward her, sure that I would find her immediately. I recognized her at once without seeing her face, and on the marble cross where shortly before I had read:

She loved, was loved, and died.

I now saw:

Having gone out in the rain one day
in order to deceive her lover,
she caught a cold and died.

It appears that they found me at daybreak, lying on the grave, unconscious.

A PAIR OF HANDS

Sir Arthur Quiller-Couch

"IT HAPPENED WHEN I lived down in Cornwall. Tresillack was the name of the house, which stood alone at the head of a valley, within sound of the sea but without sight of it; for though the valley led down to a wide-open beach, it wound and twisted on its way, and its overlapping sides closed the view from the house, which was advertised as 'secluded.' I was very poor in those days, but I was young enough to be romantic and wise enough to like independence, and the word 'secluded' took my fancy.

"The misfortune was that it had taken the fancy of several previous tenants. You know, I daresay, the kind of person who rents a secluded house in the country? 'Shady' is the word, is it not? Well, the previous tenants of Tresillack had been shady with a vengeance.

"I knew nothing of this when I first made my application to the landlord, who lived on a farm at the foot of the valley, on a cliff overlooking the beach.

"To him I presented myself fearlessly as a spinster of decent family and small but assured income, intending a rural life of seemliness and economy. He met my advances politely, but with an air of suspicion. I began by disliking him for it; afterward I set it down as an unpleasant feature in the local character. I was doubly mistaken. Farmer Hosking was slow-witted, but as honest a man as ever stood up against hard times and a more open and hospitable race than the people on that coast I never wish to meet. It was the caution of a child who had burned his fingers, not once but many times. Had I known what I afterward learned of Farmer Hosking's tribulations as landlord of a 'secluded country residence,' I should have faltered as I undertook to prove the bright exception in a long line of painful experiences. He had bought the Tresillack estate twenty years before because the land adjoined his own, but the house was a nuisance and had been so from the beginning.

"'Well, miss,' he said, 'you're welcome to look over it; a pretty enough place, inside and out. There's no trouble about keys, because I've put in a housekeeper, a widow woman, and she'll show you around. With your leave I'll step up the valley so far with you and put you on your way.' As I thanked him, he paused and rubbed his chin. 'There's one thing I must tell you, though. Whoever takes the house must take Mrs. Carkeek along with it.'

"'Mrs. Carkeek?' I echoed dolefully. 'Is that the housekeeper?'

"'Yes. I'm sorry, miss,' he added, my face telling him no doubt what sort of woman I expected Mrs. Carkeek to be, 'but I had to make it a rule after—after some things had happened. And I daresay you won't find her so bad. Mary Carkeek's a sensible, comfortable woman and knows the place. She was in service there to Squire Kendall when he sold up and went; her first place it was.'

"'I may as well see the house, anyhow,' said I dejectedly. So we started to walk up the valley. The path, which ran beside a little chattering stream, was narrow for the most part, and Farmer Hosking, with an apology, strode on ahead to beat aside the brambles. But whenever its width allowed us to walk side by side, I caught him from time to time stealing a shy, inquisitive glance under his rough eyebrows. It was clear that he could not sum me up to his satisfaction.

"I don't know what foolish fancy prompted it, but about halfway up the valley, I stopped short and asked, 'There are no ghosts, I suppose?'

"It struck me, a moment after I had uttered it, as a supremely silly question; but he took it quite seriously. 'No: I never heard tell of any ghosts.' He laid a queer sort of stress on the word. 'There's always been trouble with servants, and maids' tongues will be runnin'. But Mary Carkeek lives up there alone, and she seems comfortable enough.'

"We walked on. By and by he pointed with his stick. 'It don't look like a place for ghosts, now, do it?'

"Certainly it did not. Above an untrimmed orchard rose a terrace of turf scattered with thornbushes and above this a terrace of stone, upon which stood the prettiest cottage I had ever seen. It was long and low and thatched; a deep veranda ran from end to end. Clematis, banksia roses, and honeysuckle climbed the posts of this veranda and clustered along its roof, beneath the lattices of the bedroom windows. The house was small enough to be called a cottage and rare enough in features and in situation to confer distinction on any tenant. It suggested what in those days we would have called 'elegant' living. And I could have clapped my hands for joy.

"My spirits mounted still higher when Mrs. Carkeek opened the door. A healthy, middle-aged woman with a thoughtful but contented face and a smile, she was comfortable; and while we walked through the rooms together (for Mr. Hosking waited outside), I 'took to' Mrs. Carkeek. Her speech was direct and practical; the rooms, in spite of their faded furniture, were bright and exquisitely clean; and somehow the very atmosphere of the house gave me a sense of feeling at home and cared for; yes, of being loved. Don't laugh, my dears; for when I'm done, you may not think this fancy altogether foolish.

"I stepped out onto the veranda, and Farmer Hosking pocketed the pruning knife that he had been using on a bush of jasmine.

"'This is better than anything I had dreamed of,' said I.

"'Well, miss, that's not a wise way of beginning a bargain, if you'll excuse me.'

"He took no advantage, however, and we struck the bargain as we returned down the valley to his farm. I had meant to hire a maid of my own, but now it occurred to me that I might do very well with Mrs. Carkeek. Within the week I moved into my new home.

"I can hardly describe to you the happiness of my first month at Tresillack, because if I take the reasons that I had for being happy, one by one, there remains over something that I cannot account for. I was young, healthy; I felt myself independent and adventurous; the season was high summer, the weather glorious, the garden in all the pomp of June, yet sufficiently unkempt to keep me busy, give me a sharp appetite for meals, and send me to bed in that drowsy stupor that comes from the odors of earth. I spent most of my time outdoors, winding up the day's work with a walk down the cool valley, along the beach, and back.

"I soon found that all housework could be safely left to Mrs. Carkeek. She did not talk much; indeed, her only fault (a rare one in housekeepers) was that she talked too little, and even when I addressed her, she seemed at times unable to give me her attention. It was as though her mind strayed off to some small job that she had forgotten, and her eyes wore a listening look, as though she waited for the neglected task to speak and remind her. But, as a matter of fact, she forgot nothing. Indeed, my dears, I was never so well attended to in my life.

"Well, that is what I'm coming to. That is just it. The woman not only had the rooms swept and dusted and my meals prepared to the moment. In a hundred odd little ways this orderliness, these preparations, seemed to read my desires. Did I wish the roses renewed in a bowl upon the dining table, sure enough at the next meal they would be replaced by fresh ones. And how on earth had she guessed the very roses, the very shapes and colors I had lightly wished for? Every day, and from morning to night, I happened on others, each slight, but all bearing witness to a ministering intelligence as subtle as it was untiring.

"I am a light sleeper, with an uncomfortable knack of waking with the sun and roaming early. No matter how early I rose at Tresillack, Mrs. Carkeek seemed to have preceded me. Finally I had to conclude that she arose and dusted and tidied as soon as she judged me safely abed. For once, finding the drawing room (where I had been sitting late) 'redded up' at four in the morning and no trace of a plate of raspberries that I had carried thither after dinner and left overnight, I determined to test her and walked through to the kitchen, calling her by name.

"I found the kitchen as clean as a pin and the fire laid, but no trace of Mrs. Carkeek. I walked upstairs and knocked on her door. At the second knock, a sleepy voice cried out, and presently the good woman stood before me in her nightgown, looking (I thought) very badly scared.

"'No,' I said, 'it's not a burglar. But I've found out what I wanted, that you do your morning's work overnight. And now go back to your bed like a good soul, while I take a run down to the beach.'

"She stood blinking in the dawn. Her face was still white.

"'Oh, miss,' she gasped, 'I was so sure you must have seen something!'

"'And so I have,' I answered, 'but it was neither burglars nor ghosts.'

"'Thank God!' I heard her say as she turned her back to me in her gray bedroom—which faced the north. And I took this for a carelessly pious expression and ran downstairs thinking no more of it.

"A few days later I began to understand.

"The plan of Tresillack house (I must explain) was simplicity itself. To the left of the hall as you entered was the dining room; to the right the drawing room. The foot of the stairs faced the front door, and beside it, passing a glazed inner door, you found two others right and left, the left opening on the kitchen, the right on a passage that ran under the stairs to a neat pantry with the usual shelves and linen press, and under the window was a porcelain sink and a brass faucet. On the first morning of my tenancy I had visited this pantry and turned the faucet, but no water ran. I supposed this to be accidental. Mrs. Carkeek had to wash up, and no doubt Mrs. Carkeek would complain of any failure in the water supply.

"But the day after I had picked a basketful of roses and carried them into the pantry as a handy place to arrange them in. I chose a china bowl and went to fill it at the sink. Again the water would not run.

"I called Mrs. Carkeek. 'What is wrong with this faucet?' I asked. 'The rest of the house is well enough supplied.'

"'I don't know, miss. I never use it.'

"'But there must be a reason; and you must find it a great nuisance washing up the plates and glasses in the kitchen. Come around to the back with me, and we'll have a look at the cisterns.'

"'The cisterns'll be all right, miss. I assure you I don't find it a trouble.'

"But I was not to be put off. The back of the house stood but ten feet from a wall that was really but a stone face built against the cliff. Above the cliff rose the kitchen garden, and from its lower path we looked over the wall's parapet upon the cisterns. There were two—a very large one, supplying the kitchen and the bathroom above the kitchen, and a small one, fed by the other, obviously leading by a pipe that I could trace to the pantry. Now the big cistern stood almost full, and yet the small one, though on a lower level, was empty.

"'It's as plain as daylight,' said I. 'The pipe between the two is choked.' And I clambered to the parapet.

"'I wouldn't, miss. The pantry is only cold water, and no use to me. From the kitchen boiler I get it hot, you see.'

"'But I want the pantry water for my flowers.' I bent over and groped. 'I thought as much!' said I as I wrenched out a thick plug of cork, and immediately the water began to flow. I turned triumphantly on Mrs. Carkeek, who had grown suddenly red in the face. Her eyes were fixed on the cork in my hand. To keep it more firmly wedged in its place somebody had wrapped it around with a rag of calico print; and discolored though the rag was, I seemed to recall the pattern (a lilac sprig). Then, as our eyes met, it occurred to me that only two mornings before Mrs. Carkeek had worn a print gown of that same sprigged pattern.

"I had the presence of mind to hide this very small discovery, and presently Mrs. Carkeek regained her composure. But I felt disappointed in her. She had deliberately acted a fib before me; and why? Merely because she preferred the kitchen to the pantry faucet. It was childish. 'But servants are all the same,' I told myself. 'I must take Mrs. Carkeek as she is; and, after all, she is a treasure.'

"On the second night after this, I was lying in bed and reading myself sleepy over a novel, when a small sound disturbed me. I listened. The sound was clearly that of water trickling. A shower (I told myself) had filled the water pipes that drained the roof. Somehow I could not ignore the sound. I rose and drew up the blind.

"To my astonishment, no rain was falling; no rain had fallen. There was no wind, no clouds; only a still moon high up over the eastern slope of the valley, the distant splash of waves, and the fragrance of many roses. I went back to bed and listened again. Yes, the trickling sound continued, quite distinct in the silence of the house, not to be confused for a moment with the dull murmur of the beach. After a while it began to grate on my nerves. I caught up my candle, flung my dressing gown over me, and stole softly downstairs.

"Then it was simple. I traced the sound to the pantry.

'Mrs. Carkeek has left the water running,' said I; and, sure I found it so—a thin trickle steadily running to waste in the porcelain sink. I turned off the water, went contentedly back to my bed, and slept—

"—for some hours. I opened my eyes in darkness and at once knew what had awakened me. The water was running again. Now, it had shut easily in my hand, but not so easily that I could believe that it had slipped open again of its own accord. 'This is Mrs. Carkeek's doing,' said I; and I am afraid I added, 'Drat, Mrs. Carkeek!'

"Well, there was no help for it, so I struck a light, looked at my watch, saw that the hour was just three o'clock, and I descended the stairs again. At the pantry door I paused. I was not afraid—not one little bit. In fact, the notion that anything might be wrong had never crossed my mind. But I remember thinking, with my hand on the door, that if Mrs. Carkeek was in the pantry, I might happen to give her a severe fright.

"I pushed the door open briskly. Mrs. Carkeek was not there. But something was there, by the porcelain sink. My heart seemed to stand still—so still! And in the stillness I remember setting down the brass candlestick on a tall nest of drawers beside me.

"Over the porcelain sink and beneath the water trickling from the faucet I saw two hands.

"That was all—two small hands, a child's hands. I cannot tell how they ended.

"No; they were not cut off. I saw them quite distinctly; just a pair of small hands and the wrists, and after that— nothing. They were moving briskly—washing themselves

139

clean. I saw the water trickle and splash over them—not through them—but just as it would on real hands. They were the hands of a little girl, too. Oh, yes, I was sure of that at once. Boys and girls wash their hands differently. I can't just tell you what the difference is, but it's unmistakable.

"I saw all this before my candle slipped and fell with a crash. I had set it down without looking—for my eyes were fixed on the sink—and had balanced it on the edge of the nest of drawers. After the crash, in the darkness there with the water running, I suffered some bad moments.

"Oddly enough, the thought uppermost with me was that I must shut off that faucet before escaping. I had to. And after a while I picked up all my courage and with a little sob thrust out my hand and did it. Then I fled.

"The dawn was close upon me, and as soon as the sky reddened, I took my bath, dressed, and went downstairs. And there at the pantry door I found Mrs. Carkeek, also dressed, with my candlestick in her hand.

"'Ah,' said I, 'you picked it up.'

"Our eyes met. Clearly, Mrs. Carkeek wished me to begin, and I determined at once to have it out with her.

"'And you knew all about it. That's what accounts for you plugging up the cistern.'

"'You saw . . . ?' she began.

"'Yes, yes. And you must tell me all about it—never mind how bad. Is—is it—murder?'

"'Lord bless you, miss, whatever put such horrors in your head?'

"'She was washing her hands.'

"'Ah, so she does, poor dear! But—murder! And dear

little Miss Margaret, who wouldn't hurt a fly!'

"'Miss Margaret?'

"'Eh, she died at seven. Squire Kendall's only daughter; and that's over twenty years ago. I was her nurse, miss, and I know—diphtheria it was; she took it down in the village.'

"'But how do you know it is Margaret?'

"'Those hands—why, how could I mistake, who used to be her nurse?'

"'But why does she wash them?'

"'Well, miss, being always a dainty child—and the housework, you see—'

"I took a long breath. 'Do you mean to tell me that all this tidying and dusting—' I broke off. 'Is it she who has been taking this care of me?'

"Mrs. Carkeek met my look steadily.

"'Who else, miss?'

"'Poor little soul!'

"'Well, now'—Mrs. Carkeek rubbed my candlestick with the edge of her apron—'I'm so glad you take it like this. For there isn't really nothing to be afraid of—is there?' She eyed me wistfully. 'It's my belief she loves you, miss. But only to think what a time she must have had with the others!'

"'Were they bad?'

"'They was awful. Didn't Farmer Hosking tell you? They carried on fearful—one after another, and each one worse than the last.'

"'What was the matter with them? Drink?'

"'Drink, miss, with some of 'em. There was the major— he used to go mad with it and run about the valley in his nightshirt. Oh, scandalous! And his wife drank too—that is, if she ever was his wife. Just think of that tender child washing up after their nasty doings!

"'But that wasn't the worst, miss—not by a long way. There was a pair here with two children, a boy and a girl, the eldest scarce six. Poor mites!

"'They beat those children, miss—your blood would boil! And starved and tortured 'em, it's my belief. You could hear their screams, I've been told, away back in the main road, and that's the best part of half a mile.

"'Sometimes they were locked up without food for days together. But it's my belief that little Miss Margaret managed to feed them somehow. Oh, I can see her creeping to the door and comforting!'

"'But perhaps she never showed herself when these awful people were here, but took to flight until they left.'

"'You didn't ever know her, miss. How brave she was! She'd have stood up to lions. She've been here all the while: and only to think what her innocent eyes and ears must have took in! There was another couple—' Mrs. Carkeek sunk her voice.

"'Oh, hush!' said I, 'if I'm to have any peace of mind in this house!'

"'But you won't go, miss? She loves you, I know she does. And think what you might be leaving her to—what sort of tenant might come next. For she can't go. She's been here ever since her father sold the place. He died soon after. You mustn't go!'

"Now I had resolved to go, but all of a sudden I felt how mean this resolution was.

"'After all,' said I, 'there's nothing to be afraid of.'

"'That's it, miss; nothing at all. I don't even believe it's so very uncommon. Why, I've heard my mother tell of farmhouses where the rooms were swept every night as regular as clockwork, and the floors sanded, and the pots and pans scoured, and all while the maids slept. They put it down to the pixies; but we know better, miss, and now that we've got the secret between us, we can lie easy in our beds, and if we hear anything, say, "God bless the child!" and go to sleep.'

"I spent three years at Tresillack, and all that while Mrs. Carkeek lived with me and shared the secret. Few women, I dare to say, were ever so completely wrapped around with love as we were during those three years.

"It ran through my waking life like a song: it smoothed my pillow, touched and made my table comely, in the summer lifted the heads of the flowers as I passed, and in the winter watched the fire with me and kept it bright.

"Why did I ever leave Tresillack? Because one day, at the end of five years, Farmer Hosking brought me word that he had sold the house. There was no avoiding it, at any rate, the purchaser being a Colonel Kendall, a brother of the old squire.

"'A married man?' I asked.

"'Yes, miss, with a family of eight. As pretty children as ever you saw and the mother a good lady. It's the old home to Colonel Kendall.'

"'I see. And that is why you feel bound to sell.'

"'It's a good price, too, that he offers. You mustn't think that I'm sorry enough—'

"'To turn me out? I thank you, Mr. Hosking; but you are doing the right thing.'

"'She—Margaret—will be happy,' I said, 'with her cousins,

you know.'

"'Oh, yes, miss, she will be happy, sure enough,' Mrs. Carkeek agreed.

"So when the time came, I packed up my boxes and tried to be cheerful. But on the last morning, when they stood in the hall, I sent Mrs. Carkeek upstairs upon some poor excuse and stepped alone into the pantry.

"'Margaret!' I whispered.

"There was no answer at all. I had scarcely dared to hope for one. Yet I tried again and, shutting my eyes this time, stretched out both hands and whispered, 'Margaret!'

"And I will swear to my dying day that two little hands stole and rested—for a moment only—in mine."

THE BOYS' TOILETS

Robert Westall

THE JANUARY TERM started with a scene of sheer disaster. A muddy excavator was chewing its way across the netball court, breakfasting on the tarmac with sinuous lunges and terrifying swings of its yellow dinosaur neck. One of the stone balls had been knocked off the gateposts and lay in crushed fragments like M&Ms stepped on by a giant. The entrance to the science wing was blocked with a pile of ocherous clay, and curved glazed drainpipes were heaped like macaroni.

The girls hung around in groups. One girl came back from the indoor toilets saying that Miss Bowker was calling the council and using words that Eliza Bottom had almost been expelled for last term. She was greeted with snorts of disbelief. . . .

The next girl came back from the bathroom saying that Miss Bowker was almost crying.

Which was definitely a lie, because here was Miss Bowker now, coming out to address them in her best sheepskin coat. Though she *was* wearing fresh makeup and her eyes were suspiciously bright, her famous chin was up. She was brief and to the point. There was an underground leak in the central heating; till it was fixed, they would be using the old Harvest Road boys' school. They would march across now, by class, in good order, in charge of the hall monitors. She knew that they would behave immaculately and that the spirit of Spilsby

Girls' School would overcome all difficulties. . . .

"Takes more than school spirit," said Wendy Falstaff.

"More than a bottle of whisky," said Jennifer Mount and shuddered. Rebeccah, who was a vicar's daughter, thought of Sodom and Gomorrah, both respectable suburbs by comparison with Harvest Road. Harvest Road was literally on the wrong side of the tracks. But obediently they marched. They passed through the streets where they lived, cheery with yellow front doors, picture windows, new garages, and wrought-iron gates. It was quite an adventure at first. Staff cars kept passing them, their rear windows packed with whole classrooms. Miss Rossiter, with her brass microscopes and stuffed ducks; Mademoiselle, full of tape recorders and posters of the French wine-growing districts. Piles of *The Merchant of Venice* and "Sunflowers" by van Gogh . . .

The first time they passed, the teachers hooted cheerfully. But coming back they were silent, just their blinkers winking and frozen faces behind the wheel.

Then the marching columns came to a miserable little humpbacked bridge over a solitary railroad line, empty and rusting. Beyond were the same kind of houses, but afflicted with some dreadful disease, of which the symptoms were a rash of small windowpanes, flaking paint, overgrown, funereal hedges, and sagging gates that would never close again. And then it seemed to grow even colder, as the slum clearances started, a great empty plain of broken bricks, and the wind hit them full, sandpapering faces and sending gray berets cartwheeling into the wilderness.

And there, in the midst of the desolation like a dead sooty dinosaur, like a blackened, marooned, many chimneyed

Victorian battleship, lay Harvest Road school.

They gathered, awed, in the hall. The windows, too high up to see out of, were stained brown around the edges; the walls were dark green. There was a carved oak board, a list of prizewinners from 1879 till 1923. Victoria peered at it. "It's B.C., not A.D.," she announced. "The first name's Tutankhamen." There were posters sagging off the walls on the extreme ends of long, hairy strands of tape; things like "Tea Picking in India" and "The Meaning of Empire Day." It all felt like drowning in a very dirty goldfish tank.

A lot of them needed to use the toilet, badly. Nervousness and the walk through the cold. But nobody felt like asking till Rebeccah did. Last door at the end of the corridor and across the yard; they walked down, six-strong.

They were boys' toilets. They crept past the male mystery of the urinals, tall, white, and as rust-streaked as tombs, looking absurd, inhuman, like elderly invalid carriages or artificial limbs. In the bottom gulley, cigarette butts lay squashed and dried out, like dead flies.

And the graffiti . . . even Liza Bottom didn't know what some words meant. But they were huge and hating. . . . The whole wall screamed with them, from top to bottom. Most of the hate seemed directed at someone called "Barney Boko."

Rebeccah shuddered; that was the first shudder. But Vicky only said, practically, "Bet there's no toilet paper!" and got out her French exercise book. . . . She was always the pessimist; but on this occasion she hadn't been pessimistic enough. Not only no toilet paper, but no wooden seats either, and the toilet chains had been replaced by loops of hairy, thick, white string, like hangmen's nooses. And in the green paint of the wooden partitions, the hatred of Barney Boko had been gouged half-an-inch deep. And the locks had been busted off all the doors except the far-end one. . . .

Rebeccah, ever public-spirited and with a lesser need, stood guard stoutly.

"Boys," she heard Victoria snort in disgust. "It's a nunnery for me . . . at least in nunneries they'll have soft toilet paper."

"Don't you believe it," said Joanne, their Roman Catholic correspondent. "They wear hair shirts, nuns. Probably the toilets have *scrubbing brushes* instead of paper."

Lively squeaks, all down the line, as the implications struck home.

"Some boys aren't bad," said Liza, "if you can get them away from their friends."

"Why bother," said Vicky. "I'll settle for my poster of Duran Duran. . . ."

"It's funny," said Tracy, as they were combing their hair in the solitary cracked, fly-spotted, pocket-handkerchief-sized mirror. "You know there's six of us? Well, I heard *seven* toilets flush. Did anybody pull the chain twice?"

They all looked at each other and shook their heads. They looked back down the long, shadowy bathroom, with its tiny, high-up pebbled windows, toward the toilets. They shouted, wanting to know who was there, because nobody had passed them, nobody had come in.

No answer, except the sound of dripping.

The big attraction at break was the school boiler room. They stood around on the immense coke piles, some new, some so old and mixed with the fallen leaves of many autumns that they were hardly recognizable as coke at all. One actually had weeds growing on it. . . .

Inside the boiler room, in a red, hissing glow, two men fought to get Harvest Road up to a reasonable temperature, somewhere above that of Dracula's crypt. One was young, cheerful, cocky, with curly brown hair; they said he was from the council. The other was tall and thin, in a long, gray overall coat and a cap so old that the pattern had worn off. They said that he was the caretaker of the old school, brought out of retirement because only he knew the ropes. . . . He had such an expression on his face that they immediately called him Dracula. Occasionally, the cocky one would stop shoveling coke into the gaping red maw of the furnace and wipe his brow; that and the occasional draft of warm air, immediately swept away by the biting wind, was the only hint of heat they had that morning.

The lesson after break was math, with Miss Hogg. Miss Hogg was one of the old school; gray hair in a tight bun, tweed, gold-rimmed spectacles. A brilliant mathematician who had once unbent far enough, at the end of summer term, to tell the joke about the square on the hypotenuse. Feared but not loved, Miss Hogg made it quite clear to all that she had no time for men.

They ground away steadily at quadratic equations, until the dreary cold, seeping out of the tiled walls into their bones, claimed Rebeccah as its first victim. Her hand shot up.

"You should have gone at break," said Miss Hogg.

"I did, Miss Hogg."

Miss Hogg's gesture gave permission, while despairing

of all the fatal weaknesses of femininity.

Rebeccah hesitated just inside the doorway of the bathroom. The length of the low, dark room, vanishing into shadows; the little green windows high up that lit nothing; the alienness of it all made her hesitant, as in some old, dark church. The graffiti plucked at the corners of her eyes, dimly, like memorials on a church wall. But no "dearly beloveds" here.

JACKO IS A SLIMER
HIGGINS STINKS

Where were they now? How many years ago? She told herself that they must be grown men, balding, with wives and families and little paunches under cardigans that their wives had lovingly knitted for them. But she couldn't believe it. They were still here somewhere, fighting, snorting bubbles of blood from streaming noses, angry. Especially angry with Barney Boko. She went down the long room on tiptoe and went into the far-end cubicle because it was the only one with a lock. Snapped home the bolt so hard that it echoed up and down the concrete ceiling.

But no sooner had she settled than she heard someone come in. Not a girl; Rebeccah had quick ears. No, big boots, with steel heel plates. Walking authoritatively toward her. From the liveliness of the feet she knew that it wasn't even a man. A boy. She heard him pause, as if he sensed her, as if looking around. Then a boy's voice, quiet.

"Okay, Stebbo, all clear!"

More stamping heel-capped feet tramping in.

She knew that she had made a terrible mistake. There

must still be a boys' school here, only occupying part of the buildings. And she was in the *boys'* bathroom. She blushed. An enormous blush that seemed to start behind her ears and went down her neck over her whole body . . .

But she was a sensible child. She told herself to be calm. Just sit, as quiet as a mouse, till they'd gone. She sat, breathing softly into her handkerchief, held across her mouth.

But supposing they tried the door, shouted to ask who was in there? Suppose they put their hands on the top of the wooden partition and hauled themselves up and looked over the top. There were some awful *girls* who did that. . . .

But they seemed to have no interest in her locked cubicle. There was a lot of scuffling, scraping of steel heel plates, and panting. As if they were dragging somebody . . .

The somebody was dragged into the cubicle next door. Elbows thumped against the wooden partition, making her jump.

"Get his head down," ordered a sharp voice.

"No, Stebbo, NO! Let me go, you bastards . . ."

"Ouch!"

"What's up?"

"Little jerk bit me . . ."

"Get his head down, then!"

The sounds of heaving, scraping, panting, and, finally, a sort of high-pitched whining got worse. Then suddenly the toilet next door flushed, the whining stopped and then resumed as a series of half-drowned gasps for breath. There was a yip of triumph, laughter, and the noise of many boots running away.

"Bastards," said a bitter, choking voice. "And you've broken my pen an' all." Then a last weary pair of boots trailed away.

She got herself ready, listening, waiting, tensed. Then undid the bolt with a rush and ran down the empty, echoing place. Her own footsteps sounded frail and tiny, after the boys. Suppose she met one, coming in?

But she didn't. And there wasn't a boy in sight in the gray high-walled yard. Bolder, she looked back at the entrance of the bathroom ... it was the same one they'd used earlier; the one they'd been told to use. Miss Bowker must have made a mistake; someone should be told. ...

But when she got back to the classroom and Miss Hogg and all the class looked up, she lost her nerve.

"You took your time, Rebeccah," said Miss Hogg suspiciously.

"We thought you'd pulled the chain too soon and gone down to the seaside," said Liza Bottom, playing for a vulgar laugh and getting it.

"Let me see your work so far, Liza," said Miss Hogg frostily, killing the laughter like a partridge shot on the wing.

"What's up?" whispered Vicky. "You met a fella or something—all blushing and eyes shining . . ." Vicky was much harder to fool than Miss Hogg.

"Tell you at lunch . . ."

"The next girl I see talking . . ." said Miss Hogg ominously.

But they didn't have to wait till lunch. Liza had twigged that something was up. Her hand shot up; she squirmed in her seat almost too convincingly.

"Very well, Liza. I suppose I must brace myself for an epidemic of weak bladders. . . ."

Liza returned like a bomb about to explode, her red hair

standing out from her head like she'd back combed it for Saturday night, a deep blush under her freckles, and green eyes as wide as saucers. She opened her mouth to speak . . . but Miss Hogg had an eagle eye for incipient hysteria and a gift for nipping it in the bud.

"Shut the door, Liza—we'll keep the drafts we have." Liza sat down demurely; but even the Hogg's frost couldn't stop the idea from flaring across the class that something was excitingly amiss in the bathroom. It was droopy Margie Trawson who blew it. She went next and came back and bleated, with that air of a victimized sheep that only she could achieve.

"Miss Hogg, there's boys in the toilet . . ."

"Boys?" boomed Miss Hogg. "BOYS?" She swept out of the classroom door with all the speed that her strongly muscled legs could give her. From the classroom windows, they watched as she entered the toilets. Rebeccah, who was an expert on naval warfare in World War II, thought that she looked like an angry little frigate, just itching to depth charge any boy out of existence. But when she emerged, her frown told that she'd been cheated of her prey. She scouted on for boys lurking behind the coke piles, behind the garbage cans, behind the sagging fence of the caretaker's house. Nothing. She looked back toward her classroom windows, making every girlish head duck simultaneously, and then headed for the headmistress's office.

In turn, they saw the tall, stately figure of the headmistress inspect the bathroom, the coke piles, fence, and garbage cans, Miss Hogg circling her on convoy duty. But without success. Finally, after a word, they parted. Miss Hogg returned, with a face like thunder.

"Someone," she announced, "has been silly. Very, *very*, silly." She made "silly" sound as evil as running a concentration camp. "The head has assured me that this school has been disused for many years, and there cannot possibly be a single boy on the premises. The only . . . males . . . are the caretakers. Now, Margie, what have you got to say to *that*? Well . . . Margie . . . *well*?"

There was only one end to Miss Hogg's well-Margie-well routine: Margie gruesomely dissolving into tears. "There were boys, Miss Hogg, I heard them, Miss Hogg, honeeest . . ." She pushed back a tear with the cuff of her cardigan.

Liza was on her feet, flaming. "I heard them too, Miss Hogg." That didn't worry Miss Hogg. Liza was the class troublemaker. But then Rebeccah was on her feet. "I heard them as well."

"*Rebeccah*—you are a clergyman's daughter. I'm ashamed of you."

"I *heard* them." Rebeccah clenched her teeth; there would be no shifting her. Miss Hogg looked thoughtful.

"They don't come when you're in a crowd, Miss Hogg," bleated Margie. "They only come when you're there by yourself. They put another boy's head down the toilet an' pulled the chain. They were in the place next to me."

"And to me," said Liza.

"And to me," said Rebeccah.

A sort of shiver went around the class; the humming and buzzing stopped, and it was very quiet.

"Very well," said Miss Hogg. "We will test Margie's theory. *Come*, Rebeccah!"

At the entrance to the toilet, Rebeccah suddenly felt very silly.

"Just go in and behave normally," said Miss Hogg. "I shall be just outside."

Rebeccah entered the cubicle, bolted the door, and sat down.

"Do exactly what you would normally do," boomed Miss Hogg, suddenly, scarily, down the long, dark space. Rebeccah blushed again and did as she was told.

"There," boomed Miss Hogg, after a lengthy pause. "Nothing, you see. Nothing at all. You girls are *ridiculous!*" Rebeccah wasn't so sure. There was something—you couldn't call it a sound—a sort of vibration in the air, like boys giggling in hiding.

"Nothing," boomed Miss Hogg again. "Come along— we've wasted enough lesson time. Such nonsense."

Suddenly a toilet flushed, at the far end of the row.

"Was that you, Rebeccah?"

"No, Miss Hogg."

"Nonsense. Of course it was."

"No, Miss Hogg."

Another toilet flushed, and another, getting closer. That convinced Miss Hogg. Rebeccah heard her stout shoes come in at a run, heard her banging back the toilet doors, shouting, "Come out, whoever you are. You can't get away. I know you're there."

Rebeccah came out with a rush to meet her.

"Did you pull your chain, Rebeccah?"

"Didn't need to, Miss Hogg."

And indeed, all of the toilet doors were now open, and

all of the toilets manifestly empty, and every cistern busy refilling; except Rebeccah's.

"There must be a scientific explanation," said Miss Hogg. "A fault in the plumbing."

But Rebeccah thought that she heard a quiver in her voice as she stared suspiciously at the small, inaccessible ventilation grids.

They all went together at lunchtime, and nothing happened. They all went together at afternoon break, and nothing happened. Then it was time for Miss Hogg again. Black Monday was called Black Monday because they had Miss Hogg twice for math.

And still the cold worked upon their systems. . . .

Margie Trawson again.

"Please, Miss Hogg, I've *got* to."

Only . . . there was a secret in Margie's voice, a little gloaty secret. They all heard it; but if Miss Hogg did, she only raised a grizzled eyebrow. "Hurry, then . . . if only your *mind* was so active, Margie."

She was gone a long time; a very long time. Even Miss Hogg shifted her feet restlessly as she got on with marking the other class's quadratic equations.

And then Margie was standing in the doorway and behind her, the looming gray-coated figure of Dracula, with his mouth set so hard and cruel. He had Margie by the elbow, in a grip that made her writhe. He whispered to Miss Hogg. . . .

"Appalling," boomed Miss Hogg. "I don't know what these children think they are coming to. Thank you for telling me so quickly, Caretaker. It won't happen again. I assure you, it won't happen again. That will be all!"

Dracula, robbed of his moment of public triumph and infant humiliation, stalked out without another word.

"Margie," announced Miss Hogg, "has attempted to use the caretaker's outside toilet. The toilet set aside for his own personal use. A *man's* toilet . . ."

"Obviously a hanging offense," muttered Victoria, causing a wild but limited explosion of giggles, cut off as by a knife by Miss Hogg's glint-spectacled *look*. "How would you like it, Margie, if some strange man came into your backyard at home and used *your* toilet?"

"It'd really turn her on," muttered Victoria. Liza choked down on a giggle so hard that she almost gave herself a slipped disk.

"No girl will ever do such a thing again," said Miss Hogg in her most dreadful voice, clutching Margie's elbow as cruelly as Dracula had. A voice so dreadful and so seldom heard that the whole class froze into thoughtfulness. Not since that joke with the chewing gum in the first year had they heard that voice.

"Now, Margie, will you go and do what you have to do, in the place where you are meant to do it."

"Don't want to go no more, Miss Hogg. It's stopped . . . "

Liar, thought Rebeccah; Margie needed to go so badly that she was squirming from foot to foot.

"GO!" said Miss Hogg, in the voice that brooked no argument. "I shall watch you from the window."

They all watched her go in; and they all watched her come out.

"Sit down quickly, Margie," said Miss Hogg. "There

seems to be some difficulty with question twelve. It's quite simple, really." She turned away to the blackboard, chalk in hand. "X squared, plus two y . . ." The chalk squeaked abominably, getting on everyone's nerves; there was a slight but growing disturbance at the back of the class, which Miss Hogg couldn't hear for the squeaking of the chalk. . . . "Three x plus five y . . ."

"Oh, Miss Hogg!" wailed Margie. "I'm sorry, Miss Hogg . . . I didn't mean to . . ." Then she was flying to the classroom door, babbling and sobbing incoherently. She scrabbled for the doorknob and finally got it open. Miss Hogg moved across swiftly and tried to grab her, but she was just too slow; Margie was gone, with Miss Hogg in hot pursuit, hysterical sobs and angry shouts echoing around the whole school from both of them.

"What . . . ?" asked Rebeccah, turning. Vicky pointed silently at a wide, spreading pool of liquid under Margie's desk.

"She never went at all," said Vicky grimly. "She must have hidden just inside the doorway. She was too scared. . . ."

It was then that Rebeccah began to hate the ghosts in the boys' toilets.

She tapped on Dad's study door as soon as she got in from school. Pushed it open. He was sitting, a tall, thin, boyish figure, at his desk with the light on. From his dejectedly drooping shoulders and his spectacles pushed up on his forehead, she knew that he was writing next Sunday's sermon. He was bashing between his eyes with a balled fist as well; Epiphany was never his favorite topic for a sermon.

"Dad?"

He came back from far away, pulled down his spectacles, blinked at her, and smiled.

"It's the Person from Porlock!" This was a very ancient joke between them that only got better with time. The real Person from Porlock had interrupted the famous poet Samuel Coleridge when he was in the middle of composing his greatest poem, "Kubla Khan."

"Sit down, Person," said Dad, removing a precarious tower of books from his second wooden armchair. "Want a coffee?" She glanced at his percolator; shiny and new from Mum last Christmas, but now varnished-over with dribbles from constant use.

"Yes, please," she said, just to be friendly; he made his coffee as strong as poison.

"How's Porlock?" He gave her a sharp sideways glance through his horn-rimmed spectacles. "Trouble?"

Somehow, he always knew.

She was glad that she could start at the beginning, with ordinary things like the central heating and the march to Harvest Road. . . .

When she had finished, he said, "Ghosts. Ghosts in the toilet. Pulling chains and frightening people." He was the only adult she knew who wouldn't have laughed or made some stupid remark. But all he said was, "Something funny happened at that school. It was closed down. A few years before Mum and I came to live here. It had an evil name, but I never knew for what."

"But what can we *do*? The girls are terrified."

"Go at lunchtime—go at break—go before you leave home."

"We do. But it's so cold—somebody'll need to go sooner or later."

"You won't be at Harvest Road long—even central heating leaks don't go on forever. Shall I try to find out for how long? I know the chairman of the school board."

"Wouldn't do any harm," said Rebeccah grudgingly.

"But you don't want to wait to go that long?" It was meant to be a joke, but it died halfway between them.

"Look," said Rebeccah, "if you'd seen Margie . . . she . . . she won't dare come back. Somebody could be . . . terrified for life."

"I'll talk to your headmistress. . . ." He reached for the phone.

"NO!" It came out as almost a shout. Dad put the phone back, looking puzzled. Rebeccah said, in a low voice, "The teachers think we're nuts. They'll . . . think you're nuts as well. You . . . can't afford to have people think *you're* nuts. Can you?"

"Touché," he said ruefully. "So what do you want, Person?"

"Tell me how to get rid of them. How to frighten them away, so they leave people *alone*."

"I'm not in the frightening business, Person."

"But the church . . ."

"You mean . . . bell, book, and candle? No can do. The church doesn't like that kind of thing anymore . . . doesn't believe in it, I suppose. . . ."

"But it's *real*." It was almost a wail.

"The only man I know who touches that sort of thing has a parish in London. He's considered a crank."

"*Tell me what to do!*"

They looked at each other in silence, a very long time. They were so much alike, with their blonde hair, long faces, straight noses, spectacles. Even their hair was the same length; he wore his long; she wore hers shortish.

Finally he said, "There's no other way?"

"No."

"I don't know much. You're supposed to ask its name. It has to tell you—that's in the Bible. That's supposed to give you power over it. Then, like Shakespeare, you can ask it whether it's a spirit of health or goblin damned. Then . . . you can try commanding it to go to the place prepared for it . . ." He jumped up, running his fingers through his hair. "No, you mustn't do any of this, Rebeccah. I can't have you doing things like this. I'll call the headmistress. . . ."

"You will NOT!"

"Leave it alone, then!"

"If it leaves me alone." But she had her fingers crossed.

The headmistress came in to address them the next morning, after assembly. She put her hands together behind her back, rocked a little, head down, and then looked at them with a smile that was 100 percent caring and around 90 percent honest.

"Toilets," she said doubtfully and then with an effort, more briskly, "Toilets." She nodded gently. "I can understand you are upset about the toilets. Of all the things about this dreadful place that the council's put us in, those toilets are the worst. I want you to know that I have had the strongest possible words with the council and that those toilets will be repainted and repaired by next Monday morning. I have told them that if they fail me in this, I will close the school." She lowered her head in deep thought again and then looked up, more sympathetic than ever.

"You have reached an age when you are—quite rightly—beginning to be interested in boys. There *have* been boys here—they have left their mark—and I am sad that they have left the worst possible kind of mark. Most boys are not like that—not like that at all, thank God. But—these boys have been *gone* for more than twenty years. Let me stress that. For twenty years, this building has been used to store unwanted school furniture. You may say that there are always boys everywhere—like mice or beetles! But with all this clearance around us . . . I went out yesterday actually *looking* for a boy." She looked around with a smile, expecting a laugh. She got a few titters. "The first boy I saw was a full mile away—and he was working for a butcher on the main street." Again, she expected a laugh, and it did not come. So she went serious again. "You have been upset by the toilets—understandably. But that is no excuse for making things up—for, and I must say it, getting hysterical. Nobody else has noticed anything in these toilets. The monitors report nothing—I have watched other classes using them quite happily. *It is just this class.* Or, rather, three excitable girls in this class . . ." She looked around. At Liza Bottom, who blushed and wiggled. At the empty desk where Margie should have been sitting. And at Rebeccah, who stared straight back at her, as firmly as she could. "Two of those girls do not surprise me—the third girl does." Rebeccah did not flinch, which worried the head, who was rather fond of her. So the head finished in a rush. "I want you to stop acting as featherbrained females—and act instead as the sensible, hardheaded young women you are going to become. This business . . . is the sort of business that gets us despised by men . . . and there are plenty of men only too ready to despise us."

The headmistress swept out. A sort of deadly coldness settled over the sensible young women. It hadn't happened to the hall monitors or to the other classes. The head had just proved that there were ghosts and proved that they were only after people in 3A. . . .

It was Fiona Mowbray who bought it. It happened so swiftly, after break. They'd all gone together at break. They never realized that they'd left her there, too shy to call out. She was always the shyest, Fiona. . . .

Suddenly she appeared in the doorway, interrupting the beginning of French.

"Sit down, Feeownah," said Madamoiselle gently.

But Fiona just stood there, as pale and stiff as a scarecrow, swaying. There were strange twists of toilet paper all around her arms. . . .

"Feeownah," said Madamoiselle again with a strange panicky quiver in her voice. Fiona opened and closed her mouth to speak four times, without a single sound coming out. Then she fainted full-length, hitting the floorboards like a sack of potatoes.

Then someone ran for the headmistress, and everyone was crowding around, and the head was calling, "Stand back, give her air," and sending Liza for Miss Hogg's smelling salts. And Fiona coming around and starting to scream and flail out. And fainting again. And talk of sending for a doctor . . .

Right, you jerk, thought Rebeccah. That's *it!* And she slipped around the back of the clustering crowd, and nobody

163

saw her go, for all eyes were on Fiona.

Fiona must have been in the third toilet . . . the toilet paper holder was empty, and the yellow paper, swathe on swathe of it, covered the floor and almost buried the toilet bowl. It was wildly torn in places, as if Fiona had had to claw her way out of it. Had it . . . been trying to smother her? Rebeccah pulled the chain automatically. Then, with a wildly beating heart, locked herself in the next door and sat down with her jaw clenched and her underpants around her knees.

It was hard to stay calm. The noise of the refilling cistern next door hid all other noises. Then, as next door dropped to a trickle, she heard another toilet being pulled. Had someone else come in, unheard? Was she wasting her time? But there'd been no footsteps. Then another toilet flushed, and another and another. Then the doors of the empty toilets began banging, over and over, so hard and savagely that she thought they would splinter.

Boom, boom, boom. Closer and closer.

Come on, bastard, thought Rebeccah, with the hard center of her mind; the rest of her felt like screaming.

Then the toilet pulled over her own head. So violently that it showered her with water. She looked up, and the hairy string was swinging, with no one holding it like a hangman's noose. Nobody could possibly have touched it.

The cistern lever was pulled above her, again and again. Her nerve broke, and she rushed for the door. But the bolt wouldn't unbolt. Too stiff—too stiff for her terrified fingers. She flung herself around wildly, trying to climb over the top, but she was so terrified that she couldn't manage that either. She ended up cowering down against the door, head on her knees and hands over her ears, like an unborn baby.

Silence. Stillness. But she knew that whatever it was, it was still there.

"What . . . is . . . your . . . name?' she whispered from a creaky throat. Then a shout. "WHAT IS YOUR NAME?"

As if in answer, the toilet paper began to unroll itself, rearing over her in swirling yellow coils, as if it wanted to smother her.

"Are you a spirit of health or goblin damned?" That reminded her of Dad and gave her a little chip of courage. But the folds of paper went on rearing up, till all of the cubicle was filled with the yellow, rustling mass. As if you had to *breathe* toilet paper.

"Be gone . . . to the place . . . prepared for you," she stammered, without hope. The coils of paper moved closer, touching her face softly.

"WHAT DO YOU WANT?" She was screaming.

There was a change. The whirling folds of paper seemed to coalesce. Into a figure, taller than herself, as tall as a very thin boy might be, wrapped in yellow bands like a mummy, with two dark gaps where eyes might have been.

If it had touched her, her mind would have splintered into a thousand pieces.

But it didn't. It just looked at her with its hole eyes and swung a yellow-swathed scarecrow arm to point to the brickwork above the cistern.

Three times. Till she dumbly nodded.

Then it collapsed into a mass of paper around her feet.

After a long time, she got up and tried the door bolt. It opened easily, and her fear changed to embarrassment as she grabbed for her underpants.

It hadn't wanted to harm her at all; it had only wanted to show her something.

Emboldened, she waded back through the yellow mass. Where had it been pointing?

There could be no mistake; a tiny strand of toilet paper still clung to the brickwork, caught in a crack. She pulled it out, and the white paint crumbled a little and came with it, leaving a tiny hole. She touched the part near the hole, and more paint and cement crumbled; she scrabbled, and a whole half brick seemed to fall out into her hand. Only it wasn't all brick, but crumbly dried mud, which broke and fell in crumbs all over the yellow paper.

What a mess! But left exposed was a square black hole, and there was something stuck inside. She reached in and lifted down a thick bundle of papers. . . .

Something made her lock the door, sit down on the toilet, and pull them out of their rubber band, which snapped with age as she touched it. Good heavens . . . her mouth dropped open, appalled.

There was a dusty passport and a wallet. The wallet was full of money, notes. Pound notes and French thousand-franc notes. And a driver's license, made out in the name of a Mr. Alfred Barnett. And letters to Mr. Barnett. And tickets for trains and a cross-channel ferry . . . and the passport, dated to expire on the first of April 1958, was also made out in the name of Alfred and Ada Barnett. . . .

She sat there, and church child that she was, she cried a little with relief and the pity of it. The ghost was a boy who had stolen and hidden the loot, so well concealed, all those years ago. And after he was dead, he was sorry and wanted to make amends. But the school was abandoned by then; no one to listen to him; old Dracula would never listen to a poor lost ghost. . . . Well, she would make amends for him, and then he would be at rest, poor lonely thing.

She looked at the address in the passport. "Briardene," 12 Millbrook Gardens, Spilsby . . . Why, it was only ten minutes' walk; she could do it on her way home tonight, and they wouldn't even worry about her getting home a bit late.

She was still sitting there in a happy and pious daze at the virtue of the universe, when faithful Vicky came looking for her. Only faithful Vicky had noticed that she was gone. So she told her, and Vicky said that she would come as well. . . .

"They've taken Fiona to the hospital. . . ."

Perhaps that should have been a warning; but Rebeccah was too happy. "She'll get over it; and once we've taken this, it won't hurt anybody else again."

It all seemed so simple.

Liza came too, out of sheer nosiness, but Rebeccah was feeling charitable to all the world. It was that kind of blessed evening you sometimes get in January, lovely and bright, that makes you think of the spring before the next snow falls.

Millbrook Gardens was in an older, solider neighborhood than their own, posher in its funny old way. Walls of brick that glowed a deep rich red in the setting sun and showed their walking, blue, girlish shadows, where there wasn't any ivy or the bare strands of Virginia creeper. So it seemed that dim ghosts walked with them, among the houses with their white iron conservatories and old trees with homemade swings and garden seats still damp from the winter. And funny, stuffy names like "Lynfield" and "Spring Lodge" and "Nevsky Villa." It was hard to find "Briardene." There were no numbers on the houses. But they found it at last, looked over the gate, and saw a snowy-haired, rosy-cheeked old man turning over the rosebeds in the big front yard.

He was quite a way from the gate; but he turned and looked at them. It wasn't a nice look—a long, examining, unfriendly look. They felt that he didn't like children; they felt that he would have liked to stop them from coming in. But when Rebeccah called, in a too-shrill voice, "Do the Barnetts live here?" he abruptly waved them through to the front door and went back to his digging. Rebeccah thought that he must be the gardener; his clothes were quite old and shabby.

They trooped up to the front door and rang. There was no answer for quite a long time, and then the image of a plump, white-haired woman swam up the dark hall, all broken up by the stained glass in the door.

She looked a bit friendlier than the gardener, but not much; full of an ancient suspicion and wariness.

"Yes, children?" she said in an old-fashioned, bossy way.

Rebeccah held out her dusty package, proudly. "We found this—I think it's yours. . . ."

The woman took it from her briskly enough, the way you take a package from a postman. But when she began to take off Rebeccah's new rubber band, she suddenly looked so . . . as if she'd like to drop the package and slam the door.

"It's a passport and money and tickets and things," said Rebeccah helpfully.

The woman put a hand to her eyes, to shield them as if the sunlight was too strong; she almost fell, leaning against the doorjamb just in time. "Alfred," she called, "Alfred!" to the man in the yard. Then Rebeccah knew that the man was her husband, and she thought that the cry was almost a call for help. As if they'd been attacking the woman . . .

The old man came hurrying up, full of petty anger at being disturbed. Until his wife handed him the package. Then he, too, seemed to shrink, shrivel. The healthy high color fled his cheeks, leaving only a pattern of bright broken veins, as if they'd been drawn on wrinkled fish skin with a red pen.

"They're . . ." said the woman.

"Yes," said the man. Then he turned on the girls so fiercely that they almost ran away. His eyes were little and black and so full of hate that they, who had never been hit in their lives, grew afraid of being hit.

"*Where did you get these?*" There was authority in the voice, an ancient, cruel, utter authority. . . .

"At Harvest Road school . . . I found them in the boys' toilets . . . hidden behind a whitewashed brick . . ."

"*Which toilet?*" The old man had grabbed Rebeccah with a terrible strength by the shoulders; his fingers were savage. He began to shake her.

"Hey, watch it," said Liza aggressively. "There's a law against that kind of thing."

"I think we'll go now," said Vicky frostily.

"Which toilet?"

"The far-end one," Rebeccah managed to gasp out. Staring into the old man's hot, insane eyes, she was really

169

frightened. This was not the way that she'd meant things to go at all.

"How did you find it?" And, "What were *you* doing there?"

"We're using the school . . . till ours is fixed . . . we have to use the boys' toilets. . . ."

"*Who* showed you?" Under his eyes, Rebeccah thought that she was starting to fall to pieces. Was he a lost member of the Gestapo, the Nazi SS? So she cried out, which she hadn't meant to, "A *ghost* showed me—the ghost of a boy. It pointed to it. . . ."

"That's right," said Liza, "there *was* a ghost." Stubbornly, loyally.

It worked; another terrible change came over the old man. All of the cruel strength flowed out of his fingers. His face went whiter than ever. He staggered and clutched at the windowsill to support himself. He began to breathe in a rather terrifying, loud, unnatural way.

"Help me get him in," cried the woman. "Help me get him in quick."

Heaving and straining and panting and slithering on the dark polished floor, they got him through the hall and into a chintz armchair by the fire. He seemed to go unconscious. The woman went out and came back with a pill that she slipped into his mouth. He managed to swallow it. At first his breathing did not alter; then slowly it began to become more normal.

The woman seemed to come to herself, become aware of the little crowd, watching wide-eyed and openmouthed at what they knew was a struggle between life and death.

"He'll be all right now," she said doubtfully. "You'd better be off home, children, before your mothers start to worry." At the door she said, "Thank you for bringing the things— I'm sure you thought you were doing your best." She did not sound at all thankful, really.

"We thought you'd better have them," said Rebeccah politely. "Even though they were so old . . ."

The woman looked sharply at her, as she heard the question in her voice. "I suppose you'll want to tell your headmistress what happened? You should have handed in the stuff to her, really. . . . Well, Mr. Barnett was the last headmaster of Harvest Road—when it was boys, I mean—a junior high school. It happened—those things were stolen on the last day of the summer term. We were going on vacation in France the next day. . . . We never went; we couldn't. My husband knew the boy who had stolen them, but he couldn't prove it. He had the school searched from top to bottom. . . . The boy would admit nothing. It broke my husband's health. . . . He resigned soon after, when the school had to close. . . . Good night, children. Thank you."

She went as if to close the door on them, but Liza said sharply, "Did the boys call your husband Barney Boko?"

The woman gave a slight but distinct shudder, though it could have been the cold January evening. "Yes . . . they were cruel days, those, cruel."

Then she closed the door quickly, leaving them standing there.

They hadn't gone 50 yards when Liza stopped them, grabbing each of them frantically by the arm, as if she was having a seizure or something.

"Don't have it here," said Vicky sharply. "Wait till we get you to the hospital!"

But Liza didn't laugh. "I remember now," she said. "Listen—my Dad went to that school—it was a terrible place. Barney Boko—Dad said he caned the kids for everything—even for spelling mistakes. The kids really hated him—some parents tried to go to the school board an' the council, but it didn't do any good. There was a boy named Stebbing—Barney Boko caned him once too often—he was found dead. I think it might have been in them toilets. The verdict was he fell—he had one of those thin skulls or something. They said he fell and banged his head."

They stared at each other in horror.

"D'you think Stebbing's . . . what's in the toilets now?" asked Vicky.

They glanced around the empty streets; the lovely sun had vanished, and it had gotten dark awfully suddenly. There was a sudden rush coming at them around the corner—a ghostly rustling rush—but it was only long-dead autumn leaves, driven by the wind.

"Yes," said Rebeccah, as calmly as she could. "I think it was Stebbing. But he hasn't gotten anything against us—we did what he wanted."

"What *did* he want?" asked Vicky.

"For me to take back what he'd stolen—to make up for the wrong he did."

"You're too good for this world, Rebeccah!"

"What do you mean?"

"Did Stebbing *feel* like he was sorry?" asked Vicky. "Making Margie wet herself? Frightening Fiona into a seizure? What he did to *you*?"

Rebeccah shuddered. "He was angry. . . ."

"What we have just seen," said Vicky, "is Stebbing's revenge. . . ."

"How horrible. I don't believe that—it's too horrible. . . ."

"He used you, ducky. . . . Boys will, if you let them. . . ." Vicky suddenly sounded terribly bitter.

"Oh, I'm not going to listen. I'm going home."

They parted in a bad, silent mood with each other, though they stayed together as long as they could, through the windy streets, where the pools of light from the streetlights swayed. Rebeccah had the worst journey; she took her usual shortcut through the churchyard; before she'd realized what she'd done, she was halfway across, and there was no point in turning back. She stood paralyzed, staring at the teethlike ranks of gravestones that grinned at her in the faintest light of the last streetlight.

Somewhere, among them, Stebbing must be buried. And the worst of it was that the oldest, Victorian gravestones were behind her and the newer ones in front. She could just make out the date on the closest white one.

1956.

Stebbing must be very close.

She whimpered. Then she thought of God, who she really believed in. God wouldn't let Stebbing hurt her. She sort of reached out in her mind, to make sure that God was there. In the windy night, he seemed very far away; but he was watching. Whimpering softly to herself, she walked on, trying not to look at the names on the gravestones, but not able to stop herself.

Stebbing was right by the path, the third from the edge.

TO THE BELOVED MEMORY OF
BARRY STEBBING
BORN 11 MARCH 1944
DIED 22 JULY 1957
WITH GOD, WHICH IS MUCH BETTER

But Stebbing had nothing to say to her, here. Except, perhaps, a feeling that it was all over, and his quarrel had never been with her. Really.

And then she was running, and the lights of home were in front of her and Stebbing far behind.

She burst into the front hall like a hurricane. Daddy always kept the outside front door open, and a welcoming light glowed through the inner one, even in the middle of the winter.

Daddy was standing by the coat rack, looking at her. Wearing his dark gray overcoat and carrying a little bag like a doctor's. Instinctively, as the child of the vicarage, she knew that he was going to somebody who was dying.

"Oh," she said, "I wanted to talk to you." All breathless.

He smiled, but from far away; as God had. He always seemed far away, when he was going to see somebody who was dying.

"You'll have to wait, Person, I'm afraid. But I expect I'll be home for dinner. And all the evening. The church aid meeting's been canceled."

"Oh, *good.*" Toast made at the fire, and Daddy, and a long warm evening with the curtains drawn against the dark . . .

"I wonder," he said vaguely, "can you help? Is Millbrook Gardens the second or third turn off Windsor Road? I can never remember. . . ."

"Second from the bottom." Then, in a rush, "Who's dying?"

He smiled, puzzled. They never talked about such things. "Just an old man named Barnett . . . heart giving out. But his wife says he's very troubled . . . wants to talk about something he did years ago that's on his mind. I'd better be off, Rebeccah. See you soon." He went out. She heard his footsteps fading down the path.

She clutched the coat rack desperately, her eyes screwed tight shut so that she wouldn't see her face in the mirror.

"Come home soon, Daddy," she prayed. "Come home soon."

LEFT IN THE DARK

John Gordon

THE VILLAGE SEEMED to be stitched into the hills. A cluster of houses was held by the thread of the stream, and the stream itself was caught under a bridge and hooked around a stone barn in a fold of the heather and bracken. In the October sunshine the hills looked as soft as a quilt.

"There it is," said the big lady sitting at the front of the bus near the driver. "Lastingford."

"Me mam'll never remember that," said Alec to Jack alongside him. "She'll never have room to get it on the envelope."

"It's worse than that, man," said Jack. "I don't suppose they even get mail out here."

The lady had heard them, and she stood up and turned around so that she could talk to the whole bus. "Now, I don't want any of you to get worried," she said. "The people here are just the same as anywhere else, and I know they're going to make you welcome." She smiled down at Alec and Jack. "And you'll all be hearing from home because the mail comes quite regularly."

David, sitting by himself behind the other two, wanted her to look at him. She had been standing by the bus in Newcastle, ticking their names off on her list and watching as his mam kissed him and his dad shook his hand. Her rather large face under the green hat with the brim had had the funny little smile that women gave before they burst into tears, and she had nodded to his mother, who was quite unable to speak, as he climbed aboard. But now she had gone bossy, nursing her clipboard like a baby, so he looked out the window again and carefully, so that nobody else could see, wiped the tears away from the corners of his eyes with his fingertips.

"Missis." Jack got the lady's attention. "Do they ever have bombs here?"

"No, of course they don't. That's why you're being evacuated. You'll be as safe as houses."

David had seen a house come down. Half an hour after a bomb had landed, while the men in white helmets were climbing over fallen walls and jagged wood, the house next door had collapsed with its gray slates sliding like molten slag and the smoke from the kitchen fire still coming from the chimney pot as it plunged in a gentle roar into the soft cloud of dust. Mrs. Armstrong was dead under that, but he never saw her.

"So you've got nothing to worry about," said the lady. "There'll be cows and milk and horses."

"And duck ponds?" Alec, with the very pale face and bright red hair, looked up at her innocently. "With little ducks?"

She was not sure whether he was making fun of her and blushed as she said, "I wouldn't be surprised. You're in the countryside now, you know."

"I love fluffy little ducks," said Alec, and the lady pretended not to see as he and Jack put their heads together and choked to stop themselves from laughing. She walked past them to the back of the bus.

That smaller boy, she thought, the one behind them, he

wouldn't mind talking about ducks. But I can't say anything to him, or they'll think he's a baby. Well, he's not much more. She looked at her clipboard. He's only eight. She shook her head. It was bad enough for the other two, and they were three or four years older, but the little one should never be away from home.

They were going down into the valley now, but David could still see the hills humped like the green eiderdown on his bed at home, where, first thing in the morning, he made landscapes of it and had adventures up and down its slopes.

The bus stopped in the mouth of a stony track between the pub and a store that looked more like a house with all of the goods stacked inside somebody's living room. There were two Boy Scouts on the bus, big lads who had come to help with the evacuees, and they were each given their own little group to shepherd, but the lady picked out Alec and Jack and David to come along with her. "These three are together," she told the Scouts. "I'll just see them settled first." And then she raised her voice so that everybody could hear. "I'll be along to see every one of you and make sure you're all nice and comfy." But some of the girls were crying. "It's just like a vacation," she said. "The people here are really looking forward to having you. You'll see." She looked up and down the steep road. One woman stood on her doorstep a little way down the street; otherwise there was nobody.

"Missis." Jack caught the lady's attention. "I've never been on vacation."

A desperate gleam crossed her face. "Never mind," she said. Her voice had a tremble in it, and her accent slipped so that she spoke like their mothers. "Don't worry, pet, I'm going to take you to a really nice house. Now pick up your things."

Jack had his clothes in a bundle, but Alec and David each had small suitcases, Alec's with a strap around it, and all three wore overcoats despite the heat of the October sun. They had come to stay, and winter was not far away.

The lady led them uphill and around a sharp corner into a rough road that climbed away steeply to the high hillside where sheep were placed like puffs of antiaircraft smoke among the purple heather, but they turned sharply again, and a few paces took them to the front of a tall, plain-faced house of gray stone. Plants with broad leaves stood in the windows on each side of the door, and lace curtains hung like rain falling in the dark rooms behind. But the brass door knocker was brightly polished, and the step was scrubbed almost white. The lady's hand was still reaching for the knocker when the door opened, pulled suddenly back, and a girl of around 16 stood there, trying to see beyond the upstretched arm and at the same time saying, "Hello, have you brought them—the evacuees? There should be three, all little lads, Mrs. Prosser said. Oh, yes."

As the words came tumbling out, her eyes had been stopping on each of them in turn and counting. "Good. They're all there." Her round face beamed.

Her rosy cheeks and quick smile seemed to David to shine against the gray stone and dark hall behind her and to be quite wrong for the clothes she wore. She had a white lace cap on her brown hair, which was drawn back into a bun, and she wore a black dress buttoned high at the neck, black stockings, and black low-heeled shoes so that her body seemed in a prison from which only her face, looking over the wall, was free. She bobbed a brief curtsy to the lady. "Mrs. Prosser says I'm to take them up to their room while she sees you in the parlor."

The lady in the green hat stood to one side and let them go ahead of her, touching each on the shoulder as they went by as though what she really wanted to do was hold them back because they were barging into a place where they did not belong. "Wipe your feet," she said three times, once to each of them, and then came in behind them and stood quite still, clutching her clipboard, as the maid closed the door and shut out most of the light. The hall was dim and chilly.

Jack sniffed. "Smells of polish," he said. "Look at the shine on that floor."

A thin rug lay along the center of the hall, and Alec pushed at it with his toe so that it wrinkled over the polished wood. "Could be dangerous if you came downstairs in a rush," he said.

Jack also pushed at the carpet. "Man!" he said loudly. "You could go head over shoulders on that!"

"Shh!" The lady was horrified, but the girl gave a little strangled squeak and went past them with her lips and eyes squeezed tight. She opened a door, and they heard her mumble something and then hastily beckon the lady forward, show her through, and shut the door quickly behind her.

"You lot!" She held herself very upright, struggling not to laugh. "If that's the way you're going to carry on, you'll get me shot. Where are your manners?"

"But it's true," said Jack. "That floor's a danger."

"And it's not the only thing that's dangerous around here."

She advanced on them, and her laughter was now well under control. "If you don't watch your step, Mrs. Prosser will get you sent away home again."

"I won't mind," said Jack.

"Nor me neither." Alec backed him up.

"But what's to become of me?" She had her hands on her hips. "If you gang don't watch your p's and q's, I'll get the blame and she'll get rid of me, and then what would I do without a job?" She looked at each of them as sternly as her round face would allow. "Eh?"

David saw that the other two were going to stand dumbly, and he was suddenly afraid that they would turn the one friendly face against them. "We won't get you into trouble, miss," he said.

He stood partly behind the others and was the smallest. Her eyes rested on him fully for the first time, and her expression suddenly melted. "You don't need to call me miss," she said. "I'm not old enough for that."

Jack turned and looked down at David. "Everybody knows that," he said. "Don't be silly."

"No, he's not." The girl seemed suddenly to charge at them. "He's not silly. He's the nicest little lad of the three of you. What's your name, pet?"

"David," he said.

"Right, then, David. We'll lead the way and let them follow." She held out her hand, and he longed to hold it, but he knew that if he did, the others would call him soft, so he stood firm and looked up at her sternly. Once again she had to hold back a giggle. "Very well, then, David," she said and turned to the other two to get their names. "You can call me

Pauline, but you better not be cheeky, or else I'll tell the missis."

She turned, and her face and cap were hidden so that her figure was entirely black and merged with the deep shadows at the end of the hall so completely that David thought that she had vanished through some side doorway. Only the rustle of her dress drew him forward. Then she was climbing stairs much broader than in any house on his own street, and he hurried forward in case she should disappear again. She climbed swiftly, and his heavy case bumped against his legs as he struggled to keep up with her. But when they came to a landing, she waited for them. "Are you out of breath?" she said. "Because we've got a long way to go yet."

There was a window with colored glass. "It's just like being in a church," Jack said to her.

"And almost as cold." Alec shivered. "Do you have hymns?"

"No music." Pauline shook her head. "The missis doesn't like to hear anybody singing. She doesn't like any noise at all inside these four walls."

The unseen Mrs. Prosser could hardly have complained as they mounted the next flight and the next, because the chatter from Alec and Jack died out as they became breathless, and the only sound was their feet on the stair carpet. But David noticed that as they climbed higher, and the noise was less likely to be heard down below, the carpet became thinner and their footsteps louder. And the stairway became narrower until there was scarcely enough room for them and their luggage, and their free hands were holding a painted rail. They came to a landing of bare boards and one small window.

"Can't be any farther, can it?" said Jack. "We must be practically under the roof with the birdies."

"That's where you're wrong, hinny." Pauline imitated his Newcastle accent. "There's one more stage yet." She went to a plain door that had a latch instead of a handle. "Lift the bolt," she said as she raised the latch and pulled back the door, "and here we are. Almost."

She went into darkness, and they heard her feet on the wooden boards of uncarpeted stairs, and then another door opened and let down a gray light on the last flight. "Come on," she called, and Jack pushed to the front. Alec did not want to be left on the bare landing and went next, leaving David where he was.

The door swung to, and he was suddenly alone. The landing was like a little room, an empty closet, and no sound came from below or above, not even the scratch of a beetle. He had had a dream like this, an empty room in a house far away from anything he knew. He stood where he was and waited to wake up.

It was a full minute before Pauline, realizing that he was left behind, came clattering down the stairs.

"Oh, poor little lad!" She was immediately alongside him, bending over with her arm around his shoulders. "You'll break my heart, you will." Her tears came to the surface but did not quite brim over. "Standing there with your overcoat buttoned up and your case by your side. You look as though you're all alone at a railroad station—little boy lost." She was suddenly so motherly that she even smoothed his dark hair. "Why didn't you come after us?"

Until then he had not thought of crying, but now his mouth turned down at the corners. "There was a man," he said.

"A man? Where?"

He raised a hand and pointed toward the door. If she hadn't asked him, he was sure that he would never have remembered what had just happened. But it was true. A big man had followed Alec through the door, and that was why he had hung back and been left alone.

"There's no man here," said Pauline. "Just us."

"I saw him." The man was tall and wore a brownish suit.

Pauline studied his face for a moment and then looked carefully around the landing. "There's no man up here, David. There's no man in the whole house."

David knew that. But he had seen the broad back and the speckled, rough material of the man's jacket and pants. It was the sort of thing you see and don't see at the same time, and he would have forgotten it a moment later if it hadn't been for Pauline asking him. She was looking into his face now, as full of kindness as his mother, and his lip quivered.

"Oh," she said, crouching to hug him, "it's only your imagination, David, after all you've been through with that horrible Hitler bombing everybody. And we had to go and leave you all by yourself." She pulled a handkerchief from her sleeve and wiped his eyes. "But I can tell you this, pet, we'll never leave you alone up here again. Never, ever."

Mrs. Prosser had made sure that the three boys were going to be seen around the house as little as possible. Their room was in the attic, three iron beds in a row under a whitewashed, sloping ceiling.

"Just like a dormitory," said Jack.

"It's quite nice." Pauline was straightening the sheets. "I've tried to make it homey." She had brought two rag rugs from home to put on the cold linoleum and, without Mrs. Prosser knowing, had taken the curtains from another room at the top of the house and hung them in the single dormer window that jutted out from the slates of the roof.

"What's that?" Jack demanded, pointing to a table beneath the window.

"That's a washstand. Don't you know anything?" A jug stood in a big basin on the table's marble top. "That's where you put your soap." She pointed to a china dish. "And you hang your towels on these rails around the edge. I'll bring you up some water directly."

"All of us in the same basin?" Alec didn't believe it. "The water'll get black."

"I bags first," said Jack.

There was a chair with a cane bottom next to a huge wardrobe, but no other furniture. "You can hang your clothes up in there later," she told them, "but now you've got to go and meet the missis. Put your overcoats on your beds. No . . . " she stopped Jack from throwing his coat on the middle bed ". . . that's for the smallest one. You two big lads have got to look after him." Jack and Alec both made faces. "And you needn't be like that either."

"Has he been crying for his mam?" Jack looked carefully at David's face.

"No, I haven't!" David lunged forward suddenly, and Jack had to fend him off as Pauline gave a shriek.

"He's a real little fury when he's roused." She was delighted with him. "You'll have to watch your step." Jack put his tongue out at her. "And if there's any more of that, you'll have me to deal with."

"You're only a lass."

"We'll see about that!" Suddenly she was chasing all three of them around the room and over the beds, until she caught Jack in a corner. "Say sorry, or I'll give you a Chinese burn." She had her fist bunched, ready to rub her knuckles on his scalp. "Say sorry!"

"I won't."

They were struggling and laughing, when faintly, from far away, a bell tinkled. Through all the noise Pauline heard it and instantly pushed herself clear.

"Is my cap straight? Look at my dress—the state it's in! All crumpled up." She was pushing her hair back and pressing at the creases at the same time. "Come on now." Her attitude had changed, and she was ordering them to follow her. They even lined up before they went through the door. David was last again, and it was this that made him think of the man. He looked back. The room was empty. If there had been a man, the only place he could be was in the wardrobe. David clung to the back of Alec's jacket as he followed him down the stairs.

They came down through the house, their footsteps becoming quieter as the stair carpet thickened, and then they were in the hushed hall. Pauline smoothed her skirt once more, licked her lips, looked briefly at the three boys, and tapped at a door hidden in its own recess. They saw her bob a curtsy as she entered and then stand back and beckon them.

The light coming through the window was guillotined by the drape of the curtains, and when the door closed with a soft click behind him, David felt trapped in a dark sea cave. Tall cabinets rose to the ceiling where they lipped over in black scrolls, and pictures in ebony frames leaned from the walls like the mouths of great howling creatures held back by chains. His hand reached for Jack's and held it.

"Well?" The voice was a high-pitched yelp, and for a split second he thought that he saw a dog in a dress. The gray face against the chair back had high cheekbones and a chin so thin that it was like a dog's pointed muzzle. It barked again. "Stop fidgeting, girl."

The rustle of Pauline's dress ceased. David had half hidden himself behind Jack as they were lined up on one side of the wide fireplace, and the voice rattled again. "I can hardly see one of them. Fetch him out."

Pauline nudged him into the open.

"Are they clean?" The bony eyebrows turned away from them to the lady in the green hat who stood beside her chair.

"Of course they are, Mrs. Prosser." The lady fiddled nervously with her clipboard. "The nurse looked at their hair before we set out."

The gray face swung to Pauline. "Have they got their ration books?"

The lady said, "I've got them here."

"Have they been told about wiping their boots?"

"Yes, Mrs. Prosser," lied Pauline.

"And about noise?"

"Yes, Mrs. Prosser."

"You've taken them up and shown them their beds?"

"Yes, Mrs. Prosser."

There was a pause, and the lady said, "I'm sure they're going to be very comfortable." She smiled at them. "Aren't you?"

"We don't know yet," said Jack.

A sound like the hiss of a serpent came from Mrs. Prosser. There was a moment's silence, and then the lady beside her started to make excuses, but the gray face leaned back with the chin pulled into the thin neck, and the words fell silent. They heard the breath in Mrs. Prosser's nostrils before she spoke.

"I want them out of my sight," she said. "At once."

Pauline would not let them say a word until they had climbed to the top of the house.

"Oh," she said, "I'll just plonk meself down here till I get me breath back." She sat in the single chair looking down into her lap, and after a moment her shoulders began shaking. It was more than David could bear to see her sobbing, and he went and stood in front of her, wanting to touch her but not daring. She looked up, and her face was red, but not with tears. She was giggling. "That young scamp Jack," she said. "I don't know how he dares!"

David had made a mistake. He tried to grin, but knew that there was too much alarm in his face, and he tried to move away. Pauline reached and grasped his hand. "No. Don't go away. Somebody's got to protect me from those two demons."

"I only spoke the truth," Jack protested. "We don't know if we're going to like it yet." He turned to Alec. "Do we?"

Alec's pale brow was wrinkled. "Her downstairs," he said. "If that's what *she's* like, what's going to happen when Mr. Prosser comes home?"

"Oh, hell," said Jack. "I hadn't thought."

"Well, you don't need to." Pauline got to her feet. "And don't let me hear you using language like that anymore."

"I only said hell."

"That's enough!" She went briskly to the big wardrobe.

"You don't need to worry about Mr. Prosser coming home. He's dead."

"Phew!" Jack let out his breath. "That was a narrow squeak. I couldn't bear two like that."

Pauline suddenly turned on him. "That's just where you're wrong, clever clogs. He wasn't anything like the missis. Never a bit. Mr. Prosser was a lovely man. He was so gentle you felt you always wanted to talk to him, and . . ." Her voice rose. "I won't have a word said against him."

Jack was taken aback, but only for a moment. "But he married *her*," he said.

Pauline sighed, and they could hear her mother and all of the other village women talking as she said, "It's such a shame they never had any children. But she never would, never in a million years. He wanted them, you could tell that. He was a bit shy like, even with lads and lasses, but he had such a lovely, big, kind face and eyes just like little Davey's here." She was teasing now. "He's going to be a lady-killer, aren't you, Davey?"

"I wish you'd shut up," he said.

"Look, I've made him blush. But it is true—you have got nice big eyes."

"What about mine?" said Jack.

"You! You're too cheeky by half. Yours are wicked," and she turned to open the wardrobe door. "Now, here's where you've got to hang your clothes. There's plenty of room."

"Smells of mothballs," said Jack, "and it looks as though somebody's already using it."

"It's only just one old suit," she said. "You three don't look as though you're going to need much space."

"Whose suit is it?"

Pauline turned to face them. "It's Mr. Prosser's, and I don't want you saying a word about it, any of you, or you'll get me fired just as sure as night follows day. When he died, she made me throw everything out. Every single thing that was his. I don't think she'd ever wanted him—not him, not children, nothing. All she wants is to sit in state and have the whole village think she's bloody royalty."

"Who's swearing now?"

Pauline had reddened. "Well, she makes you. And she wasn't going to have everything her own way, not if I had anything to do with it. So I kept his suit, the old one he wore every day. He used to keep candy in the pockets for all us kiddies in the village." She turned back to the open wardrobe. "Anyway, it's still his house, and he has a right to be here."

She reached to move the coat hanger along the rail, and, as it slid, the suit swung around so that the back of the jacket was toward them. It was broad and reddish. David had seen it before.

The village school was smaller than the one they were used to, but not so very different. The coke stove had the same breathless fumes, and the blackboard chalk had the same dry taste when you put it on your tongue. Jack found new friends and fought with them in the playground, Alec felt the cold as the winter came on, and David tried to keep up with the big lads and not be homesick, but the ache was with him most of the time.

They hardly ever saw Mrs. Prosser. She made sure of that. Once a day a woman came up from the village to cook lunch for her, but they had to stay at school and eat the sandwiches that Pauline made for them. And by the time school was over and they climbed the hill and turned the corner, the house was bleak and dark and already closed down for the night. Except for the kitchen. They were not allowed to use the front door, and they would not have wanted to, because it was easier to get to the kitchen through the yard at the back, and they knew the fire would still be burning and Pauline waiting for them. David used to think it was like coming out of the dark into a secret burrow, with the yellow light of the oil lamp in the center of the table gleaming on the plates set out for them and showing the steam curling from the kettle on the stove.

"Something hot," said Pauline. "You need it when the nights draw in." Generally, it was soup. "I'm not the world's best cook," she said, but she would roast potatoes at the edge of the fire and bring bread her mother had baked and sent up to the house because she "couldn't bear the thought of young lads going to bed on an empty stomach."

It was the best part of the day. They lived in the kitchen, and gradually it began to feel as though they had always been there. The two bigger boys tried to make it belong to them. They never quite succeeded.

They had not been there long when Jack said one night, "Where's the radio? I like that when I'm at home."

Pauline shook her head. "We haven't got electricity, and she won't have it in the house, anyway."

"What does she do, then?"

"She sews. She does beautiful embroidery."

"Her?" He didn't believe it. "I bet she catches beetles and eats them."

Pauline laughed, but she hushed him and glanced at the door to the hall. "You never quite know where she is," she whispered. "She moves so quiet."

They were noisy enough most nights playing board games, which Pauline had brought from home, or they drew pictures, especially David, or sometimes Pauline read to them, mostly stories about murder and love from little books with gray pages that she smuggled into the house.

But by seven o'clock the fire was only a few red coals in the grate, and it was time for her to go home and for them to go to bed. Every night she lit a candle and went ahead of them into the dark hall. They moved quietly in the silent house, because boots were forbidden, and the boys were in their socks. There was always a scuffle, because nobody wanted to be the last in line with the darkness creeping at their heels as they went higher, and David always lost until Pauline saw what was happening and made either Jack or Alec go alongside him—in case he stumbled, she said.

But still the great whispering well of the stairs surged around them, and the little light made tall shadows lean into walls and doorways and wait for them on the landings above.

"Be quick, then," she always said as she put the candlestick on the floor and left them as they got undressed. She had to come back, once they were in bed, and take the candle because Mrs. Prosser would not allow it to be left. David was clumsy with his clothes, and often she had to help put on his pajamas, but it gave her the chance to tuck him in, which she always wanted to do because he looked so small and forlorn.

"Sleep tight." She would take one last look around the room, and they would see the cracks of light fade around the edges of the door as her steps clattered down the bare stairs.

They huddled under their blankets, talking in the dark about home. David listened. He never said very much, but as the other two talked, he walked with them from the lamppost where they always met at night until the blackout came and along the street until he saw his mother waiting, and then he realized that his eyes were wet and his pillow was damp, and he curled tighter and screwed up a corner of the sheet until it was the shape of the limp toy dog he always took to bed at home. He had been afraid to bring it with him.

One night he was almost asleep when Alec said into the darkness, "I wouldn't like to be left here alone. I bet there are ghosts."

"Don't be silly," said Jack. "Who needs ghosts when we've got her downstairs?"

"But I bet there are. I bet David thinks there are."

They asked him. He hardly heard them because he had the sheet to his lips and was far away. Alec insisted. "Are there any ghosts in this house, David?"

"I don't know," he said, but the thought of the man on the landing drifted into his mind. He let it fade. It was too long ago and too misty, and he did not want the misery of that day to come back. "I don't know."

"You're hopeless, you are. Anyway," Alec turned over with a lot of noise, "nothing would ever make me stay here by meself."

"Nor me," said Jack. "Never."

Christmas was a few days away, and it brought an excitement that had nothing to do with packages and presents.

Christmas cards came from Newcastle with letters tucked inside from mothers saying that as there had been no raids for quite a while, it was safe to come home for a short time. Everybody's cheeks seemed to be glowing with the same good news.

"And me Dad's on leave," Jack shouted in the kitchen. "Man, it's going to be great!"

Alec had a letter saying that he was to catch the same bus as Jack, but David's letter was slow in coming. It was the day before Christmas Eve, and Jack and Alec were already packed, ready to leave that afternoon, when the mail came with David's letter. They all crowded around to find out when he was leaving.

It was Pauline who told her mother what had happened. "His little fingers were so clumsy that he could hardly get it out of the envelope. Just like a baby he looks sometimes. And there was a letter and a postal order. 'That'll be for your fare home,' said one of the lads, but Davey was reading what his mam said. I've never seen a look on a boy's face quite like I seen then. It was a lovely letter, I read it, but his mam told him she didn't think it was safe and that he wasn't going to go home after all. I had to turn me back. The look in that little lad's eyes was something I never want to see again."

David did not cry. Jack, watching him carefully, said, "You're a good lad, Davey," and then he and Alec whispered in the corner, and Pauline heard the chink of pennies. When they put on their coats and boots and went out secretively, she knew that they were going down to the store to buy him a present before their bus left. It was all they could do to cheer him up.

To prevent her own tears from welling up again, Pauline said, "That's a pretty card your mam sent, Davey. Nice little red robin." He nodded. It was a tiny card, very small, like his mother. "But I don't believe you've sent one to her."

"I did."

"But not a real one. Not one you made yourself. Anyone can send an old store-bought card."

She knew he liked drawing. "Tell you what," she said as she led him to the window. "See that old tree behind the yard? It's still got some lovely leaves on it, all red and yellow. Why don't you go and get some while I get a big piece of paper and make some flour paste, and then you can stick them onto your picture and send them to your mam. There's still time; it's not Christmas Eve till tomorrow."

She watched him cross the yard, and then she smoothed her dress and bit her lip. His letter had been bad news for her, too, and the bell that suddenly rang meant that she had to face up to it.

Mrs. Prosser's few Christmas cards were of the dark kind, and they stood among the black ornaments on the mantel as a reminder that Christmas was midwinter and cold and hard. Pauline felt their chill as she told Mrs. Prosser that not all the boys were leaving for the holiday.

"Why's that? Has his mother no feelings?" The thin voice did not wait for an explanation. "These people ought never to have children. They can't wait to saddle other people with them." She waved Pauline away. "Get the other two ready. I can't wait to see the back of them."

Pauline fled. For the next hour there was bustle, and when Jack and Alec had given her David's present to hide, she went with them down to the village to make sure that they caught the bus.

David was alone in the kitchen. All he could do now was pretend. He pretended he was going home and he had to hurry to finish the big Christmas card he was making for his mother. He was drawing on the sheet of paper that Pauline had given him when he heard the door to the hall open. He did not want to look up, but he slowly raised his eyes. Mrs. Prosser stood there with her monkey fingers clasped in front of her black dress.

For a long moment neither moved, and then her voice snapped at him. "Stand up!" He slid off his chair. "Stand up when a lady comes into the room!"

She swished forward so smoothly that she seemed not to have legs under her long dress. "So you're the one that's staying." He saw that her lips had bluish blisters. "Your mother expects me to provide your Christmas dinner, I suppose. Oh, does she, indeed!" Her breath hissed as she sucked it in. "There will be no heathen feast in this house. No Christmas dinner, so don't expect it. The very idea!"

Indignation raged inside her, and she was turning away when quite suddenly she stopped. Her chin was pulled in so tightly that it seemed to be part of her neck, and she was looking down at the table. "What on earth is that?"

The red leaves were spread out in front of him, and for the first time David had a question he could answer. "I'm going to stick them on a picture for me mam."

His voice was no more than a murmur, and her action was equally silent. She leaned forward and scraped the leaves into one bony hand, crunched them like wastepaper, and threw them into the back of the fire.

"That for your mother!" she said. "I will not have my kitchen made into a Newcastle slum." The door slammed.

When Pauline came back, David's picture was also on the fire. "I didn't feel like doing it," he said. He wanted to cry, but he did not dare, and she did not question him.

She gave him all of his favorite things for dinner and stayed with him late, reading a story to him as he lay in bed, something that she had never done when the others were there.

When she tucked him in, she whispered, "I'll leave you the candle, Davey, but don't let on to the missis."

At the door she turned and smiled at him, and then the latch dropped. He heard her footsteps on the stairs, another door opened and closed, and he was in a silence so deep that he thought he heard the flutter of the candle flame.

He lay as she had left him, curled up on his side, looking at Alec's empty bed. Behind him, Jack's bed would be the same—flat and empty. He was alone in the long room, and the frosty night crept in and held the candle flame stiff—as smooth as an almond. No sound, and all that emptiness at his back.

He turned his head on the pillow until he could see the wardrobe towering against the wall. From where he lay the long mirrors of its doors were blank, but the columns on either side shone in the candle flame, as though they guarded a yawning gateway.

Then deep inside it something moved, and at the same instant a voice from almost alongside him dragged him around. The door to the stairs was open, and the tall figure of Mrs. Prosser was in the room. She made no noise. It was her reflection that he had seen in the mirror.

"I knew it!" Her voice was as bitter as the icy air as she swept to the foot of his bed and pointed at the candle. "Who gave you this?"

Words did not come. From his pillow he looked up at her. In the candlelight the blue flecks on her lips were black.

"Am I going to wait all night for an answer?"

The pointing hand suddenly clenched, and he drew himself into a ball, ready for her to reach over and strike. But the blow did not come. Her hand came down, and something that may have been a smile pushed at her wrinkles. Even her voice was softer.

"But I don't suppose you like being on your own, do you, sonny?" He shook his head. "And I suppose you are afraid of the dark." He nodded. "Very, very afraid, I expect."

He watched the wrinkles at the corner of her mouth deepen, and now she was definitely smiling. "After all," she said, "it's almost Christmas."

He tried to smile.

"Well," she said, and her voice was still soft, "you know you deserve a thrashing, don't you?" She waited for his nod. He had to give it. "Worse than a thrashing, in fact." Her voice rose. "And worse than a thrashing you shall have!"

As she spoke, she snatched at the candle and turned for the door. "You will stay in this room all night and all tomorrow until I tell you to come out!"

The flame streamed and dipped in front of her as she swept out. The door closed with a bang and then the next, but even before he heard it slam, he had scrabbled at the sheets and pulled them tight around himself as he crouched.

He heard himself sob, but the echo made the black room emptier, and he stifled the sound. The sheets seemed clammy, as though they were never intended to be laid over a living creature, and his shivers made the iron bed frame give out little sounds like beetles' feet until he clamped his arms around his knees and controlled the trembling.

He heard a night bird shriek briefly on the hillside above the house, and then it, too, was swallowed in the silence of the night, and everything was utterly still. He could not hear even the sound of his own breathing, but as his eyes stared into the darkness and the silence in the room became more dense, he gradually saw the shape of the window against the stars.

It was then, in the corner beyond the foot of the bed, that he heard something shift. His bones were rigid, as cold as iron. He was clamped motionless.

Silence. His breath crept into his mouth. Then the sound came again. His eyes were as wide as an owl's, and in the starlight he saw the wardrobe door sigh open.

He flung himself across the empty bed, and his feet were on cold linoleum as his fingers fumbled for the latch. It bit his fingers, but the door was open, and he plunged into the blackness of the stairs. His foot missed the step. He clutched for the handrail, but missed it and fell, twisting in the rushing darkness until his shoulder and back crashed into the door at the bottom. The catch burst, and he fell out on to the bare boards of the landing.

There was a glimmer of light downstairs. Mrs. Prosser had stopped and was looking up. Her face halted him. The candle, gleaming like a star, made her mouth a pitiless shadow and her eyes two dark pits. But he had to go down to escape from whatever had swung the wardrobe door. He was too late. Something large and dark moved out from the burst doorway and brushed past him. He could see it against the whitewashed wall—the shape of a man, blocking his way.

David shrank. He was no more than a fistful of fear, and the man looked down at him. In the faint light from below, the man's face was hardly visible. It was no more than a blur of heavy mustache and eyebrows, which threw a deep shadow over its eyes, but David felt their gaze, and his blood slowed, and the silence stiffened until it seemed like nothing would move again.

It was then that the figure turned away. He watched it as it began to descend, seeming to tread heavily, but no sound came. The well of the stairs was a column of silence, with the spark of the candle shining faintly. Mrs. Prosser's head was still tilted upward. She saw what was coming, and the candle trembled, but she did not move. Fear held her motionless until it was too late.

The figure of the man was only two steps above her, when, in a sudden stab of terror, she thrust the candle at him as though to scorch him out of the air. But his big hand reached and closed over hers. It was then that she cried out and began to struggle. She could not save herself. The candle flared, fell, and went out.

As darkness engulfed the whole staircase, David ran down into it, sliding his hand down the banister. Nothing would keep him alone at the top of the house. He heard Mrs. Prosser fall. She did not cry out or even moan. He heard the thud of her arms, hips, and head on the stairs, a soft slither, and then silence.

He remembered the sole of his foot stepping on something warm that yielded beneath it, but then he was over it and crossing the cold floor of the kitchen to the back door.

His mother came that day, not to fetch him but to stay that night and the next, over Christmas. They were in Pauline's house down in the village with the stream outside the door, where she had found him standing on the ice.

"I don't know how we are ever going to thank you," said his mother for the tenth time. She was still shy, sitting very upright in the easy chair by the big fire as Pauline bustled around making tea. "It was such a terrible shock when I got your message."

Pauline's mother, round-cheeked like her daughter, smiled. "Now, just you put your mind at rest. Davey stays with us from now on. He could hardly go back there, could he?"

The two women looked at each other. They understood one another. David, in the warmth of the fire, with the tinsel of the Christmas tree trembling at his elbow, bowed his head over the drawing notepad on his knee and pretended that he was not listening as all three lowered their voices.

"Poor soul. What a terrible way to go."

"And that little lad in the house all on his own. He hasn't said much about it, and I don't like to ask."

Pauline glanced at him, and he started to hum to himself and bent further over his drawing. She turned her back to him and lowered her voice even further. "She must have been up in his room. Must have been. I'm just sure one of those boys told her what was up there, because she had it with her when we found her at the foot of the stairs. It must have been the last thing she saw before she died."

David's mother did not understand.

"Mr. Prosser's old suit," said Pauline. "It was wrapped around her. Tight. Really tight."

David's picture had a house standing in the snow, and you could see firelight through the windows. He would give it to his mother in the morning.

THE MONKEY'S PAW

W. W. Jacobs

OUTSIDE, THE NIGHT was cold and wet, but in the small parlor of Laburnum Villa the blinds were drawn and the fire burned brightly as father and son played chess.

"Hark at the wind," said Mr. White.

"I'm listening," said his son, Herbert, grimly surveying the board as he stretched out his hand. "Check."

"I should hardly think that he'd come tonight," said his father, with his hand poised over the board.

"Mate," replied the son.

"That's the worst of living so far out," bawled Mr. White, with sudden and unlooked-for violence. "Of all the beastly, slushy, out-of-the way places to live in, this is the worst. Path's a bog, and the road's a torrent."

"Never mind, dear," said his wife soothingly. "Perhaps you'll win the next one."

"There he is," said Herbert White as the gate banged loudly and heavy footsteps came toward the door.

The old man rose with hospitable haste and welcomed in a tall, burly man, beady of eye and rubicund of visage.

"Sergeant Major Morris," he said, introducing him.

The sergeant major shook hands and, taking the proffered seat by the fire, watched contentedly while his host got out whiskey and tumblers.

At the third glass the sergeant major's eyes got brighter, and he began to talk, the little family circle regarding with eager interest this visitor from distant parts, as he squared his broad shoulders in the chair and spoke of wild scenes and daring deeds; of wars and plagues and strange peoples.

"Twenty-one years of it," said Mr. White, nodding at his wife and son. "When he went away, he was a slip of a youth in the warehouse. Now look at him."

"He doesn't look to have taken much harm," said Mrs. White politely.

"I'd like to go to India myself," said the old man, "just to look around a bit, you know."

"Better where you are," said the sergeant major, shaking his head.

"I should like to see those old temples and fakirs and jugglers," said the old man. "What was it that you started telling me the other day about a monkey's paw or something, Morris?"

"Nothing," said the soldier hastily. "Leastways nothing worth hearing."

"Monkey's paw?" said Mrs. White curiously.

"Well, it's just a bit of what you might call magic, perhaps," said the sergeant major offhandedly. "To look at," he said, fumbling in his pocket, "it's just an ordinary little paw, dried to a mummy."

He took something out of his pocket and proffered it.

"And what is there special about it?" inquired Mr. White, examining it.

"It had a spell put on it by an old fakir," said the sergeant major, "a very holy man. He wanted to show that fate ruled people's lives and that those who interfered with it did so to their sorrow. He put a spell on it so that three separate men could each have three wishes from it."

His manner was so impressive that his hearers were conscious that their light laughter jarred somewhat.

"Well, why don't you have three, sir?" said Herbert White cleverly.

"I have," he said quietly, and his blotchy face whitened.

"And did you really have the three wishes granted?" asked Mrs. White.

"I did," said the sergeant major, and his glass tapped against his strong teeth.

"And has anybody else wished?" persisted the old lady.

"The first man had his three wishes, yes," was the reply. "I didn't know what the first two were, but the third was for death. That's how I got the paw."

His tones were so grave that a hush fell upon the group.

"If you've had your three wishes, it's no good to you now then, Morris," said the old man at last. "What do you keep it for?"

The soldier shook his head. "Fancy, I suppose," he said slowly. "I did have some idea of selling it, but I don't think I will. It has caused enough mischief already."

"If you could have another three wishes," said the old man, eyeing him eagerly, "would you have them?"

"I don't know," said the other. "I don't know."

He took the paw and, dangling it between his forefinger and thumb, suddenly threw it upon the fire. Mr. White, with a slight cry, stooped down and snatched it off.

"Better let it burn," said the soldier solemnly.

"If you don't want it, Morris," said the other, "give it to me."

"I won't," said his friend doggedly. "I threw it on the fire.

If you keep it, don't blame me for what happens. Pitch it on the fire again like a sensible man."

The other shook his head and examined his new possession closely. "How do you do it?" he inquired.

"Hold it up in your right hand and wish aloud," said the sergeant major, "but I warn you of the consequences."

Mr. White drew the talisman aloft, but the sergeant major, with a look of alarm on his face, caught him by the arm. "If you must wish," he said gruffly, "wish for something sensible."

Mr. White dropped it into his pocket. In the business of supper the talisman was partly forgotten, and afterward the three sat listening in an enthralled fashion to a second installment of the soldier's adventures in India.

"If the tale of the monkey's paw is not more truthful than those he has been telling us," said Herbert, as the door closed behind their guest, "we shan't make much out of it."

"Did you give him anything for it, Father?" inquired Mrs. White, regarding her husband closely.

"A trifle," said he, coloring slightly. "He didn't want it, but I made him take it. And he pressed me again to throw it away."

"Likely," said Herbert, with pretended horror. "Why, we're going to be rich, and famous, and happy. Wish to be an emperor, Father."

Mr. White took the paw from his pocket and eyed it dubiously. "I don't know what to wish for, and that's a fact," he said slowly. "It seems to me I've got all I want."

"If you only cleared the house, you'd be happy, wouldn't you?" said Herbert, with his hand on his shoulder. "Well, wish for two hundred pounds, then; that'll just do it."

His father, smiling shamefacedly, held up the talisman, as his son, with a solemn face, sat down at the piano and struck a few impressive chords.

"I wish for two hundred pounds," said the old man distinctly.

A fine crash from the piano greeted the words, interrupted by a shuddering cry from the old man. His wife and son ran toward him.

"It moved," he cried, with a glance of disgust at the object as it lay on the floor. "As I wished, it twisted in my hand like a snake."

"Well, I don't see the money," said his son as he picked it up and placed it on the table, "and I bet I never will."

"It must have been your fancy, Father," said his wife, regarding him anxiously.

He shook his head. "Never mind, though; there's no harm done, but it gave me a shock all the same."

They sat down by the fire again while the two men finished their pipes. Outside, the wind was higher than ever, and the old man startled nervously at the sound of a door banging upstairs. A silence unusual and depressing settled upon all three, which lasted until the old couple rose to retire for the night.

"I expect you'll find the cash tied up in a big bag in the middle of your bed," said Herbert as he bade them good night, "and something horrible squatting up on top of the wardrobe watching you as you pocket your ill-gotten gains."

He sat alone in the darkness, gazing at the dying fire and seeing faces in it. The last face was so horrible and so simian that he gazed at it in amazement. It got so vivid that, with a little uneasy laugh, he felt on the table for a glass containing a little water to throw over it. His hand grasped the monkey's paw, and with a little shiver, he wiped his hand on his coat and went up to bed.

In the brightness of the wintry sun the next morning he laughed at his fears. The dirty, shriveled little paw was pitched on the sideboard with a carelessness that betokened no great belief in its virtues.

"I suppose all old soldiers are the same," said Mrs. White. "The idea of our listening to such nonsense! How could wishes be granted in these days? And if they could, how could two hundred pounds hurt you, Father?"

"Might drop on his head from the sky," said the frivolous Herbert.

"Morris said that the things happened so naturally," said his father, "that you might if you so wished attribute it to coincidence."

"Well, don't break into the money before I come back," said Herbert as he rose from the table.

His mother laughed and, following him to the door, watched him down the road.

"Herbert will have some more of his funny remarks, I expect, when he comes home," Mrs. White said later to her husband as they sat at dinner.

"I daresay," said Mr. White, "but for all that, the thing moved in my hand; that I'll swear to."

"You thought it did," said the old lady soothingly.

"I say it did," replied the other. "There was no thought

about it; I had just . . . What's the matter?"

His wife made no reply. She was watching the mysterious movements of a man outside, who, peering in an undecided fashion at the house, appeared to be trying to make up his mind to enter. Three times he paused at the gate and then walked on again. The fourth time he stood with his hand upon it and then with sudden resolution flung it open and walked up the path. Mrs. White brought the stranger, who seemed ill at ease, into the room. She waited as patiently as she could for him to broach his business, but he was at first strangely silent.

"I—was asked to call," he said at last. "I come from Maw and Meggins."

The old lady started. "Is anything the matter?" she asked breathlessly. "Has anything happened to Herbert? What is it? What is it?"

"I'm sorry—" began the visitor.

"Is he hurt?" demanded the mother wildly.

The visitor bowed in assent. "Badly hurt," he said quietly, "but he is not in any pain."

"Oh, thank God!" said the old woman, clasping her hands. "Thank God for that! Thank—"

She broke off suddenly as the sinister meaning of the assurance dawned upon her. There was a long silence.

"He was caught in the machinery," said the visitor at length in a low voice.

"Caught in the machinery," repeated Mr. White in a dazed fashion. "Yes."

He sat staring blankly out the window and took his wife's hand between his own. "He was the only one left to us," he said, turning gently to the visitor. "It is hard."

The other coughed and, rising, walked slowly to the window.

"The firm wished me to convey their sincere sympathy to you in your great loss," he said.

There was no reply; the old woman's face was white, her eyes staring, and her breath inaudible; on the husband's face was a look such as his friend the sergeant might have carried into his first action.

"I was to say that Maw and Meggins disclaims all responsibility," continued the other. "They admit no liability at all, but in consideration of your son's services, they wish to present you with a certain sum as compensation."

Mr. White dropped his wife's hand and, rising to his feet, gazed with a look of horror at his visitor. His dry lips shaped the words. "How much?"

"Two hundred pounds," was the answer.

Unconscious of his wife's shriek, the old man smiled faintly, put out his hands like a sightless man, and dropped, a senseless heap, to the floor.

In the huge new cemetery, some two miles distant, the old people buried their dead and came back to the house steeped in shadow and silence.

It was around a week after that the old man, waking suddenly in the night, found himself alone and heard the sound of subdued weeping coming from the window.

"Come back," he said tenderly. "You will be cold."

"It is colder for my son," said the old woman and wept afresh.

The sound of her sobs died away on his ears. The bed was

warm, and his eyes were heavy with sleep. He dozed fitfully until a sudden wild cry from his wife awoke him with a start.

"*The paw!*" she cried wildly. "The monkey's paw!"

He started up in alarm. "Where? Where is it? What's the matter?"

She came stumbling across the room toward him. "I want it," she said quietly. "You haven't destroyed it?"

"It's in the parlor," he replied. "Why?"

"I only just thought of it," she said hysterically. "Why didn't I think of it before? Why didn't *you* think of it?"

"Think of what?" he questioned.

"The other two wishes," she replied rapidly. "We've only had one."

"Was that not enough?" he demanded fiercely.

"No," she cried triumphantly. "We'll have one more. Go down and get it quickly and wish our boy alive again."

The man sat up in bed and flung the sheets from his quaking limbs. "Good God, you are insane!" he cried, aghast.

"Get it," she panted. "Get it quickly and wish. Oh, my boy, my boy!"

Her husband struck a match and lit a candle. "Go back to bed," he said unsteadily. "You don't know what you are saying."

"We've had the first wish granted," said the old woman feverishly. "Why not the second?"

"A coincidence," stammered the old man.

"Go and get it and wish," cried his wife, quivering with excitement.

The old man turned and regarded her, and his voice shook. "He has been dead ten days, and besides he—I would not tell you else, but—I could only recognize him by his clothing. If he was too terrible for you to see then, how now?"

"Bring him back," cried the old woman and dragged him toward the door. "Do you think I fear the child I have nursed?"

He went down in the darkness and felt his way to the parlor and then to the mantelpiece. The talisman was in its place, and a horrible fear that the unspoken wish might bring his mutilated son before him ere he could escape from the room seized upon him, and he caught his breath as he found that he had lost the direction of the door. His brow cold with sweat, he felt his way around the table and groped along the wall until he found himself in the small passage with the unwholesome thing in his hand.

Even his wife's face seemed changed as he entered the room. It was white and expectant and to his fears seemed to have an unnatural look upon it. He was afraid of her.

"*Wish!*" she cried in a strong voice.

"It is foolish and wicked," he faltered.

"*Wish!*" repeated his wife.

He raised his hand. "I wish my son alive again."

The talisman fell to the floor, and he regarded it fearfully. Then he sank trembling into a chair as the old woman, with burning eyes, walked to the window and raised the shade.

He sat until he was chilled with the cold, glancing occasionally at the figure of the old woman peering through the window. The candle end was throwing pulsating shadows on the ceiling and walls, until, with a flicker larger than the rest, it expired. The old man, with an unspeakable sense of relief at the failure of the talisman, crept back to his bed, and a minute or two afterward the old woman came silently and apathetically beside him.

Neither spoke, but lay silently listening to the ticking of the clock. A stair creaked, and a squeaky mouse scurried noisily through the wall. The darkness was oppressive, and after lying for some time screwing up his courage, he took the box of matches and, striking one, went downstairs for a candle.

At the foot of the stairs the match went out, and he paused to strike another; and at the same moment a knock, so quiet and stealthy as to be scarcely audible, sounded on the front door.

The matches fell from his hand and spilled in the passage. He stood motionless, his breath suspended until the knock was repeated. Then he turned and fled swiftly back to his room and closed the door behind him. A third knock sounded through the house.

"*What's that?*" cried the old woman, starting up.

"A rat," said the old man in shaking tones. "A rat. It passed me on the stairs."

His wife sat up in bed, listening. A loud knock resounded through the house.

"It's Herbert!" she screamed. "It's Herbert!"

She ran to the door, but her husband was before her and, catching her by the arm, held her tightly.

"What are you going to do?" he whispered hoarsely.

"It's my boy; it's Herbert!" she cried. "What are you holding me for? Let go. I must open the door."

"For God's sake don't let it in," cried the old man, trembling.

"You're afraid of your own son," she cried, struggling. "Let me go. I'm coming, Herbert; I'm coming."

There was another knock and another. The old woman, with a sudden wrench, broke free and ran from the room. Her husband followed to the landing and called after her appealingly as she hurried downstairs. He heard the chain rattle back and the bottom bolt drawn slowly and stiffly from the socket. The old woman's voice was strained and panting.

"The bolt," she cried. "Come down. I can't reach it."

But her husband was on his hands and knees groping wildly on the floor in search of the paw. If he could only find it before the thing outside got in. He heard the scraping of a chair as his wife put it down in the passage against the door. He heard the creaking of the bolt as it came slowly back, and at the same moment he found the monkey's paw and frantically breathed his third and last wish.

The knocking ceased suddenly, although the echoes of it were still in the house. He heard the chair drawn back, and the door opened. A cold wind rushed up the staircase, and a long, loud wail of disappointment and misery from his wife gave him courage to run down to her side and then to the gate beyond. The streetlight flickering opposite shone on a quiet and deserted road.

LOST HEARTS

M. R. James

IN SEPTEMBER OF the year 1811, a post chaise pulled up before the door of Aswarby Hall, in the heart of Lincolnshire. The little boy who jumped out as soon as it had stopped looked around him with the keenest curiosity during the short interval between the ringing of the bell and the opening of the hall door. He saw a tall, square, red-brick house, built in the reign of Anne; the windows of the house were many, tall, and narrow, with small panes and thick white woodwork. An evening light shone on the building, making the windowpanes glow like so many fires. Away from the hall in front stretched a flat park studded with oaks and fringed with firs, which stood out against the sky. The clock in the church tower, buried in trees on the edge of the park, only its golden weathervane catching the light, was striking six, and the sound came gently beating down the wind. It was altogether a pleasant impression, though tinged with melancholy.

The post chaise had brought the boy from Warwickshire, where he had been left an orphan. Now, owing to the generous offer of his elderly cousin, Mr. Abney, he had come to live at Aswarby. The truth is that very little was known of Mr. Abney's pursuits or temper. The professor of Greek at Cambridge had been heard to say that no one knew more of the religious beliefs of the later pagans than did the owner of Aswarby. Certainly his library contained all the then available books bearing on the mysteries. In the marble-paved hall stood a fine group of Mithras slaying a bull, which had been imported from the Levant at great expense. He was looked upon as a man wrapped up in his books, and it was a matter of great surprise among his neighbors that he should even have heard of his orphan cousin, Stephen Elliott, much more that he should have volunteered to make him an inmate of Aswarby Hall.

Whatever may have been expected by his neighbors, it is certain that Mr. Abney—the tall, the thin, the austere—seemed inclined to give his young cousin a kind reception. The moment the front door was opened he darted out of his study, rubbing his hands with delight.

"How are you, my boy? How are you? How old are you?" said he. "That is, you are not too much tired, I hope, by your journey to eat your supper?"

"No, thank you, sir," said Master Elliott. "I am pretty well."

"That's a good lad," said Mr. Abney. "And how old are you, my boy?"

It seemed a little odd that he should have asked the question twice in the first two minutes of their acquaintance.

"I'm twelve years old next birthday, sir," said Stephen.

"And when is your birthday, my dear boy? Eleventh of September, eh? That's well—that's very well. Almost a year hence, isn't it? I like—ha, ha!—I like to get these things down in my book. Sure it's twelve? Certain?"

"Yes, quite sure, sir."

"Well, well! Take him to Mrs. Bunch's room, Parkes, and let him have his tea—supper—whatever it is."

"Yes, sir," answered the staid Mr. Parkes; and he conducted

Stephen to the lower regions.

Mrs. Bunch was the most comfortable and human person whom Stephen had as yet met at Aswarby. She made him completely at home; they were great friends in a quarter of an hour; and great friends they remained. Mrs. Bunch had been born in the neighborhood some 55 years before; consequently, if anyone knew the ins and outs of the house and the area, Mrs. Bunch knew them.

Certainly there were plenty of things about the hall and the hall gardens that Stephen, who was of an adventurous and inquiring turn, was anxious to have explained. "Who built the temple at the end of the laurel walk? Who was the old man whose picture hung on the staircase, sitting at a table with a skull under his hand?" These and many similar points were cleared up by the resources of Mrs. Bunch's powerful intellect. There were others, however, of which the explanations furnished were less satisfactory.

One November evening, Stephen was sitting by the fire in the housekeeper's room.

"Is Mr. Abney a good man, and will he go to heaven?" he suddenly asked, with the peculiar confidence that children possess in the ability of their elders to settle these questions.

"Good?—bless the child!" said Mrs. Bunch. "Master's as kind a soul as ever I see! Didn't I never tell you of the little boy he took in out of the street, as you may say, this seven years back? And the little girl, two years after I first came here?"

"No. Do tell me all about them, Mrs. Bunch!"

"Well," said Mrs. Bunch, "the little girl I don't seem to recollect so much about. I know Master brought her back with him from his walk one day and gave orders to Mrs. Ellis, who was the housekeeper then, that she should take every care with. And the poor child hadn't no one belonging to her—she telled me so her own self—and here she lived with us a matter of three weeks it might be; and then, whether she were something of a gypsy in her blood or whatnot, but one morning she out of her bed afore any of us had opened a eye, and neither track nor yet trace of her have I set eyes on since. Master was wonderful put about and had all the ponds dragged; but it's my belief that she was had away by them gypsies, for there was singing around the house for as much as an hour the night she went, and Parkes, he declare as he heard them a-calling in the woods all that afternoon. Dear, dear! An odd child she was, so silent in her ways and all, but I was wonderful taken up with her, so domesticated she was—surprising."

"And what about the little boy?" said Stephen.

"Ah, that poor boy!" Mrs. Bunch sighed. "He was a foreigner—Jevanny, he called hisself—and he come a-tweaking his hurdy-gurdy around and about the drive one winter day, and Master had him in that minute, and asked all about where he came from, and how old he was, and how he made his way, and where were his relatives, and all as kind as heart could wish. But it went the same way with him. They're a unruly lot, them foreign nations, I do suppose, and he was off one fine morning just the same as the girl. Why he went was our question for as much as a year after; for he never took his hurdy-gurdy, and there it lays on the shelf."

The remainder of the evening was spent by Stephen in efforts to extract a tune from the hurdy-gurdy.

That night he had a curious dream. At the end of the passage at the top of the house, in which his bedroom was situated, there was an old, disused bathroom. It was kept locked, but the upper half of the door was glazed, and, since the muslin curtains that used to hang there had long been gone, you could look in and see the lead-lined bathtub affixed to the wall on the right-hand side, with its head toward the window.

On the night of which I am speaking, Stephen Elliott found himself, as he thought, looking through the glazed door. The moon was shining through the window, and he was gazing at a figure that lay in the bathtub.

His description of what he saw reminds me of what I once beheld in the famous vaults of St. Michan's Church in Dublin, which possess the horrid property of preserving corpses from decay for centuries. A figure inexpressibly thin and pathetic, of a dusty leaden color, enveloped in a shroudlike garment, the thin lips crooked into a faint and dreadful smile, the hands pressed tightly over the region of the heart.

As he looked upon it, a distant, almost inaudible moan seemed to issue from its lips, and the arms began to stir. The terror of the sight forced Stephen backward, and he awoke to the fact that he was indeed standing on the cold boarded floor of the passage in the full light of the moon. With a courage that I do not think can be common among boys of his age, he went to the door of the bathroom to ascertain if the figure of his dream was really there. It was not, and he went back to bed.

Mrs. Bunch was much impressed the next morning by his story and went so far as to replace the muslin curtains over the glazed door of the bathroom. Mr. Abney, moreover, to whom he confided his experiences at breakfast, was greatly interested and made notes of the matter in what he called "his book."

The spring equinox was approaching, as Mr. Abney frequently reminded his cousin, adding that this had been always considered by the ancients to be a critical time for the young: that Stephen would do well to take care of himself and to shut his bedroom window at night. Two incidents that occurred around this time made an impression upon Stephen's mind.

The first was after an unusually uneasy and oppressed night that he had passed—though he could not recall any particular dream that he had had.

The following evening Mrs. Bunch was occupying herself in sewing his nightgown.

"Gracious me, Master Stephen!" she broke forth rather irritably. "How do you manage to tear your nightdress all to flinders this way? Look here, sir, what trouble you do give to poor servants that have to darn and mend after you!"

There was indeed a most destructive and apparently wanton series of slits or scorings in the garment. They were confined to the left side of the chest—long, parallel slits, around six inches in length, some of them not quite piercing the texture of the linen. Stephen could only express his entire ignorance; he was sure that they were not there the night before.

"But," he said, "Mrs. Bunch, they are just the same as the scratches on the outside of my bedroom door; and I'm sure I never had anything to do with making *them*."

Mrs. Bunch gazed at him openmouthed and then snatched up a candle, departed hastily from the room, and was heard making her way upstairs. In a few minutes she came down.

"Well," she said, "Master Stephen, it's a funny thing to me how them marks and scratches can come there—too high up for any cat or dog to 'ave made 'em, much less a rat: for all the world like a Chinaman's fingernails, as my uncle in the tea trade used to tell us of when we was girls together. I wouldn't say nothing to Master, not if I was you; just turn the key of the door when you go to your bed."

"I always do, Mrs. Bunch, as soon as I've said my prayers."

"Ah, that's a good child, always say your prayers, and then no one can hurt you."

This was on a Friday night in March, 1812.

On the following evening the usual duet of Stephen and Mrs. Bunch was augmented by the sudden arrival of Mr. Parkes, the butler, who as a rule kept himself to himself in his own pantry. He did not see that Stephen was there; he was, moreover, flustered.

"Master may get up his own wine, if he likes, of an evening. Either I do it in the daytime or not at all, Mrs. Bunch. I don't know what it may be: very like it's the rats or the wind got into the cellars; but I'm not so young as I was, and I can't go through with it."

"Well, Mr. Parkes, you know it is a surprising place for the rats, is the hall."

"I'm not denying that, Mrs. Bunch; and to be sure, many a time I've heard the tale from the men in the shipyards about the rat that could speak. I never laid no confidence in that before; but tonight, if I'd demeaned myself to lay my ear to the door of the further bin, I could pretty much have heard what they was saying."

"Oh, there, Mr. Parkes, I've no patience with your fancies! Rats talking in the wine cellar, indeed!"

"Well, Mrs. Bunch, I've no wish to argue with you; all I say is, if you choose to go to the far bin and lay your ear to the door, you may prove my words this minute."

"What nonsense you do talk, Mr. Parkes—not fit for children to listen to! Why, you'll be frightening Master Stephen there out of his wits."

"What! Master Stephen?" said Parkes, awaking to the consciousness of the boy's presence. "Master Stephen knows well enough when I'm a-playing a joke with you, Mrs. Bunch."

In fact, Master Stephen knew much too well to suppose that Mr. Parkes had in the first instance intended a joke. He was interested, not altogether pleasantly, in the situation.

We have now arrived at March 24, 1812. It was a day of curious experiences for Stephen: a windy, noisy day, which filled the house and the gardens with a restless impression. As Stephen stood by the fence of the grounds and looked out into the park, he felt as if an endless procession of unseen people were sweeping past him on the wind, borne on resistlessly and aimlessly, vainly striving to stop themselves, to catch at something that might arrest their flight and bring them once again into contact with the living world of which they had formed a part. After luncheon that day, Mr. Abney said, "Stephen, my boy, do you think you could manage to come to me tonight as late as eleven o'clock in my study? I shall be busy until that time, and I wish to show you something connected with your future life that it is most important that you should know. You are not to mention this matter to Mrs. Bunch nor to anyone else in the house; and you had better go to your room at the usual time."

Here was a new excitement: Stephen eagerly grasped at the opportunity of sitting up till 11 o'clock. He looked in at the library door on his way upstairs that evening and saw a brazier, which he had often noticed in the corner of the room, moved out before the fire; an old silver-gilt cup stood on the table, filled with red wine, and some written sheets of paper lay near it. Mr. Abney was sprinkling some incense on the brazier from a round silver box as Stephen passed, but did not seem to notice his step.

The wind had fallen, and there was a still night and a full moon. At around ten o'clock Stephen was standing at the open window of his bedroom, looking out over the country. Still as the night was, the mysterious population of the distant moonlit woods was not yet lulled to rest. From time to time strange cries as of lost and despairing wanderers sounded from across the mere. They might be the notes of owls or water birds, yet they did not quite resemble either sound. Were not they coming closer? Now they sounded from the closer side of the water, and in a few moments they seemed to be floating around among the shrubberies. Then they ceased; but just as Stephen was thinking of shutting the window and resuming his reading of *Robinson Crusoe*, he caught sight of two figures standing on the graveled terrace that ran along the garden side of the hall—the figures of a boy and girl, as it seemed; they stood side by side, looking up at the windows. Something in the form of the girl recalled irresistibly his dream of the figure in the bathtub. The boy inspired him with more acute fear.

While the girl stood still, half smiling, with her hands clasped over her heart, the boy, a thin shape with black hair and ragged clothing, raised his arms in the air with an appearance of menace and of unappeasable hunger and longing. The moon shone upon his almost transparent hands, and Stephen saw that the nails were fearfully long and that the light shone through them. As he stood with his arms thus raised, he disclosed a terrifying spectacle. On the left side of his chest there opened a black and gaping hole; and there fell upon Stephen's brain, rather than upon his ear, the impression of one of those hungry and desolate cries that he had heard resounding over the woods of Aswarby all that evening. In another moment this dreadful pair had moved swiftly and noiselessly over the dry gravel, and he saw them no more.

Inexpressibly frightened as he was, he determined to take his candle and go down to Mr. Abney's study, for the hour appointed for their meeting was near. The study opened out of the front hall on one side, and Stephen, urged on by his terrors, did not take long in getting there. To effect an entrance was not so easy. The door was not locked, he felt sure, for the key was on the outside of it as usual. His repeated knocks produced no answer. Mr. Abney was engaged: he was speaking. What! Why did he try to cry out? And why was the cry choked in his throat? Had he, too, seen the mysterious children? But now everything was quiet, and the door yielded to Stephen's terrified and frantic pushing.

★★★

On the table in Mr. Abney's study certain papers were found that explained the situation.

"It was a belief very strongly held by the ancients that by enacting certain processes, a very remarkable enlightenment of the spiritual faculties in man may be attained; that by absorbing the personalities of his fellow creatures, an individual may gain a complete ascendancy over the elemental forces of our universe.

"It is recorded of Simon Magus that he was able to fly in the air, to become invisible, or to assume any form he pleased by the agency of the soul of a boy whom he had 'murdered.' I find it set down, moreover, in the writings of Hermes Trismegistus, that similar happy results may be produced by the absorption of the hearts of not less than three human beings below the age of twenty-one years. To the testing of the truth of this I have devoted the greater part of the last twenty years, selecting as my experiment such persons as could conveniently be removed without occasioning a gap in society. The first step I effected by the removal of one Phoebe Stanley, a girl of gypsy extraction, on March twenty-fourth, seventeen ninety-two. The second, by the removal of a wandering Italian lad named Giovanni Paoli, on the night of March twenty-third, eighteen oh-five. The final 'victim'— to employ a word repugnant in the highest degree to my feelings—must be my cousin, Stephen Elliott. His day must be this March twenty-fourth, eighteen twelve.

"The best means is to remove the heart from the *living* subject, to reduce it to ashes, and to mingle them with around a pint of some red wine, preferably port. The remains of the first two subjects, at least, it will be well to conceal: a disused bathroom or wine cellar will be found convenient for such a purpose. Some annoyance may be experienced from the psychic portion of the subjects, which popular language dignifies with the name of ghosts. But the man of philosophic temperament—to whom alone the experiment is appropriate—will be little prone to attach importance to the feeble efforts of these beings to wreak their vengeance on him. I contemplate with the liveliest satisfaction the emancipated existence that the experiment will confer on me; not only placing me beyond the reach of human justice (so-called), but eliminating to a great extent the prospect of death itself."

Mr. Abney was found in his chair, his head thrown back, his face stamped with an expression of rage, fright, and mortal pain. In his left side was a terrible lacerated wound, exposing the heart. There was no blood on his hands, and a long knife that lay on the table was perfectly clean. A savage wildcat might have inflicted the injuries. The window of the study was open, and it was the opinion of the coroner that Mr. Abney had met his death by the agency of some wild creature. But Stephen Elliott's study of the papers I have quoted led him to a very different conclusion.

THURNLEY ABBEY

Perceval Landon

Alastair Colvin has been invited down to Thurnley Abbey by the owner, an old friend from Far Eastern days named John Broughton, and his wife. Something is badly wrong at the Abbey; there is talk of the ghost of a nun. At dinner, Colvin sees the other guests watching him and talking about him, in a way that suggests that he may be the object of mysterious speculation.

"BY ELEVEN, ALL the guests were gone, and Broughton, his wife, and I were alone together under the fine plaster ceiling of the Jacobean drawing room. Mrs. Broughton talked about one or two of the neighbors, and then, with a smile, said that she knew I would excuse her, shook hands with me, and went off to bed. I felt that she talked a little uncomfortably and with a suspicion of effort, smiled rather conventionally, and was obviously glad to go. I had throughout the faint feeling that everything was not square. Under the circumstances, this was enough to set me wondering what on earth the service could be that I was to render—wondering also whether the whole business was not some ill-advised jest in order to make me come down from London for a mere shooting party.

"Broughton said little after she had gone. But he was evidently laboring to bring the conversation around to the so-called haunting of the Abbey. As soon as I saw this, of course, I asked him directly about it. He then seemed at once to lose interest in the matter. There was no doubt about it:

Broughton was somehow a changed man, and to my mind he had changed in no way for the better. I reminded him that he was going to tell me what I could do for him in the morning, pleaded my journey, lighted a candle, and went upstairs with him. At the end of the passage leading into the old house he grinned weakly and said, 'Mind, if you see a ghost, do talk to it; you said you would.' He stood irresolutely a moment and then turned away. At the door of his dressing room, he paused once more: 'I'm here,' he called out, 'if you should want anything. Good night,' and he shut his door.

"I went along the passage to my room, undressed, switched on a lamp beside my bed, read a few pages of *The Jungle Book*, and then, more than ready for sleep, turned the light off and went fast asleep."

"Three hours later I woke up. There was not a breath of wind outside. There was not even a flicker of light from the fireplace. As I lay there, an ash tinkled slightly as it cooled. An owl cried among the silent Spanish chestnuts outside. I idly reviewed the events of the day, but at the end I seemed as wakeful as ever. There was no help for it. I must read my *Jungle Book* again till I felt ready to go off, so I fumbled for the pear at the end of the cord that hung down beside the bed, and I switched on the bedside lamp. The sudden glory dazzled me for a moment. I felt under my pillow for my book with half-shut eyes. Then, growing used to the light, I happened to look down to the foot of my bed.

"I can never tell you really what happened then. Nothing I could ever confess in the most abject words could even faintly picture to you what I felt. I know that my heart stopped dead, and my throat shut automatically. In one instinctive movement I crouched back up against the headboard of the bed, staring at the horror. The movement set my heart going again, and the sweat dripped from every pore. I am not a particularly religious man, but I had always believed that God would never allow any supernatural appearance to present itself to man in such a guise and in such circumstances that harm, either bodily or mental, could result to him. I can only tell you that at that moment both my life and my reason rocked unsteadily on their seats.

"Leaning over the foot of my bed, looking at me, was a figure swathed in a rotten and tattered veiling. This shroud passed over the head, but left both eyes and the right side of the face bare. It then followed the line of the arm down to where the hand grasped the bed end. The face was not entirely that of a skull, though the eyes and the flesh of the face were totally gone. There was a thin, dry skin drawn tightly over the features, and there was some skin left on the hand. One wisp of hair crossed the forehead. It was perfectly still. I looked at it, and it looked at me, and my brain turned dry and hot in my head. I had still the pear of the electric lamp in my hand, and I played idly with it; only I dared not turn the light out again. I shut my eyes, only to open them in a hideous terror the same second. The thing had not moved. My heart was thumping, and the sweat cooled me as it evaporated. Another cinder tinkled in the grate, and a panel creaked in the wall.

"My reason failed me. For twenty minutes, or twenty seconds, I was able to think of nothing else but this awful figure, till there came, hurtling through the empty channels of my senses, the remembrance that Broughton and his friends had discussed with me furtively at dinner. The dim possibility of it being a hoax stole gratefully into my unhappy mind, and once there, one's pluck came creeping back along a thousand tiny veins. My first sensation was one of blind, unreasoning thankfulness that my brain was going to stand the trial. I am not a timid man, but the best of us needs some human handle to steady him in times of extremity, and in the faint but growing hope that after all it might be only a brutal hoax, I found the fulcrum that I needed. At last I moved.

"How I managed to do it I cannot tell you, but with one spring toward the foot of the bed I got within arm's length and struck out one fearful blow with my fist at the thing. It crumbled under it, and my hand was cut to the bone. With a sickening revulsion after the terror, I dropped, half fainting across the end of the bed. So it was merely a foul trick after all. No doubt the trick had been played many a time before: no doubt Broughton and his friends had had some large bet among themselves as to what I should do when I discovered the gruesome thing. From my state of abject terror I found myself transported into an insensate anger. I shouted curses upon Broughton. I dived rather than climbed over the bed end onto the sofa. I tore at the robed skeleton—how well the whole thing had been carried out, I thought—I broke the skull against the floor and stamped upon its dry bones. I flung the head away under the bed and ripped the brittle bones of the trunk into pieces. I snapped the thin thighbones across my knee and flung them in different directions. The shinbones I set up against a stool and broke with my heel. I raged like a berserker against the loathly thing and stripped the ribs from the backbone and slung the breastbone against the cupboard. My fury increased as the work of destruction went on. I tore the frail rotten veil into twenty pieces, and the dust went up over everything, over the clean blotting paper and the silver inkstand. At last my work was done. There was but a raffle of broken bones and strips of parchment and crumbling wool. Then, picking up a piece of the skull—it was the cheek and the temple bone of the right side, I remember—I opened the door and went down the passage to Broughton's dressing room. I remember still how my sweat-dripping pajamas clung to me as I walked. At the door I kicked and entered.

"Broughton was in bed. He had already turned on the light and seemed shrunken and horrified. For a moment he could hardly pull himself together. Then I spoke. I don't know what I said. Only I know that from a heart full and overfull with hatred and contempt, spurred on by shame of my own recent cowardice, I let my tongue run on. He answered nothing. I was amazed at my own fluency. My hair still clung lankily to my wet temples, my hand was bleeding profusely, and I must have looked a strange sight. Broughton huddled himself up at the head of the bed just as I had. Still he made no answer, no defense. He seemed preoccupied with something besides my reproaches and once or twice moistened his lips with his tongue. But he could say nothing, though he moved his hands now and then, just as a baby who cannot speak moves his hands.

"At last the door into Mrs. Broughton's room opened, and she came in, white and terrified. 'What is it? What is it?

Oh, in God's name! What is it?' she cried again and again, and then she went up to her husband and sat on the bed in her nightdress, and the two faced me. I told her what the matter was. I spared her husband not a word for her presence there. Yet he seemed hardly to understand. I told the pair that I had spoiled their cowardly joke for them. Broughton looked up.

"'I have smashed the foul thing into a hundred pieces,' I said. Broughton licked his lips again, and his mouth worked. 'By God!' I shouted. 'It would serve you right if I thrashed you within an inch of your life. I will take care that not a decent man or woman of my acquaintance ever speaks to you again. And there,' I added, throwing the broken piece of the skull upon the floor beside his bed, 'there is a souvenir for you, of your damned work tonight!'

"Broughton saw the bone, and in a moment it was his turn to frighten me. He squealed like a hare caught in a trap. He screamed and screamed till Mrs. Broughton, almost as bewildered as myself, held onto him and coaxed him like a child to be quiet. But Broughton—and as he moved I thought that ten minutes ago I perhaps looked as terribly ill as he did—thrust her from him and scrambled out of bed onto the floor and, still screaming, put out his hand to the bone. It had blood on it from my hand. He paid no attention to me whatsoever. In truth I said nothing. This was a new turn indeed to the horrors of the evening. He rose from the floor with the bone in his hand and stood silent. He seemed to be listening. 'Time, time, perhaps,' he muttered and almost at the same moment fell at full length on the carpet, cutting his head against the fender. The bone flew from his hand and came to rest near the door. I picked up Broughton, haggard and broken, with blood over his face. He whispered hoarsely and quickly, 'Listen, listen!' We listened.

"After ten seconds of utter quiet, I seemed to hear something. I could not be sure, but at last there was no doubt. There was a quiet sound as of one moving along the passage. Little regular steps came toward us over the hard oak flooring. Broughton moved to where his wife sat, white and speechless, on the bed and pressed her face into his shoulder.

"Then, the last thing that I could see as he turned the light out, he fell forward with his own head pressed into the pillow of the bed. Something in their company, something in their cowardice, helped me, and I faced the open doorway of the room, which was outlined fairly clearly against the dimly lighted passage. I put out one hand and touched Mrs. Broughton's shoulder in the darkness. But at the last moment, I, too, failed. I sank on my knees and put my face in the bed. Only we all heard. The footsteps came to the door, and there they stopped. The piece of bone was lying inside the door. There was a rustle of moving stuff, and the thing was in the room. Mrs. Broughton was silent; I could hear Broughton's voice praying, muffled in the pillow; I was cursing my own cowardice. Then the steps moved out again on the oak boards of the passage, and I heard the sounds dying away. In a flash of remorse, I went to the door and looked out. At the end of the corridor I thought I saw something that moved away. A moment later the passage was empty. I stood with my forehead against the jamb of the door, almost physically sick.

"'You can turn the light on,' I said, and there was an answering flare. There was no bone at my feet. Mrs. Broughton had fainted. Broughton was almost useless, and it took me ten minutes to bring her to. Broughton only said one thing worth remembering. For the most part he went on muttering prayers. But I was glad afterward to recollect that he had said that thing. He said in a colorless voice, half as a question, half as a reproach, 'You didn't speak to her.'

"We spent the remainder of the night together. Mrs. Broughton actually fell off into a kind of sleep before dawn, but she suffered so horribly in her dreams that I shook her into consciousness again. Never was dawn so long in coming. Three or four times Broughton spoke to himself. Mrs. Broughton would then just tighten her hold on his arm, but she could say nothing. As for me, I can honestly say that I grew worse as the hours passed and the light strengthened. The two violent reactions had battered down my steadiness of view, and I felt that the foundations of my life had been built upon the sand. I said nothing, and after binding up my hand with a towel, I did not move. It was better so. They helped me, and I helped them, and we all three knew that our reason had gone very close to ruin that night. At last, when the light came in pretty strongly and the birds outside were chattering and singing, we felt that we must do something. Yet we never moved. You might have thought that we should particularly dislike being found as we were by the servants; yet nothing of that kind mattered a straw, and an overpowering listlessness bound us as we sat, until Chapman, Broughton's man, actually knocked and opened the door. None of us moved. Broughton, speaking hardly and stiffly, said, 'Chapman, you can come back in five minutes.' Chapman was a discreet man, but it would have made no difference to us if he had carried his news to the 'room' at once.

"We looked at each other, and I said that I must go back. I meant to wait outside till Chapman returned. I simply dared not reenter my bedroom alone. Broughton roused himself and said that he would come with me. Mrs. Broughton agreed to remain in her own room for five minutes if the blinds were drawn up and all the doors left open.

"So Broughton and I, leaning stiffly one against the other, went down to my room. By the morning light that filtered past the blinds, we could see our way, and I released the blinds. There was nothing wrong in the room from end to end, except smears of my own blood on the end of the bed, on the sofa, and on the carpet where I had torn the thing to pieces."

NOT AT HOME

Jean Richardson

THERE WERE NO lights in the bike shed, and the bushes roundabout, which in daylight were an insignificant school-uniform green, loomed menacingly and cast fingers of shadows over the path.

Fetching her bike was the thing that Alison hated most about staying late at school, though she usually had Joanne's cheerful company, and the two of them together were brave enough to enjoy a few shivers. But Joanne had a sore throat, and although she had insisted on coming to school because it was English class and she wanted her essay back, she had no voice for choir practice.

"But it was worth it," she told Alison, her face flushed with pleasure and a temperature. "'A minus and a nice feeling for words.'"

It would have been showing off in anyone else, but Alison knew how much being good in English mattered to Joanne. It made up for not being good at sports and a coward at vaulting and climbing a rope.

"You'd be up it fast enough if there was a fire," Miss Barry had said unsympathetically, and several girls who were jealous of Joanne had tittered.

But Joanne didn't care. She felt that she was the wrong shape to climb a rope and saw herself, in an emergency, being saved by a handsome fireman. She was always making up stories. It was she who referred to the old bike at the far end of the shed as a skeleton and suggested that the school caretaker lurked there after dark, hoping to catch a nice, plump little girl for his supper.

It was nonsense, of course. Old Trayner didn't look very attractive, with decayed teeth that you couldn't help noticing when he smiled, but he was probably lonely and only wanted someone to talk to.

Nevertheless, Alison was in a greater hurry than usual to find the key to her padlock. She had been late that morning, and the only space had been at the far end, next to the "skeleton." No one knew whose bike it was nor why it had been abandoned, but the mudguards and chain were gone, and the rust and cobwebs had moved in. Cobwebs . . . spiders . . .

Alison jerked her bike free. In her hurry she had forgotten to remove her front light, and someone had taken it. Blast! It was fatal to leave a light or a pump behind. Trayner probably had a thriving business in lights and pumps, though most people suspected Finn's gang, who all had sticky fingers. Oh, well, perhaps Dad would get her a dynamo at last.

She fumbled in her backpack for her safety belt. Books, ruler, pens, and something that felt like crumbs or sand. No, it wasn't there. Then she remembered that it had wrapped itself around a book, and she had put it in her desk. The door was probably still unlocked, but she didn't fancy crossing the dark hall and going upstairs and along the corridor to 2B. Schools were designed to be full of people; empty, they were scary places, unnaturally quiet, as though everyone was dead. She'd have to do without her belt. It surely wouldn't matter just this once, though she had promised to wear it every day. It was something her mother had insisted on when she agreed to let Alison cycle to school.

She wedged her backpack in her basket and patted her saddle. Although she wouldn't have admitted it to Joanne, Alison thought of her bike as a trusty steed, and it was comforting to feel that she had an ally who would help her make a quick getaway.

She decided to risk cycling down the drive. They were not supposed to, but there were no lights in the headmistress's study, and she doubted whether Miss Cliffe, who lived across from the school and was fond of keeping an eye on things even when off-duty, would be glued to her window on a winter evening. More likely she'd be toasting her sturdy legs in front of the fire.

It seemed much darker without a front light, though its light was only small and wavering. The damp air tangled Alison's hair into frizzy curls, and she shivered. They didn't have real fogs nowadays, not the kind you read about in Dickens, where people had to grope their way through the streets, but there were rags of mist, and the streetlights had garish yellow haloes.

Alison sang to herself as she cycled along. "The holly bears a berry as red as any blood. And Mary bore sweet Jesus Christ for to do poor sinners good."

They had been practicing for the end-of-term concert, and her head rang with glorias and tidings of comfort and joy. It was less than a month to Christmas, and the very thought warmed her.

She reached a crossroad and now had to turn right onto the main road. It was always a moment she dreaded, because the traffic raced along, and she didn't have the nerve to take a quick chance.

She looked to the right, to the left, and then to the right again and stuck her arm out, though it seemed silly to signal when she wasn't very visible. She was halfway across when a car shot out impatiently from the other side of the crossroad. Startled, Alison swerved and then wobbled as her shoe slipped off the pedal and grazed the road, and at that moment a truck as tall as a house and as long as a train came hurtling toward her. It was going fast, and the swish of its hot breath seemed to suck her in toward the giant tires. It happened so quickly: she felt as though she was being drawn into a black void, while two red eyes, which she realized afterward must have been the brake lights of the car, blazed fiercely before being extinguished by the mist.

And then Alison found herself alone in the road. She was trembling, and she felt off balance and as though her body didn't quite belong to her. Her heart was still pounding as she began to push her bike along, but it was too far to walk all the way. "It's like falling off a horse," she told herself. "I must get on again, or I will lose my nerve."

If only Mum would be there when she got home, but her mother worked part time and had a late meeting. Peter might be home, but he wasn't prepared to say what he was up to these days, at least not to a sister. Alison enjoyed getting her own dinner, but having the house all to herself was a bit creepy, especially at first, when it was so still she thought that someone was there and holding his breath.

She turned into the Avenue and took the third turn on the right and then down Fernhead. The houses there had bay windows and stubby front yards behind privet hedges. Mum had promised to leave the light on, but she must have forgotten, for the house was in darkness.

Alison pushed open the gate with her bike. The hedge seemed taller than usual and showered her with raindrops. It really was time Dad cut it, though he always said as an excuse that hedges didn't grow in the winter. She scrabbled in her pocket for the key. Soggy tissues . . . wallet . . . the button off her raincoat . . . here it was. She felt for the lock and opened the door. The light switch was halfway along the wall, which meant that she had to plunge into blackness.

In her haste she banged her knee on something hard with a sharp corner. It took her by surprise, and her heart thumped as she felt for the switch and pressed it down.

She had banged her knee on a large carved wooden chest that she had never seen before. She sensed at once that the hall was different. The carpet was the same. And there was that mark on it where Peter had upset a can of paint. The walls were the same color, but the two watercolors that her gran had done on vacation were missing, and in their place was a poster advertising a railroad museum.

Alison looked around in bewilderment. She was in two minds about shutting the front door, because it seemed more frightening inside than out. Was she seeing things? Was she in the right house? She looked down at the telephone standing on the mysterious wooden chest and checked. Yes, it was the right number. Of course it was. Her mother was fond of saying that they needed a change, and switching the pictures was just the sort of thing she liked doing. And it was just like her to forget to tell them that she'd bought a chest, because her father would then point out that they didn't need a chest because they'd got enough old junk of their own already. Yes, that must be what had happened.

She shut the front door and went upstairs to her room.

Only it wasn't her room anymore. It belonged to someone who could have been around her age, but this person had a scarlet chest of drawers and a wardrobe with a desk unit slotted between them. They were so much what Alison herself would have liked that for a moment she wondered whether her parents had gotten rid of the old wardrobe that had belonged to Gran and the rickety table that she used as a desk and bought these smart units as a giant Christmas present.

But what had they done with her things? The clothes spilling out of the wardrobe weren't hers. She didn't wear long skirts or that vivid shade of pink. And what had Mum done with her books and the old toys that she couldn't bear to throw away . . . ?

She went along the landing into Peter's room. It was even messier than usual: there were stacks of computer magazines and a workbench scattered with little cans of paint and brushes and glue and a half-finished model airplane. That was something Peter would never have the patience to make.

Alison was standing in the doorway of her parents' transformed bedroom when she heard the front door open.

It must be Peter, and she was about to call out and run downstairs to him when something stopped her. Everything was so different, so unexpected, that perhaps Peter might have changed in some dreadful way too.

She tiptoed across to the stairs, aware that she didn't want to be seen. She heard voices, and then someone slammed the front door.

"Danny! You've let out the cat." It was a woman's voice.

"It wasn't my fault. He ran out before I could stop him." The boy sounded younger than Peter.

"Well, don't blame me if he gets run over. You know how dangerous that road is. The Walkers' cat was killed last week, and the traffic shoots along now that it's one way."

"It doesn't make any difference if you let him out at the back. He's learned how to get around." This was a girl, who went into the living room and turned on the television while the boy and the woman disappeared into the kitchen. Alison heard water running and then the sound of a kettle being plugged in.

She felt like an intruder. They sounded like a normal family coming back to their own home, and what would they do when they found a stranger there? Would they believe that it had been her home that morning, that she and her brother and her parents had lived there for the past seven years? More likely they'd think she'd broken in and send for the police. And would *they* believe her? Alison saw herself trying to convince a disbelieving, unsympathetic officer that she had left the house that very morning and that the key that opened the front door was hers. . . .

No, she must get out of the house as quickly as possible.

"It's upstairs. I'll go and get it." The boy appeared in the hall, and Alison ducked back into her bedroom. She held her breath as she heard him run up the stairs. Please let whatever he wanted be in his own room!

The door was just open, and she saw the boy go past with a sweater. There was a smell of frying, and Alison thought longingly of her own dinner. She had been planning to have fish sticks and baked beans with oven fries.

"In here or in there?" called the woman.

"In here. I want to watch TV."

"Well, come and get it."

There was a clatter of knives and forks, and people went to and from the kitchen. Alison moved to the top of the stairs. The living room door was shut, and they all seemed to be in there having their dinner. Please don't let them have forgotten the salt or the ketchup!

She slid down the stairs, ran to the front door, and out into the night. Something jumped on her, and she half screamed before she realized that it was the cat. It was as startled as she was and fled under the hedge.

At least her bike was still there, invisible in the shadows. She grabbed it and stumbled out into the street. There seemed to be more traffic than usual, coming toward her on both sides of the road, and she remembered the woman saying that it was a one-way street. But it hadn't been. Not that morning.

I must have made a mistake, she told herself. It's the wrong street, but somehow my key fit their front door. Was it possible? But the phone number was the right one, and the sign at the end of the street, when she reached it, said unmistakably, "Fernhead Road."

Alison was close to tears. She was cold and frightened and alone, and she longed for her mother and the safety and security of her own home. Even Peter would have been welcome. He must be due home, whatever he'd been up to, and he would find everything as changed as she had.

She cycled past the little public park that always closed

243

early in the winter. That at least looked the same. She was now approaching the main street, where there was a straggling parade of stores. There was Aziz, where they bought candy and newspapers, the Chinese takeout, a fish and chips restaurant, and a pub called The Frog and Nightdress. There couldn't be another pub with a name like that! Home must be somewhere nearby. Perhaps if she was to go back to Fernhead Road she would find that it had all been some horrible mistake or a bad dream.

And then Alison saw that something had changed. On Saturday she had noticed a new billboard that had gone up on some empty lot at one end of the stores. It said that the site had been acquired by a chain of supermarkets, and now, only four days later, there was the new supermarket.

Wonderingly, she wheeled her bike toward it. There was even a rack of bicycles outside, and as though in a dream, she parked hers and went in.

It was the largest supermarket that she had ever seen. Avenues of shelves stretched away into the distance, and frozen cabinets half a mile long were stacked with regiments of turkeys, ducks, and geese. Boxes of mince pies and Christmas puddings were stacked in a pyramid crowned by a plastic Christmas tree with winking lights, and a carol, arranged for some vast invisible orchestra, wafted through the air as though on the wings of an angel.

Most of the customers wheeled carts piled so high that they might have been shopping for expeditions to the North Pole or the Andes, while boys in holly-green aprons replenished the shelves or hurried up and down the aisles checking queries relayed to them by walkie-talkie. Some of them didn't look much older than Alison, and she tried to pluck up the courage to speak to a boy who was shoveling Brazil nuts into a container. There was something familiar about him, she realized. He reminded her of Sean Maloney, who was in her class, but it couldn't be him because they weren't allowed to take jobs, even part time. She knew that there were lots of Maloneys, so he must be an older brother with the same tight, coppery curls.

But what could she say? He'd think that she was crazy if she asked him how they could possibly have built, stocked, and staffed a supermarket in four days!

She had just decided to ask him, as an opener, where the milk was, when she saw a familiar face farther down the aisle. It was Joanne's mother, Mrs. Cullen, and she was reaching for some mince pies.

It was better than the best Christmas present. Everything was going to be all right, even if it was quite puzzling. She would tell Mrs. Cullen about the house and perhaps go back and have dinner with Joanne while it was all sorted out.

She ran down the aisle. Mrs. Cullen had her back to Alison, so she didn't see her coming.

"Mrs. Cullen, am I glad to see you. I don't know what's happened—"

Alison got no further, because when Joanne's mother saw her, she made a funny little choking noise and crumpled up as though Alison had shot her. She fell against the display, and mince pies and Christmas puddings skated along the aisles, while the tree lurched forward, its lights flashing a wild signal of distress.

"She's having a seizure," said one woman. "I think she's

fainted," said another, but neither of them made any move to help. A girl from the checkout, who had done a course in first aid, propped up Mrs. Cullen and asked for a glass of water.

Mrs. Cullen opened her eyes. She seemed dazed.

"I think she's only fainted," said the checkout girl. "Can someone get a chair?"

Sean Maloney, looking a mixture of embarrassed and inquisitive, brought one.

Mrs. Cullen recognized him. "Did you see her?" she asked faintly.

"See who?"

"That girl. The one who came up to me. She . . . she . . ." Mrs. Cullen was crying.

"I didn't see any girl." Several customers were looking at Sean as though he was somehow to blame.

"It wasn't *any* girl. You must remember her. She was in your class. She was Joanne's friend. Alison Potter."

"Alison Potter!" Sean Maloney backed away. "But it couldn't have been her. She was . . ." He didn't like to say it.

"Killed," said Mrs. Cullen with a shudder. "That's right. She was run over and killed on the way home from school. The Potters lived on our street, but they moved after the accident."

"You must have imagined it," said Sean. "Or seen someone who looked like her."

He looked around at the shoppers, most of whom had moved away now that there was nothing to see but a frightened-looking woman on a chair. He remembered Alison Potter, but there was no sign of her or of any girl who looked remotely like her.

THE SHEPHERD'S DOG

Joyce Marsh

CHAUVAL LIFTED HIS head sharply; his sensitive, upstanding ears twitched as he listened intently. From outside the window a little twig scraped against the pane, and the big white dog recognized it as the sound that had roused him from his uneasy sleep. His body relaxed as he allowed his shaggy head to drop down onto his forepaws.

He did not sleep again, however, as his olive-green eyes, lightly flecked with little pinpoints of golden light, stared fixedly at the still form on the bed. For two long days he had watched that figure, waiting to see the tiniest movement of life, although by now his every sense told him that he hoped in vain.

On that morning when the Master had not risen as he usually did at first light of day, Chauval had been impatient and slightly irritable. Even through the closed window, his sensitive nose had picked up the exhilarating scent of the new day. His limbs almost ached in their eagerness for that glorious, rushing scamper over the heather with which every morning began.

Restlessly, he had padded around the room, scratched at the closed door, and lifted his head to savor the fresh, clean smell of a new day. Then a long, deep growl had begun low in his throat, but still the Master had not moved. The growl had become a whine, anxiety replaced impatience, and Chauval had crept closer to the bed. He had thrust his nose beneath the Master's shoulder and nudged him violently. The man's head rolled on the pillow, but he had not opened his eyes nor made a sound. One still hand dangled from the bed; Chauval licked it—it was so cold.

Then the big, shaggy white dog had jumped onto the bed, covering the man with his body, licking his face and hands as he tried to drive out that dreadful cold with the warmth of his own body.

It was then that the vague anxiety had become a sickening fear, for the Master's well-known scent had gone, and in its place was a smell that Chauval knew and dreaded.

So many times in his long working life the sheepdog had found a sheep that had wandered too close to the edge and had fallen to its death on the rocky beach below or a straying lamb that had become stranded on a ledge to die of fear and hunger. All of these animals had the smell of death on them, and now that same hateful scent was upon the Master.

Chauval, in his panic, had leaped from the bed and rushed first to the door and then to the window, his head lifted in a long, despairing wail. Instinctively, he knew that with his great strength and size, he could, if he chose, break out of the room, but without direct orders from the Master, he dared not try.

All of his life, ever since he had first come as a tiny puppy to the lonely cliff-top cottage, the Master had ordered and directed his every action. It was the Master who had taught him how to guard sheep; it was he who had told the dog what to do and when to do it. Even in those carefree, happy moments when work was done and the shepherd's dog was at liberty to rush pell-mell over the springy turf and wind-scorched heather, Chauval never forgot the law of instant obedience, for his playtime began on the Master's command and ended with his whistling call.

Chauval had been happy and secure in his trusting devotion, but now the Master's voice was still, and the dog was alone and desolate. In his bewilderment and confusion, there was only one thing of which he could be certain. When he was alone, his duty was to stay on guard, so for two long days and nights he had been in this room. Even the gnawing hunger and thirst was forgotten as he crouched low, every muscle of his body tense and alert to protect his Master and his home.

Suddenly, Chauval's head lifted again as another, much louder noise came from outside, and the draft, blowing in through a broken pane, carried the scent of a human. Silently, but with his lip lifted in the beginnings of a snarl, Chauval moved to the window and raised himself on hind legs to look out.

On the path, a few yards from the cottage, stood a man. His head was thrown back as he shouted loudly. "Are ye in there, Will? Are ye all right then, Will?"

Chauval looked back quickly toward the bed, half hoping that the sound of a voice might have called the Master back to life; but still there was no movement from the bed.

The dark-haired man, still calling the Master's name, had come very close to the cottage and was rapping on the door with his heavy stick. Chauval's snarl became more menacing, and the hairs on his back stood up stiffly. He knew that man, and he knew that stick. Once, a very long time ago, he had felt its weight upon his back; the man had come into the cottage while Chauval was alone and had walked into rooms and looked into places where only the Master was allowed to go. The dog had barked once in warning, and the man had hit him with the stick. Now that man was an enemy—never to be allowed inside.

The knocking on the door had ceased as the man walked around the cottage, looking in at all the windows. He came to Chauval's window and stopped to peer inside. For a brief moment the man and the dog stared into each other's eyes. The sound of the dog's angry barking echoed in the room, and the man leaped back in startled fear.

But he realized that he was protected by the glass between them, and he came forward again to look past the frantic dog into the room. He stared in for a moment, and then, turning quickly, he ran off. Chauval fell silent. In the distance he could hear the soft, melancholy bleating of the sheep and, farther away still, the wild rushing of the sea hurling itself against the barren, rocky beach.

Stiffly, he dropped down from the window and crept back to resume his vigil by the bed, but weakened by lack of food and little sleep, the spate of barking had exhausted him, and his eyes closed again in slumber.

A long time must have passed, for the room was almost dark when Chauval was once more roused by the sound of footsteps and loud voices.

There was a violent banging on the cottage door, and Chauval heard it fly open with a crash. Swiftly, he leaped onto the bed, crouching over the defenseless Master. He was sweating with fear, and the perspiration ran off his tongue to hang in wet, sticky streams from his mouth.

The voices came closer and closer; the bedroom door flew open, and in the opening was the man with the stick. The huge white dog remained motionless, hunched protectively and tense above his Master's body. His lip curled upward, showing long, yellow teeth, and the whites of his eyes gleamed through the dusk.

"The great ugly brute will ne'er let us come near. We'll have to shoot him first."

It was that harsh, rough voice of the man with the stick. Chauval gathered himself to spring, but suddenly someone else spoke, softly and gently.

"Poor thing, he must have been locked in here for days; he's half starved. Maybe I can coax him out."

The cruel voice muttered and mumbled, but the man stood aside, and his place in the doorway was taken by a stranger.

"Good dog, come on, then, we won't hurt you, good boy, that's a good dog."

The stranger's voice was kind and reassuring. He held out the back of his hand with the fingers hanging limply down.

"Good dog, come here, then."

With infinite slowness, Chauval eased himself off the bed. Never taking his eyes from the stranger's face, the dog crawled slowly across the floor. With all of his heart he wanted to trust this man.

"For heaven's sake, get on wi' it. We haven't got all night to mess around wi' yon vicious brute."

The harsh voice spat out the words, and out of the corner of his eye Chauval saw the stick raised above him. With a powerful spring, he leaped up, and his teeth fastened on the hand holding the stick. He felt the warm taste of blood in his mouth as his body thudded into the man's chest and bore him backward to the floor.

The room was full of noise and the smell of human fear. The stranger's voice, no longer gentle, was raised above the other's, and his was the hand that snatched up the stick and brought it down hard on the dog's back. With a yelp of pain and anger, Chauval turned to snarl a brief defiance at the stranger who was now another enemy, and then he sprang past the man toward the open door. Frantic hands grabbed at his long fur, but snapping and snarling, the dog pulled himself free and leaped outside. With a few bounding strides, he reached the cover of the bushes and threw himself down in the tangled bracken.

In an agony of confusion and fear, he stared at the cottage. He wanted to go back inside to continue his guard over the Master, but he dared not. Lights had sprung up in the windows, and the sound of voices drifted out. The front door stood open, and suddenly two men came out carrying something wrapped in white. Instinctively, Chauval knew that it was the Master.

The man with the stick had brought the stranger, and Chauval had been driven out. They had forced him to abandon his post, and now his enemies were taking away the Master. The big dog raised himself up onto his haunches, his green eyes glittered in the twilight darkness, and he began to whimper softly. Then he flung back his head, the long snout pointing directly upward toward the pale moon, and the whimper became a long howl of desolation and despair.

"There he is, over there! Shoot him, someone, while ye've got the chance. He'll be no good now that old Will's gone, and if he turns rogue, he'll be a menace to all of us."

It was the harsh, cruel voice, and close upon the words came a sharp crack, and a singing bullet passed close to the dog's ear.

Chauval began to run as he had never run in his life before. Leaping, bounding, with lolling tongue and eyes bulging until they were almost bursting from the sockets, he crashed through the bracken and undergrowth.

The lights in the cottage receded to pinpoints, and the shouts of the men were borne away on the night breeze, and still Chauval ran. The scrubby trees and bushes thinned, and the ground beneath his feet became more sharp and rocky as he fled up the steep, craggy hill that rose sharply from the cliff-top pasture. At last he could run no more, and he flung himself down onto a flat rock.

His sides heaved, and the breath rasped in his throat. The pounding of his heart quieted at last, and he breathed more easily, but now he was tormented by thirst.

The big dog raised his head, and the sensitive nostrils quivered as he explored the night wind for the longed-for scent of water. His senses told him that water was not far away, but he did not immediately go to find it. Instead, he peered anxiously down the slope and listened intently. In his headlong flight he had taken no care to hide his trail, and his enemies could easily track him down.

To his relief he could hear only the sound of rushing wind; for the moment he was safe. Gleaming wraithlike in the darkness, the dog weaved a cautious zigzagging course toward the water. The clear mountain stream flowed abundantly. Bursting out from a fissure in the rock, it cascaded first into a deep pool before it ran off down the hillside. Chauval thrust his muzzle into the icy water and greedily drank his fill.

He was ravenously hungry, but the wild, rushing escape up the steep hill had drained the last of his strength, and he was too exhausted to search for food. A flat, jutting shelf of rock offered him some shelter, and he crept beneath it. Wearily, he buried his nose into the long, warm hairs on his flank and slept.

Chauval awoke at the first light of day and at once felt the gnawing, agonizing hunger. He had never in his life needed to find his own food; no one had ever taught him how, and now he had no idea where to begin. He whimpered and whined, calling for the Master. Even now he could still desperately hope to hear a whistle or the beloved voice calling his name, but all was silent except for the tinkling water and the lonely singing of the wind.

His green eyes flicked restlessly as he surveyed the barren hillside—there was no food here. There would be food in the cottage if only he dared to go to find it. Hunger overcame fear at last, and moving carefully with his body close to the ground, he crept down the hill.

The cottage was deserted, the strangers had gone, and the Master had not returned. In the pale light of dawn the dog moved around the house, scratching at the closed doors, but there was no way to get in. The sheep, left unguarded, had strayed into the tangled undergrowth near the cottage, where they bleated dismally. Instinctively, Chauval moved around them, expertly gathering them into a little flock and herding them back to the grazing land. Enviously, he watched them eat their fill of the succulent grass.

Suddenly he heard the sound of a sheep in distress, and behind a large rock he found a young ewe with her lamb stretched out on the ground beside her. It had fallen from the top of the rock, and its fleece was streaked with blood. The mother bleated pathetically, but the lamb was dead. With an expert little rush, Chauval drove the ewe away and nudged the lamb with his nose. It was still warm, and the sickly sweet smell of the fresh blood made the juices flow in his mouth; but it was forbidden to eat the flesh of a dead sheep, and Chauval would not disobey the Master's law—he would die first.

"Good dog, you may eat the lamb."

The well-known voice sounded loud and clear in his ear. With a little yelp of joyful surprise, Chauval looked around. The breeze blew in off the sea, and the sheep called softly to each other, but there was neither scent nor sight of the Master, and yet his voice came again urgently.

"Eat, Chauval—eat, or you will die."

The pangs of desperate hunger gnawed agonizingly at his insides, but there was no need now to hesitate. Somehow and from somewhere far off the Master had spoken.

The long, yellow teeth ripped and tore at the soft flesh as, with ravenous haste, the dog wolfed down the fresh meat. So intent was he upon satisfying his hunger that he did not immediately notice that he was no longer alone on the cliff top. A man, a woman, and their son were running toward him. They were shouting and waving their arms, and Chauval heard them at last and looked up from his meal. He gave a quick welcoming bark; he knew them, and they were his friends. Suddenly the boy bent down and picked up something from the ground, and the next moment a sharp, hard rock flew through the air to hit the dog a stinging blow on the head. He yelped in pain and surprise; there was no doubting now the menace in their voices and gestures. Suddenly and inexplicably, even these friends had become his enemies. Once more he fled upward to safety. The full and satisfying meal had restored his strength, and he moved swiftly.

The people stood by the bloody remnants of the lamb and watched him go.

"That was Will's old dog," the boy said.

"Ay, an' I shoulda had my gun handy. He'll have to be shot now; he's turned sheep killer."

The woman answered her husband, and there was pity in her voice. "Poor thing, 'twill be a mercy to put him down, or like as not he'll starve to death, for he'll not let us near him, that's for sure."

And so the barren, rocky hill became Chauval's home and refuge. Water he had in abundance, but food was a constant nagging problem. Once or twice he managed to catch a young rabbit, but mostly he lived by what he could scrounge or steal from the scattered cottages on the cliff top. He always had to take care to search for his food when the people were asleep, for at the very sight of him they drove him off with sticks and stones and even guns.

At night or in the light of early dawn he slunk down the hill, moving cautiously with his body close to the ground. The Master's voice had never come again to give him leave, so he would not touch the sheep. In the pale light he moved like a great white shadow through the flock, and they, knowing him to be their friend, never ceased their constant nibbling at the grass as he passed.

While the cottagers slept, he padded silently around their homes, sniffing and searching for the scraps that they had thrown away. Sometimes he ate the foul-smelling mash that the good wives had put out for their chickens. At other times he found a clutch of eggs laid in the undergrowth by a straying hen. Once in his maraudings he was attacked by a little, half-wild cat; he had killed it and in his desperation had eaten even that.

In the weeks since the Master had gone, the sheepdog had grown thin and gaunt. His long coat, wetted by the rain and dried by the sun and salt breezes, was filthy and matted. Twigs, thorns, and brambles had become entangled in the long hairs, where they fretted and scratched his skin when he lay down.

At night, especially when the moon rode high in the heavens, he yearned so desperately for the Master that he lifted his snout to the stars and let forth a long, desolate howl. Below, in the little village, the people would hear his mournful wail and shudder in their warm, cozy beds.

One morning he had been particularly unsuccessful in his search for food; the sun had risen, and the cottagers were stirring, yet his ravenous hunger would not allow him to abandon his scavenging. Suddenly he heard a door opening nearby, and in a quick, panicky scamper, he made for a clump of bracken, where he pressed his body close to the ground and trembled.

The cheerful sound of a woman's voice drifted out through the open door, and a few minutes later, a tiny child, tottering on unsteady legs, came out into the yard. Chauval pressed down even further into the concealing bracken, and his heart thudded painfully. The little boy was coming closer, and the dog dared not move, for he could not escape without being seen.

With the casual curiosity of the very young, the child was peering into the bushes. Suddenly he saw the white dog, and his eyes opened wide in surprise. For a moment he swayed uncertainly on chubby little legs and then plumped down in front of Chauval.

"Hello, doggy," he lisped. "Do you want thum buppy?"

With trusting friendliness, he offered a thick crust of bread liberally spread with butter. Chauval took the food gently in his front teeth and wolfed it down. The boy gurgled his pleasure and stretched out his little hand to scratch and tickle at the sensitive spot behind the dog's ears. It was so long since Chauval had felt a loving, friendly touch, and his delight in it now made him forget even his hunger. He crept forward and rested his head on the child's lap.

"Does doggy want thum more buppy?"

The little boy scrambled clumsily to his feet.

"Come on, doggy, let's get more buppy."

He set off toward his home, encouraging his new friend to follow. Longing to feel again that loving, friendly touch, Chauval crawled out of his hiding place. With tail tucked between his legs and head hanging low, he slunk after the boy, but his progress was slow, and the child grew impatient.

"Come on, silly doggy."

He grasped the dog's ears in both his little hands and tugged with all his strength. In an excess of grateful affection, Chauval reached up and licked the baby's face, and it was at that moment that a piercing shriek rang out from the cottage doorway. A woman's voice shouted urgently.

"Husband, come quickly, the killer dog's got our Ian."

Chauval leaped sideways, and the child, startled by the note of fear in his mother's voice, ran to hide himself in her skirts. The woman was thrust aside, and her place in the doorway was taken by a man—it was the man with the stick, only now it was not a stick but a gun that he held in his hand.

The terrified dog raced for the concealing cover of the undergrowth, but he was too late. The shot sounded almost in his ear and the searing bullet ran along his side, gouging a deep, bloody weal in its path.

For a moment or two Chauval ran on and felt no pain, but after a while his limbs stiffened, and every thudding step was an agony. He knew he could never reach the safety of his rocky retreat, and he veered off toward the only other hiding place he knew—the tall rock on the cliff, behind which he had found and eaten the lamb.

He reached the rock and crept gratefully into its concealing shadow, pressing himself as close as he could to the cool hardness.

The bullet wound was painful, and for a long while he diligently licked it until his rough tongue had cleaned it and soothed the pain. Weakened by the lack of food, the effort exhausted him, and he fell into a deep sleep.

When he awoke, the sun had long since reached its peak and had begun its slow slide down toward the sea. Chauval was thirsty, his nose felt hot and dry, and the inside of his mouth burned feverishly. He longed for the cool waters of his mountain stream, and he peered cautiously out of his hiding place. The sound of human voices drifted over to him, and the dog drew back in alarm.

Not far away, across the rich green pasture, a man, a woman, and several children were playing with a ball. They laughed and shouted in their play, but their gaiety brought neither comfort nor reassurance to Chauval. He knew that he had but to show himself, and their happy voices would become rough and harsh as they came at him with their sticks and their guns.

Behind him the cliff dropped down sheer to the sea; there was no escape that way, and the only way to safety was barred by the group on the cliff top.

Patiently, the big white dog settled down to wait for his opportunity to slip past his enemies. As he watched, one of the children wandered away from the group and, unnoticed by the others, came toward Chauval and the cliff edge.

The breeze carried his scent to the dog's sensitive nose, and he recognized the tiny boy who had befriended him that morning. The child tottered to the very edge; with all the strength in his fat little arms, he threw a pebble out over the cliff and chuckled as it rattled and clattered onto the beach below.

So many times Chauval had seen the Master's sheep venture too close to the crumbling edge of the cliff—he knew what should be done. Like the sheep, this human child should be herded back to safety, and yet if he was to venture out, he would be seen, and the man would attack.

The boy swayed out dangerously on the very edge, and Chauval could not decide what to do. In his anxiety he whimpered softly.

As he watched the child with an ever-increasing confusion, there came upon him an icy chill; he began to tremble violently. A small, misty cloud had drifted in from the sea, enveloping him in its clammy touch. The hairs on his neck bristled, and then, from somewhere in the vapor that hung over him, came the voice that he had so longed to hear.

"Chauval, my good Chauval," it called. "Go, then, boy, fetch him back."

There was no hesitation now. The Master had spoken, and Chauval leaped to obey.

"Steady boy, easy now," the voice called from behind, and the good sheepdog lay down in the grass. Then quietly, so as not to startle the child, he moved forward in a series of little rushes. As soon as he was able, the dog placed himself between the boy and the cliff edge. The child, unafraid, lunged toward him, gurgling his pleasure; but with a warning snarl, Chauval forced him back. Again the child came on, and this time the dog herded him away from the edge with a little nip on the fatty part of his leg. More startled than hurt, the boy gave a loud, indignant wail and ran at his protector with his clenched fists—but again Chauval urged him backward from the cliff.

The man and the woman had heard their son's cry and were hurrying to his rescue. Chauval paid them no heed as, with all the skill that he had learned from guarding sheep, he forced the child to safety. It was the man who reached the child first and snatched him up in his arms.

"Get away, you evil brute."

He lashed out with his heavy boot. Chauval leaped back,

but the blow caught him full in the chest, forcing him closer to the edge. The man aimed yet another vicious kick, and the dog felt his back legs slip away into space. The weight of his body dragged down, and he clawed frantically at the soft turf with his front feet. For a brief moment he hung suspended, but his grip was too tenuous, and he fell.

Tumbling and twisting, Chauval hurtled down. The seagulls got up from their rocky perches, and their shrieks mingled with the screams of the doomed dog. His body smashed down onto the rocks and earth; sea and sky were blotted out in one final stab of pain.

The blood-streaked flanks heaved once, twice, and were still. The birds settled back on the rocky ledges, and from above the man and the woman looked down on the still shape so far below them.

"Well, that's the last trouble we'll get from that vicious dog," the man said with cruel satisfaction.

"Aye," said his wife, "an' it might have been our Ian lyin' doon there. We've only the dog to thank that it isn't."

The man looked askance.

"You're a fool, husband," she went on. "You've seen a dog work sheep often enough. Could ye no see that it weren't attacking our boy; he were herdin' him back from the edge just like he would sheep."

The man hung his head. "Well, he's gone wild; he's better off this way anyhow," he said sulkily.

"Aye," she said, and they moved off while the child in his father's arms whined, "Nice doggy, where's 'at nice doggy gone?"

All was now very quiet upon the beach. The sun had dipped its rim into the sea, and the shadows grew long and dark. A shrill whistle sounded in the breeze, and a mist at the water's edge trembled like the heat haze of high summer. The misty cloud steadied and darkened and took shape. The whistle came again, and a soft, white vapor hung over the body of the dead dog.

The cloud by the water's edge took on the shape of a man, and he stretched forth his hand.

"Chauval."

The name was a soft sigh on the sea breeze. A great shaggy dog bounded forward, leaving behind the dead, bloodstained thing on the rocks.

The man moved off over the sand, and the dog by his side leaped and danced in a transport of delight.

Few people now will venture down onto that part of the beach; for it is said that, in the late afternoon, just as the sun is about to slide into the sea, a man and his dog walk the sand. Those who have seen them say that the dog's olive-green eyes forever glow with a loving devotion while the man smiles his contentment, and as they pass, the air turns cold and is filled with soft sounds. Even the little waves breaking on the shore sing out the name: "Chauval, Chauval . . ."

ACKNOWLEDGMENTS

For permission to reproduce copyright material, acknowledgment and thanks are due to the following:

Schocken Books for "The Knock at Manor Gate" by Franz Kafka, from *The Complete Stories* edited by Nathum N. Glatzer, copyright 1946, 1947, 1948, 1949, © 1958, 1971 by Schocken Books, published by Pantheon Books, a division of Random House, Inc.; Blackie and Son Ltd. Glasgow and London for "Yesterday's Witch" by Gahan Wilson from *Spectre 1* edited by Richard Davis; Souvenir Press Ltd. for "School for Ghosts" from *Fifty Great Ghost Stories* adapted by Vida Derry and edited by John Canning; William Kimber & Co. Ltd. for "The Little Yellow Dog" by Mary Williams from *Chill Company*; Methuen Children's Books for "The Lilies" by Alison Prince from *The Ghost Within*; Don Gongdon Associates Inc. and Ray Bradbury for an excerpt from Ray Bradbury's story *The Emissary*; David Higham Associates for "John Pettigrew's Mirror" by Ruth Manning-Sanders from Philippa Pearce, 1977; the Random Century Group for "Was it a Dream?" by Guy de Maupassant, translated by Marjorie Laurie; A. P. Watt Ltd. on behalf of John Gordon for "Left in the Dark" from *Shades of Dark* by John Gordon; Joyce March for "The Shepherd's Dog" from *Spectre 2* edited by Richard Davis.